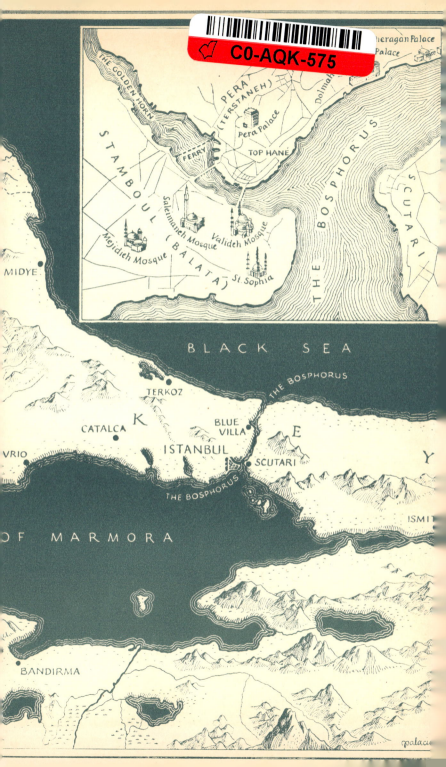

C0-AQK-575

THE GOLDEN HORN

PERA (TERSTANEH)

Dolma

Pera Palace

FERRY

TOP HANE

STAMBOUL

Suleimaneh Mosque

Valideh Mosque

Mejidieh Mosque

(BALATA)

St. Sophia

THE BOSPHORUS

SCUTARI

heragan Palace

Palace

BLACK SEA

THE BOSPHORUS

TERKOZ

MIDYE

CATALCA

K

BLUE VILLA

E

ISTANBUL

SCUTARI

VRIO

THE BOSPHORUS

Y

ISMIT

OF MARMORA

BANDIRMA

palaci

Dardanelles Derelict

Books by
VAN WYCK MASON

Dardanelles
Derelict

A MAJOR NORTH STORY BY
VAN WYCK MASON

Garden City, New York
DOUBLEDAY & COMPANY, INC.
1949

The characters and the incidents in this book are entirely the product of the author's imagination and have no relation to any person or event in real life.

For those most hospitable of friends
CHARLES *and* HELEN CLIFFORD

Contents

CONTENTS

Dardanelles Derelict

CHAPTER I

Search

OVER the scarred and bulbous bow of one of those dingy little diesel ferries which ply between Terstaneh on the Pera Shore of Istanbul and Balata across the Golden Horn, Major Theodore Stoddard's bright blue eyes anxiously surveyed lights beginning to wink and blink by the hundreds over in Stamboul. He started nervously when the slender young woman at his side made a sudden grab at her pert brown felt hat. It had been all but torn from her head by a sudden icy blast which, roaring up the estuary, crisped the dirty waves and wrenched ragged streamers of smoke from the soot-streaked funnels of various vessels anchored to either side of the main channel.

Major Stoddard, G-2 to the Military Attaché's staff on duty at the United States Embassy at Ankara, tightened the belt of his trench coat. "Well, Jingles," he growled, "if we don't find him at the Three Moons I guess we'll have to admit he's got away again. You'd think that anybody as soused as he is would be a cinch to locate but, dammit, he's easy to find—like coal dust in an ink well!"

Miss Haïdi Lawson nodded, fetched a small, thoroughly exasperated sigh. "Hugh'd be far better off if he hadn't such a confounded long hollow leg." The girl's wide, rather full lips quivered momentarily at their corners. Moodily, she added, "During my brief but sparkling journalistic career I've known not a few lads who could tuck away corn squeezings, but never in my born days have I known such a zinc-lined, two-fisted drinker."

She fell silent because, whistling stridently, the Balata ferry suddenly churned close under the stern of a towering Greek freighter, then darted across the bows of a rusty Egyptian tanker before chugging on among moored vessels of every registry known to the Mediterranean and to the Black Sea.

"I still can't understand what's come over Hugh," Stoddard commented more to himself than to his companion, and his gloved fingers commenced to drum irritably on the deeply scarred rail.

The Lawson girl turned in his direction a squarish, rather dark-complexioned face. "I think I can, Ted. Let's diagnose his trouble as a case of aggravated disillusionment. After all, our pal North has fought hard in two wars and between them has been handed God-knows-how-many tough assignments. All of them he accepted because—because——"

"Because why?"

"Because, in his clever but charming way, he's sold himself on the idea of trying to help make this sinful old globe a more decent planet to live on."

"How d'you know?"

The Lawson girl dropped her gaze, flushed a little. "Because he told me so—among other things."

"And he's fed up, you think?"

"Yes. 'Now look at the damn' thing,' was what he said the last time I saw him."

Slowly the Intelligence Officer nodded. "Crack-ups like his follow every war, I expect, and the delayed action ones are the worst."

The November wind, veering suddenly, whipped over the rail a tantalizing whiff of curry, mutton and garlic from the galley of a little, broad-beamed Syrian felucca lying to port.

"As you say, Ted, it's a terrible thing, this crack-up of Hugh's. Praise God, I've never before seen anybody go so completely to pieces; and believe you me, around Trans-World Press and similar syndicates you can note some pretty spectacular mental and moral crashes."

Stoddard turned angular, wind-whipped features in her direction. "It's none of my business—I know, but you are, well, sort of gone on Hugh? Or is it my over-active imagination?"

Under the restless breeze light brown curls lashed softly at the smooth curve of Jingles Lawson's strong cheekbones as she started a quick reply, but instead, paused and smiled a taut little smile. "If you weren't poor Hugh's oldest friend in these latitudes I'd swear, Ted, that you, and only you, raise this gal Thursday's blood pressure, but—but cuss it, I guess I—I kind of get unglued inside when Hugh's around, and me a growed-up gal of near thirty. Silly isn't it? Silly, silly!"

Softly the girl's muscular but well-proportioned hand beat upon the rail, causing a bracelet heavily adorned by various golden charms to jingle softly to each impact. At grimy marks resultant on her brown suede glove, she frowned.

Fixedly, Stoddard considered the jet waters below. "Then I'm doubly unhappy over this miserable, bad business. Damn it, Jingles, come hell or high water, we—well, we'll somehow straighten him out." Almost savagely he added, "I've *got* to!"

"Yes, Ted, one way or another, Hugh must be persuaded, must be sold the idea of pulling himself together," Jingles agreed, wide blue-gray eyes suddenly meeting Stoddard's blue ones. "He's too damned fine, too kind and—and valuable. Well, you know."

"Yes, I know. I suppose you're aware that Hugh North's peculiar genius is for understanding how the minds of various foreigners work? He's invaluable, especially right now." Stoddard smiled a tight smile and pulled closer his faded trench coat. "Personally speaking, I've never served under a superior in this Army that I couldn't respect, even if sometimes it was quite a job; but there've been precious few I—I have cared about so damn' much!"

A group of passengers came wandering forward, among them a Persian in a round lambskin hat, a couple of khaki-clad soldiers, a pair of thick-ankled, black-browed Armenian girls and a gaunt *hamal*. The porter looked anxiously at the landing lights, hawked noisily and shivered under the cold wind. In the twilight the handful of passengers aboard the ferry looked chilled, impatient and hungry.

With exception of the soldiers and the two Americans, the passengers all appeared to be desperately poor. After all, neither the suburb of Balata nor Terestoni, its twin slum across the Golden Horn, could be described as better than sordid, urban drains designed to catch that polyglot riff-raff which came drifting towards Istanbul not only from the Black Sea, but from the Sea of Marmora, the Aegean and the more distant Mediterranean.

Presently Jingles tightened soft, brilliantly tinted lips, inquired, "When did you first notice signs of poor Hugh's cracking-up?"

Stoddard thought a moment. "Why, almost immediately after he turned up here in Istanbul, I guess. If only he weren't on leave, his sense of responsibility would help. Haven't you any notion of what's biting him?" Glancing sidewise he studied his companion more carefully than she might have suspected. "A gal, maybe?"

Her bracelet tinkled as, instantly, came the answer. "No. I—I'm very sure of that. Hugh's not the type to go over-board for a skirt, worst luck, no matter how fascinating—and he's seen the pick of the crop, I'm told."

"It's baffling." Unseeingly, Stoddard continued to gaze on this slender, straight-backed young woman. "For instance, long as I've known him Hugh has never gambled seriously—for money that is—now he's stupidly throwing away his pay and allowances. In case you don't know, the man hasn't any money he doesn't earn the hard way—'you'll never get rich,' as the song goes. Believe it or not, he's getting sloppy about his dress and drinking five times as much as he used to.

"As you say, Jingles, we've got to consider him as a—a sort of delayed war casualty. You won't believe it, but within the last two weeks he has insulted, offended or otherwise alienated all his old friends, except me and that's only because I won't let him." Stoddard's big gloved hands closed spasmodically. "Damned if he can shake me off without one hell of a battle. You see, I figure he's drunk himself really off his rocker."

"I agree. Sometime or other I expect all of us go through spells of disillusionment," Jingles observed, her gaze on the silhouettes of many slender minarets dominating the heights above the ferry landing. "I have. When my fiancé waltzed off with another gal I wanted to live in Portofino with an abstractionist painter, then I was all for eloping, sans wedding ring, to Ecuador with a flyer-of-fortune; all kid stuff, of course. Hugh's different, though. I tell you, Ted, suddenly something's gone sick inside of his nature."

"Playing around with the high brass and under terrific pressure long enough will drive anybody crackers," Stoddard commented. "I expect he's suffered just one too many double-cross from those amateur 'international experts' at the State Department and so-called policy makers in Washington."

In belated caution Stoddard cast a quick look about and was relieved to perceive that no one stood within earshot, but well away from the dilapidated craft's dangerously low rail.

When, presently, the ferry's whistle emitted a bronchial screech and the little vessel slid awkwardly into its slip,

various ragged figures materialized from among the shadows
of Balata shore and prepared to make fast the ferry's haw-
sers.

Incurious and indifferent to anything save their own affairs, the dozen or more other passengers pushed past the
two Americans, crowded down the gangplank and promptly
became lost among tall, crazily canting structures lining the
shore in disreputable array. It was Haïdi Lawson who, in
fluent Turkish, quickly established that Three Moons, a
café owned by one Vasil, was situated not very far away,
in the Street of the Red Pomegranate.

Stoddard stared at the trim figure in the brown tweed
suit, neat alligator shoes and small close-fitting felt hat,
the severity of which was relieved by a crisp little panache
of partridge feathers.

"Where'd you learn Turkish like that?" he demanded.

Her white and nearly even teeth flashed through the
gloom beyond the ferry slip.

"My father was a professor here at Roberts College—
and my grandmother was Turkish," she explained smoothly.
"I spoke no English till I was nine. Then I came home
with Dad."

As they swung along over slippery, ill-matched cobbles
he inquired, "What else do you speak?"

Quite serious was her manner as she countered, "If you
mean fluently, I speak Greek, Armenian, Bulgarian and
Serb—French of course." She shrugged. "Don't look so impressed. I'll bet yonder *majonaji* speaks at least three languages. Most watermen do."

"Well, I'm damned, and me proud of French and a res-
taurant-and-railway knowledge of Spanish and Turkish!"

"Bon soir." Beneath the dull patent-leather peak of his
képi a gendarme's heavy brows merged and below mustaches, as black and curving as a buffalo's horns, thick lips
contracted. He saluted carelessly. "What might the Effendi

and the Bayan be seeking in so squalid a quarter as Balata?"

"A friend," Stoddard informed in French tinged with a Nebraskan twang. "Have you seen anything of a tall, dark-haired American? He wears a close-clipped mustache, has a straight, thin nose and high cheekbones. He's quite lean and walks very straight." The Intelligence Officer's description was terminated by a snort.

"Vallahi! Have I not!" The policeman's manner underwent a noticeable change. *"Ey!* So you know of this wild man who is cursed by Shaitan with an insane passion for liquor?"

"Yes. We have come to bring him home. Where is he?"

In the light of a dim street lamp the gendarme's expression hardened. "At the Inn of the Three Moons, a most evil resort."

"Merci, then we'll be on our way." Stoddard smiled. It was a relief to learn that North was still at Vasil the Greek's.

"One moment, Effendi. To conduct so pretty a bayan into such a place as this Greek's café is no part of wisdom." Silver numerals on the police officer's shoulder straps glinted to a shrug. "None but riff-raff, *frengues* and rascals frequent this place. To gain admittance to the Three Moons will prove no problem," he predicted, "but to leave it is another matter."

Major Stoddard nodded. "I expect he's right. Wait for me at the ferry landing, will you?"

"Nothing doing." The Lawson girl's objection was as prompt as it was emphatic. "I've got into, and out of, worse joints than Three Moons plenty of times. Besides, Ted, my pet, Baby knows some useful, if nasty, tricks which come in handy come the goin' gets rough. Let's shove."

Watched by the gendarme, they set off among shadows, which grew ever deeper, and pungent odors of cooking— olive oil, fish, saffron, mutton and, above all, garlic. These had become mingled with a sour reek from open sewers and the unmistakable smell of rotting wood when Jingles pointed to a blue enamel sign.

"This is it—the Street of the Red Pomegranate." Stoddard found himself wishing for a certain well-weighted swagger stick at the moment reposing in his quarters over in Pera.

Every yard the pair advanced along the alley—no longer accurately to be described as a street—it grew muddier, narrower and darker. Only occasional rays of light penetrated behind the sagging jalousies of houses which canted so far out over this noisome passage that their roofs threatened to touch eaves. Numbers of mangey cats, angular through hunger and battered by warfare, darted across the couple's path or entered into querulous debates over desirable items of garbage. In a nearby dwelling a woman shrieked as in sudden pain until a volley of curses delivered in some dialect, unidentifiable to Stoddard, cut her short.

The wide-shouldered young officer halted. "Enough is enough. That cop was right. I'm going to take you back to the ferry."

In a small hard voice the girl demanded, "Since when has G-2 taken over the management of Trans-World Press correspondents? Besides, with or without you, Ted, I aim to find Hugh North."

"But Jingles, for God's sake—you can't; the risk's too great. You really mustn't go any further," he argued and placed an urgent hand on her arm. "Don't be foolhardy. Please listen——"

The felt hat swung in firm negation; once, twice. "I'm going on and you'll not stop me. You see, I've an awful presentiment that something bad has happened to Hugh."

Hard-faced, ragged and round-shouldered passersby, Albanians, Serbs, Greeks, Italians and Egyptians were among those nationalities which lurched or glided past the tall young man in the trench coat and this girl so trim in her brown tweeds. The former's eyes roved ceaselessly, probing the more dangerous-appearing entries and doorways.

Jingles cried suddenly, "There it is—that's the place."

"Where? I don't see any sign."

"There," came the impatient explanation. "Can't you see three moons painted on the wall beside yonder door?"

Stoddard drew a deep breath, squared his shoulders and, after a momentary hesitation, pushed open the café's portal. Immediately the ear-splitting blare of a radio playing pseudo-American jazz reverberated in the Street of the Red Pomegranate and a glare of over-strong and naked electric light bulbs dazzled the couple on the threshold.

"Sweet attar of roses!" grunted the Lawson girl when a rank miasma composed of patchouli, musk and extremely bad tobacco billowed into their faces. Unable for the moment to see anything, Major Stoddard halted, his large and compact figure nearly filling the inn's battered blue and white painted doorframe, and his strong features very red and shiny in this blaze of light.

The Three Moons Café proved to be quite small but crowded to overflowing by a clientèle which appeared as polyglot as it looked unsavory. Obviously, most of the brown-faced and uncombed patrons were sailors, fishermen and watermen of varying sorts.

Wreckage littering a small, zinc-covered bar suggested that, recently, it had suffered a furious assault; shards of broken pottery and brilliant splinters of glass dotted its dull surface or lay heaped in generous quantities about its base.

The first thing Stoddard saw clearly was a garish advertisement of "All-Nu-Fly Spray" before which stood a heavy, jowled individual in a striped blue apron. Every lineament of his shiny fat features was eloquent of suspicion and hostility. So deafeningly loud was the radio tune that those patrons who sat near it were forced to cup their ears in order to hear one another.

Almost without exception, everyone present turned and

stared. Stoddard's muscles tightened when, as his pupils readjusted themselves from the exterior gloom, he glimpsed, secured above the bar by Scotch tape, not only the usual crude and flyblown portraits of Kemal Ataturk and President Inonu, but also yellowed newsprint photographs of Marshal Tito, Gottlieb, Dimitrov and Ana Pauker. Everywhere scowls and frowns were in evidence, and several ragged figures muttered asides. Evidently Stoddard's American Army trench coat wasn't improving his welcome.

The patrons' pitch of interest increased, but a measure of their animosity subsided, when Jingles' handsome squarish face materialized on a level with Stoddard's shoulder. The dozen-odd, shapeless and raddled females present narrowed kohl-darkened eyes and stared. Some of these shabby creatures merely spat but a Cypriote harlot wearing huge brass rings in her ears deliberately flicked a cigarette butt at the girl in the doorway.

Stoddard strode forward and gazed calmly about him before demanding, "I am looking for the proprietor. Which of you is Vasil?"

Finally a gap-toothed French seaman grunted, *"Voilà,"* and jerked a spatulate, tar-spotted thumb towards a hairless, flat-featured fellow leaning over the far end of the small bar.

"Is there here an American, a black-haired man who drinks greatly?" suddenly demanded the Lawson girl in low-pitched Greek.

Vasil, a beetle-browed Levantine Greek—he spoke with a Smyrna accent she judged, denied having seen anything of an American of any description.

The patron of the Three Moons, Jingles quickly decided, would have won no beauty prizes even in a wrestling ring. Once upon a time he had suffered a blow so terrific that it had crumpled in one whole side of his saddle-hued countenance. In fact, because of a huge and pointed nose, flaring gray mustaches and tiny, bright black eyes, Vasil suggested nothing so much as a vicious and gargantuan rat.

As she stood there trying to choke down a series of smoke-induced coughs, the newspaper woman realized that the gendarme had not exaggerated. Lascars, Senegalese, Syrians and Egyptian merchant sailors were staring, casting frankly speculative glances that started at her ankles and climbed upwards. Faugh! The air was really vile. Could Hugh North really have gravitated into such a sink?

"Hi, you-all. How's about buyin' us a drink?" greeted an unmistakably American voice. "We're about broke."

Even while belatedly concealing the gold bracelet in her jacket's side pocket, Haïdi Lawson turned unhurriedly, noticed a scrawny fellow in a greasy sweat shirt entering from a side door.

"Sure thing." Stoddard was entirely companionable. "What'll you have? It's colder outside than a witch's bra."

"Is this old home week?" Jingles demanded. "What gives around here?"

"Anything. Call the tune, Sister, pay for it, and you can have it. 'Course Vasil's joint ain't no Ritz," called he who first had spoken, "but I've seen worse. Alberoni's the name, Sis, Sam Alberoni—from Hackensack, New Jersey." He beckoned with a grimy hand. "Come over and join us, we ain't proud."

"—That's mighty hospitable of you," Jingles cut in before Stoddard could object.

Followed by curious and often hostile eyes, the new arrivals, clean and distinctive as a pair of cedar waxwings among a flock of cowbirds, made their way among a scattering of unwiped tables upon which sheep's ear soup, pilav and *borek* noisily were being consumed. Alberoni commenced bowing in exaggerated cordiality from the corner table he was sharing with a powerful, light-haired young fellow who balanced a battered accordion on his knees.

"Jesus, it's sure swell to meet folks from home," Sam declared. "This lug with the squeeze box calls himself Pete Kuzak—he's from San Diego."

Kuzak nodded but made no effort to rise, only kicked forward a chair for Jingles' occupancy. Steadily, with neither approbation nor disapproval, the accordionist regarded the new arrivals.

Stoddard smiled, gave his name and offered his hand. "This is Miss Lawson—we're taking a look around."

"Slumming, eh?" Alberoni suggested. "Well, you've landed in the right place." Then, in an undertone, he added, "For Gawd's sake w'yn't you hide that bracelet sooner?" He beckoned Vasil. "Okay, Pop, set 'em up, five arracks, and see you pour 'em outa the good bottle, see?"

"Five?" Jingles queried. "The extra, I suppose, is for the Little Man Who Isn't Here?"

"That's fer Cap Larkin, he's went to the head——"

"Well, here's blood on the moon."

To Major Stoddard's lively but carefully concealed surprise there presently appeared, not the merchant skipper he had been half expecting, but a sharp-eyed, swarthy young man of about thirty. Curiously enough, he wore in the buttonhole of a gray flannel jacket an enamelled bar indicating his possession of the Distinguished Flying Cross.

"Howdy," he greeted then slid onto a chair and raised his glass. "Unexpected pleasure, Miss—Miss——?"

"Lawson. Quite a bistro, isn't it?"

"Sure is. Worst hellhole I've found this side of Port Said," agreed the red-haired young man, then relapsed into silence.

"Cap'n Larkin's a painter," Alberoni explained waving his glass, "when he ain't teachin' th' goddam Turks how to fly."

Stoddard was at pains to appear only mildly intrigued. "Oh, then I expect you'll belong to our Military Mission?"

"You expect correctly, Major," the flyer admitted, a trifle embarrassed it seemed to Jingles. "Off duty I like to drift around the seamy sections of this burg and sketch. You on duty here?"

Stoddard evaded a direct answer and was about to advance a cautious inquiry concerning North when Jingles said, "Say, Pete, you any good on that squeeze box?"

"They say so," grinned the young fellow in faded blue denims. "Why?"

"When it comes to a hot accordion I'm a real gone gal."

"Pete's the McCoy," Alberoni supplied, reaching for the dark green arrack bottle. "You've played with the best, ain't you, Pete?"

"That's so. I've played at the Plaza in New York, the Blackstone in Chi—lots of such joints, no kidding." His pale blue eyes sought Jingles' friendly gray ones. "Say, Miss, you don't know of a band could use me? I play the alto sax and trumpet, too."

"How come you're in a crum joint like this?"

Kuzak's broad shoulders rose under a grimy skivvy shirt. "Just tough luck, I guess. My old outfit got stranded in Athens and broke up. I signed on as steward on a Jewish refugee ship and hit the beach here."

"Hearing's believing. Let's hear you play," Jingles invited. "Maybe I *could* put you onto something—I know a few big wheels hereabouts." Stoddard could sense that, for all her careless manner, she was none-the-less working on the main problem.

Kuzak slipped tattooed arms through the accordion's support straps. He grinned and exposed a double row of strong white teeth. "Call the turn, Sister, and let's drown out these damn' foreigners."

"Suppose you hit me with 'Faraway Places'?"

Despite Stoddard's impatient glare, Jingles first listened attentively then enthusiastically, and ended by attracting the attention of the whole café by singing, and not at all badly, a couple of verses.

"Say," cried Alberoni, "know what? You've earned yer-self a drink. You're near as good as Lena Horne. Know that?"

"Thanks, Sam. How was I, Larkin?"

"Wonderful. Maybe you'll sing for our mess dance some night."

"Only if you hire Pete," she laughed. "By the way, Pete, suppose I land you an audition, where would I find you?"

After a nearly imperceptible pause the accordionist mumbled, "Why, here, I guess. I sure hope you can job me. I hate sea-sick passengers to hell and back."

"No promises, but I'll try. You know, Ted? Old Melek Effendi is throwing a plushy shindig for some of our Military Mission's top brass, come Wednesday."

Alberoni leaned forward, a half-rolled cigarette poised. "Who'd you say?"

"Melek Effendi, the tobacco exporter. It should——"

"—Say, Miss Lawson," Captain Larkin interrupted. "I've seen you before. Aren't you with a news syndicate, a newspaper, or something like that?"

"Yes. Right now I'm working for Trans-World Press, and have the last five years. At present I'm busy doing a series of articles about the emancipation of Turkish women. As if the world cared."

Kuzak was casual in the extreme while beckoning forward a slovenly, starved-looking waiter the hair of whose chest sprouted in dark handfuls through the front of a collarless and deplorably unclean shirt.

"This round had better be on me, boys," Captain Larkin announced over the renewed blaring of the radio. "I've got to catch the next ferry; damned bus back to the field won't wait."

Stoddard found himself wondering whether some subtle

signal had not been given, so promptly did Kuzak commence to secure the straps of his well-travelled accordion. He gulped his arrack then grinned at Jingles, sitting small and darkly handsome, before a dusty, whitewashed wall. "Guess I'll be drifting along, too. If it ain't too late I generally pick up a few piastres at those gin mills over in Galata. Sure hope I hear from you, Miss."

Presently the two pushed their way across the café and disappeared, but Alberoni lingered, fingering his glass. "Coupla nice Joes."

"Yes, nice Joes. Does Captain Larkin come in often?"

"I suppose so. He's nuts on waterfront night life. He wants to write a novel about it, sometime—so he says."

Stoddard now was more willing to linger because a rather sinister-appearing *yadekdji,* or boatman, clumsily was trying on a gray, snap-brim felt hat which, in its band, sported teal and pintail feathers very similar to those so favored by Hugh North.

After Major Stoddard had ordered a round of incredibly evil-tasting cocktails, Alberoni hunched far over the table and, through a miasma of arrack, muttered, "Bud, you look like a right guy—and you, Miss, are the swellest-lookin' dame I've seen in years so I'll tell yer somethin'. A while ago that damn' dogface, Vasil, lied to you. That guy you asked after is here, all right. He calls himself 'Nelson' and he's upstairs right now, and drunker'n ten boiled owls." Alberoni grimaced. "Don't know what's bitin' him, but for three days now he's been tryin' to drink this sink-hole dry and, till his dough began to give out, standin' drinks to all comers."

In Jingles' warmly brown cheeks spots of color appeared and brightened.

Alberoni's unshaved dark features contracted and he shot a quick glance about. "Yer friends of his?"

"Yes. We've come to fetch him away."

"If this Nelson guy ain't ready to go you'll have fun doing that. Jesus, I never seen a guy so damn' handy with his dukes!" Reminiscently, the seaman rubbed a set of skinned knuckles. "This afternoon some dicks and a gendarme tried to take away our pal, but Vasil and the rest wouldn't let 'em, account of, like I said, Nelson's generous and he still had some jack."

"Where is he?"

"What's it worth?" came the instant query.

"Two pounds Turkish enough?"

"Check. Come along, I'll show you."

"All right, Jingles, let's go." Stoddard picked up his hat pleased to notice that, so far as he could tell, the Three Moons' patrons had lost interest in his companion and himself.

The girl hesitated. "Before you try any rough stuff, you'll let me talk to him?"

"Sure." Stoddard smiled. "I'm bigger and younger, but I'd sure hate to risk a fast fall with him."

The Derelict

ANYONE who had known the invariably neat and healthily tanned Major Hugh North at all well would, at first glance, never have identified him with that unshaven and haggard spectre which glowered at the intruders across a greasy, crumb-strewn and bottle-littered table.

"Oh, no! It can't be——"

"Can't be wha'?" Panting a little, the apparition arose, attempted a little bow, then collapsed rather than sat back in its chair. " 'M honored, if it isn' the delectable Miss Lawson hersel'. Siddown, Ted—wha' for you bring Jingles to m' little party? Takin' up gate crashin', eh?"

Jingles gasped—and a small sound not unlike a moan escaped her. Obviously North's crisp, brown-black hair had not experienced the pressure of a brush for days on end, nor had he shaved any more recently. The tall and muscular figure's shirt was deplorable; it suggested that also it had served its owner as napkin, towel and handkerchief and had been slept in not one, but many, nights. Of the derelict's coat or vest there was no visible trace and, in place of a belt, a piece of dirty twine was knotted about North's abdomen. Dully, the drunkard's deep-set eyes swung towards that oddly assorted group crowding the doorway. No longer of their usual clear blue-gray, North's eyes more suggested pink than any other color and their lids were granulated, red and bloated.

The air in this sordid little room proved even more foul than that of the café. Hot and lifeless, it was heavy with a stench of stale alcohol fumes, cigarette butts and the reek of long unwashed clothing. A fat little man with a ginger-colored beard lay snoring in sodden slumber across a disordered and sagging bedstead.

At North's left, and eyeing the intruders with the furtive attention of a surprised alley cat, sat one of the dirtiest and most obscenely handsome females Ted Stoddard could recall having seen. On this Kurdish woman's forehead had been tattooed the conventionalized hand of Fatima; whatever else had chanced, North's companion had preserved an erect though heavy-waisted figure. Her wrists and ankles were slim and well formed.

"Please, Hugh, look at me." The Lawson girl's voice sounded a little choked. "Do you know me? I'm Jingles."

Slowly North's head raised itself, the silver patches above his ears glistening dully in the light of a feeble electric bulb. He got up once more, shivered violently two or three times, then remained swaying gently above the glass-littered table. Uncertainly, the renegade's gaze wavered from Stoddard, to the Lawson girl, and finally over to Alberoni.

"T' be sure, Jingles, darlin'—wan' you meet Yildiz—well-name' Star—Yildiz, meet Jingles—old pal of mine."

"Hugh——"

"Wha' you want?"

"Hugh, I want you to come with us——" Jingles cried. "You didn't let me finish what I wanted to say the other night."

"Tol' you and tol' you I'm finish' with you——" A small belch escaped the haggard figure. "—And all that. So wipe that silly hurt look off your puss."

"For God's sake, Hugh, don't talk like that!" Stoddard cried then started forward, but halted when North's hand shot out and closed over a bottle's neck.

"Ge' back! I like it here, an' I'm stayin'!"

A strained smile curving her wide, dark red lips, Jingles

motioned back Stoddard. "Please, Hugh, listen, for my sake and your own."

"Go 'way."

"I won't. You don't know what you're saying. You—you're sick."

"Sick?" A peal of dreadful laughter broke from the derelict, made the dark-faced slut recoil and clutch at her tarnished brass necklace. "Sure I'm sick—sick of so-call' democracy—sick of th' selfish hypocrites in high places—sick of our self-righteous American sham. Why don' we quit tryin' to buy respect from the worl'?"

"Easy does it, Hugh." Stoddard soothed and gathered himself. "You're coming with us."

Underneath the grimy shirt North's long and muscular figure contracted. "The hell you preach! Now get to the devil out o' here 'fore I throw you out."

For the first time desperation entered the younger man's manner. "Hugh, please listen. I simply *must* talk with you."

Waving his arms, the derelict shouted, "Talk! Talk! Tha's all us Amer'cans ever do—till it's too late. Me, I've struggled an' struggled—lots of times alone, to pull the U.S.A. out o' some bloody mess any idiot could ha' foreseen—and for what? Contempt, criticism and a general pushin' around. Now I'm tired, fed up. Nossir, ladeez and gentlemen, there'll be no more duty for li'le Hughie. Nossir, I'm just not goin'. 'Sno use. America's finish'—done for, only she don't know it yet." He shook a trembling fist. *"Now get out!"*

The Kurdish woman slipped off her chair in silence and, on blunt bare feet, darted past Alberoni to patter off down the corridor.

"Put down that bottle, Hugh." Jingles Lawson pushed by Stoddard, gray-blue eyes large with pity. "I'm your friend. Haven't I always been?"

"Sure—an' a damn' neat parcel, too."

The derelict lurched sidewise but recovered, straight black brows merging in a confused single line. "Why, wha' for you follow me 'round like this? Haven' I tol' you and tol' you I'm *fini, kaput, ausgespielt,* fed up?"

"Sure, but I don't believe it." Jingles laid slim, red-nailed fingers on his forearm. "Where's your pride? I thought you West Pointers had a lot of it."

"Sorry. Report it—Senior Cadet Cap'n——" He giggled a little. "Miss Lawson, an' you too, Ted," he waved a loose hand at the still motionless sleeper—an unlovely sight in sweaty suspenders, ragged trousers and horny bare feet, "wan' you to meet my good ol' friend, Hermann. Sing us a song, Hermann. *Ein Bruder Habe Ich Gehabt!* Wha's matter? Oh, still in the land of Nod. Pity, usually ol' Hermann's life of the party. Le's have drink, what say?"

He swayed under the orange-yellow bulb. They saw his grimy hand waver out and pick up a bottle which, proving empty, North hurled violently into a corner so forcefully as to shatter it among the jagged remains of several predecessors. "Ha! Here's one—you'll like this, Jingles—'s anisette—always liked anisette didn' you?" He lurched suddenly. "Damn' ship's rolling—mus' be in trough of the waves."

Casting Stoddard a single agonized look, Jingles ran around the table to steady the now violently swaying figure. "No, I don't want a drink—you've had enough for the three of us. Oh, Hugh, for God's sake stop it. *Stop it!* I simply can't bear this any longer."

Feet grated on the gritty flooring of the corridor. Kuzak's big, brutally handsome blond head thrust itself through the doorway. "Missed the damn' ferry," he announced. "What's going on?"

Stoddard turned impatiently. "He's gone ugly drunk. Either lend me a hand or leave us alone, will you?"

"Sure, sure!" agreed the accordionist. "But we won't get

anywhere. Old Nelson's been like this before—soused to the ears and ready to scrap like a stack of black tomcats."

"Darling, please come with us," pleaded Jingles, fighting down a violent revulsion at the foulness of his breath and unkempt condition. Softly she murmured, "Hugh dear, let's go away from here. We'll have grand fun—same as before. Remember the wonderful times we used to have in Washington and in Paris?"

The squalid figure steadied, then North's head inclined. "Sure I do; but—damn it, Jingles, as the cartoonist said, 'Them days is gone forever!'—along with truth, decency and American backbone. 'S no use—'sides nobody loves me." A tear slipped out of the drunkard's eyes and dripped off the strong black bristles on his chin.

"Oh, but Hugh, you're wrong—so very wrong! I—I'll prove it. Come back to Pera with Ted and me, won't you?"

"Like hell I will, *ma petite*. Me, I'm finish' with sham, stuffed shirts and protocol an' the goo' old U.S. Army. Me, I'm for real people—the—the"—he wavered, grinned vacuously at Alberoni and Kuzak—"people who really do the worl's work. So, my lovely, pale-handed scribe, you can take all your white ties, embassy dinners and—and stuff 'em. I been wrong; I been wastin' my life a long, long time, yessir, Ted. An' you, Jingles, you can write in your nex' dispatch—only place a fellow can find real truth, friendship or honesty is—is in a joint like this."

He hiccoughed, cast a blear-eye look at the sleeper who suddenly rolled over and commenced a stertorous snoring. "Sure, at the Three Moons Vasil and his boys cheat and rob, but at least they le' you know what to expect. If Alev there on the bed aims to knock your block off, or Murat downstairs figures to carve you up a bit, why they set right out to do it—don' claim it's all in interests of science or some God-given mission. That's proletarian honesty—an' I like it. Tha' right, Sam?"

"Yes—that's right. They call their shots 'round here," Kuzak agreed.

The drunk mumbled on the bed and his mouth fell uglily open. The Lawson girl was trembling now, and her eyes filled.

"Looks as if Alev really shouldn' have put *raki* on top of *kidusch,* even if he has lived in Brooklyn," North gravely assured Jingles.

The accordionist up-ended the last bottle containing any liquor and, grinning, said, "Jeeze, Mac, gotta hand it to you. Sam and me seen you drink four guys down and yer still kicking."

The line of Stoddard's jaw hardened as he crossed to North's side, took him by the forearm and said in a low and urgent tone, "Hugh, you must listen. Something's come up —something terribly, *vitally,* important. Do you hear? I —I've got to talk with you for about five minutes—out in the open."

"Well, go ahead—we' all frien's here."

"No, it must be in private——"

"The hell with you, Mister." Alberoni's heavy black brows merged. "Leave Mac alone. He's enjoyin' himself here."

"Oh, Hugh dear—please, please do as Ted asks," Jingles pleaded, mouth held near to North's ear. "Can't you see Ted's right? Please, you used to, well, to like me so, didn't you?" The shaggy head inclined. "Well, if I count for anything with you, please come and listen to Ted." She forced a tremulous smile to her shiny dark red lips. "Besides, you promised to beau me to Melek Effendi's party—remember?"

"Get somebody else. There's plenty of men ready and eager."

"No. I am counting on you, Hugh; you gave me your word, you know."

North stared into Jingles' steady gray-blue eyes—so nearly

the color of his own—as if he had never seen her before, then seized the anisette bottle, shook it and took a tremendous swallow. Said he, wiping his mouth on the back of a trembling and unwashed hand, "Jingles, m'dear, hope your chances of gettin' into Heaven are better'n my showing up for tha' rat race you're talkin' about. Can't you understand? I'm through—tired, disgusted and sick to death with the old racket."

The Lawson girl flashed Stoddard a fleeting wink. "Okay, then you're through with the Service and your old friends." She slipped a slim arm through his. "But I'm not going to go without saying 'goodbye'—the way I want it said. No harm in that, is there?"

"No, I guess not," sighed the scarecrow figure. "I—I guess I'm—kind of in love—or was."

"Then come with me, Hugh. I won't keep you from your friends here very long."

"Don't listen to the broad," Alberoni growled, but Jingles paid him no heed.

"Just five minutes, dear. I promise I won't keep you any longer. Okay?"

"Okay." North shrugged and swayed in Sam Alberoni's direction. "Sam, you order up some more anisette—Kuzak, le's have some more sweet melodies when I ge' back. An', an' see'f you can fin' that black-eyed wench I was talkin' to. She suits me fine. Everything in its proper place, eh, Kuzak? Cheerio! Cheerio! Cheerio!"

He reeled towards the door.

CHAPTER 3

Shadows beside the Golden Horn

ON A PIER piled high with lumber and estimated by Stoddard to jut sufficiently far out into the water to eliminate any chance of eavesdropping, the three halted. Being coatless, North began to shiver under that cold wind now blowing steadily up the Golden Horn from the Sea of Marmora. "Le's get in the lee o' that shed."

"Thanks for coming along." Haïdi Lawson summoned a tight smile, pressed North's hand, then through the starless gloom cast Stoddard a significant glance. "Well, boys, have fun."

"Wha'? You're not goin', Jingles?"

"Me, I've got to get back over to Pera and cable a dispatch before eight. Hugh, I'll expect you to escort me to Melek Effendi's dinner dance. No. No excuses. Remember the 'officer and gentleman' stuff. Goodbye, Hugh dear. Hope your hangover won't be too God-awful." Hurriedly her lips brushed the long bristles darkening his lean jaw.

Viciously the wind whipped North's dark hair about his forehead while his hand described a loose semi-circle.

"See you later!" Trim, silken ankles flashing, the girl's straight young figure set off towards that cluster of glaring electric bulbs marking the ferry slip.

"As a certain wise old *hodja* observed th' other day, '*Wallahi ajaib*'. 'Man is but a frail caïque gripp' by th' irresistible currents of Fate.'" He giggled, then sat down rather heavily on a stringer and briefly concealed his be-whiskered face between grimy hands, but, through his fingers, North's gaze followed that slender, brown-clad form.

Stoddard watched Haïdi Lawson out of sight, grunted, "Yonder goes an extra-fine sample of what we raise by way of women in America. Incidentally, Hugh, you'd do right well to remember so."

"I do, but—but, but damn it, there aren't enough like her." Slowly the derelict passed a trembling hand over his forehead, pushing aside the wild black locks. By the light of a distant street lamp Stoddard was dismayed to see how thick and swollen were his companion's eyelids, and that the familiar sharp outlines of his almost Indian-like cheekbones had become blurred by dissipation.

The sound of a native orchestra's tinkling *ude* and deeptoned *darml*—drum—reverberated in that restless blackness beyond the pier.

"Well, Hugh—will you listen to me?"

"You're wastin' your time, Ted," North grunted, at the same moment staring dully over his shoulder at a tangle of lumber beyond the shed; he was quite sure that something considerably larger than a stray cur had settled into position there. "'S cold here, colder'n a Congressman's conscience an' I'm gettin' thirsty. Wha' you want?"

Incredulous, profoundly shocked, Stoddard stared on his companion. "Great God, Hugh. Where's your pride, your decency? Your patriotism?"

The older man's voice grew harsh and carrying as he struggled to his feet. "If all you're goin' to do is preach I'm goin'. Already told you I'm through with th' Army, with th' States and that poor decadent joke of a thing called democracy."

"For God's sake, man, don't raise your voice."

"Why?"

"We're too close to shore. Mustn't be overheard. There's tremendous—critically important news."

The thin wail of a ferry whistle, followed by a dull churning as of backed propellers, reached the two men on the timber wharf.

"Maybe you've been out of the picture long enough not to know that, during the past week, the Soviets have been raising holy hell in the United Nations." The Intelligence Officer lowered his voice. "Yesterday their representative threatened an ultimatum to the Security Council."

"'United Nations?' Tha' poor, pitiful symposium of stuffed shirts and starry-eyed idealists! Ha! Ha! and ha again. Th' Soviets believe wha' they preach, know wha' they want and—and—how to get it."

"Shut up, you damn' disgusting sot!" snarled the Intelligence Officer in sudden exasperation. "I'm trying to tell you that an outbreak of World War III is entirely possible at any hour. We've been so warned at the Embassy. Dear God, the pressure is becoming unbearable; from the Ambassador down, our Embassy staff hasn't had any rest in days; our Military Mission went on twenty-four-hour duty three days ago. Our fleet in the Dardanelles is being reinforced by every available vessel."

"Wha's at th' bottom of all this excitement?"

Nearby a dog set up a startled yapping, yapping that caused every cur in the nieghborhood to raise a sympathetic clamor.

"It's a new and very deadly weapon the Russkie's are known to have perfected just recently."

"Deadly?" North's gaze again sought the lumber pile.

"It moves the atom bomb down to second place. You recall the great purge of the Red Army top brass last September?"

"Yes. Joe's buddies made th' mistake of figuring him too old, an' tried to take over." North coughed, blew his nose between his fingers and stared dully at a freighter nosing into her berth at the Naval Arsenal docks across the river.

"Well, they didn't pull it off. Marshal Stalin's a wonderful man—greates' leader in the world."

Stoddard's hands closed convulsively. "Better stow that kind of talk. Remember you still hold a commission in the United States Army."

"Th' more fool I. Well, wha' about th' purge?"

"Remember Air Marshal Vassily Kravenko—the one they liquidated about the twenty-second of September?"

"Kravenko got what he deserved," North declared emphatically. "He was a Trotzkyite."

"For God's sake keep your voice down," rasped Stoddard. "In Washington, before you went on leave, were you briefed concerning 'W' weapons the Soviets have been developing?"

" 'W'—weapons?" For the first time a trace of interest appeared on North's haggard, dimly-seen countenance. "Oh, yes—they're a series of—of long-range, guided missiles, aren't they?"

"Check. They're all dangerous, damnably so, but one of them designated as 'W-3b' is reported to be the deadliest engine of destruction ever invented. The 'b' you'll recall stands for bacteriological?" Stoddard's gloved hands tightened again and he peered anxiously at the shadowy outlines of his companion sitting slumped on a decaying log. "As you know, we've already developed our own 'W-b' missiles which are generally conceded to be superior—with the exception of one all-important element; it's called a vari-phase, multi-jet ejector unit. Our designs are reported fair but not satisfactory."

"Tha's too bad; an' all those bright boys at Aberdeen an' down in th' Virginias drawin' their pay ever so reg'lar."

Stoddard's breath came in with a rush. "Good God, can't your damned, rum-soaked brain work any more? You know even better than I that, in the next war, bacteriological is going to leave gas and the atom bomb far behind. They're both comparatively localized weapons, whereas these new cultures can kill everything for miles in all directions—crops, animals and people."

North's narrow head swayed. "Look, we're being spied on—see yonder? Biggest damn'd proletarian cat I ever seen. Ho! Ho!" Sure enough, a large tomcat appeared, scuttling in startled fashion out of that pile of lumber which previously had attracted the derelict's attention.

Desperately, Stoddard continued. "Yesterday the Military Attaché received a signal saying that, beyond question, Soviet engineers have completed satisfactory tests on their vari-phase multi-jet unit. Their 'W-3b' missiles are expected to be put into mass production immediately. You know their estimated range? It's *four thousand miles!*"

The Intelligence Officer's voice grew harsh. "So now you see why we need you so damned badly. You're just about our last and only hope of securing a certain set of their multi-jet drawings." The Intelligence Officer's fingers closed hard on North's forearm. "Hugh, if we can't lay hands on that set of drawings, and apply them to our otherwise superior missiles in one damn' big hurry, we feel certain Russia will launch an attack on the West. She's been having too much trouble in the Satellite countries—and at home—to wait any longer. Her attitude in the U.N. proves what I say. Right now we won't stand the chance of a snow bird in hell of stopping her before she rapes and ruins France, England and the Benelux countries."

"Yours is a ver' interestin' an' pathetic appeal," North grunted, blinking owlishly. "Used to fall for a spiel like tha' —but never no more. Me, I'm tired." North delved in his back trousers pocket and produced a small bottle from which he drank thirstily. "Here's to sense an' social justice." When he waved the flask under Stoddard's nose, the younger man's temper so flared that he slapped the bottle far out over the jet waters.

"Why, damn you for a meddlesome bastard!" North snarled and tried to rise. Stoddard, however, easily pushed him back, then bent menacingly over the sprawled figure.

"I hate to admit I was wrong about you, but I am. You're a damned disgrace to your country and a traitorous son-of-a-bitch to boot. You can go to hell and stay there!"

Casting on the fallen figure a final furious glance, Stoddard wheeled, swung off towards the ferry far too angry to note that, from behind a stack of lumber sidled a furtive figure. Stealthily, the shadow commenced to close in upon him.

Once the two men had become lost to sight a second shadowy form emerged from the gloom behind the shed and paused, bending over the babbling, inert figure there. Presently the new arrival squatted on his heels and, over the steady droning of the wind, urged softly, *"Tovarich,* let me help you back to the Three Moons."

CHAPTER 4

Signals from Washington

A SUBTLE yet recognizable atmosphere of tension pervaded the Consulate General of the United States high on its hill in the Pera Quarter of Istanbul. Clearly revealed by the briefly bright sunlight of mid-November, four persons sat in Consul-General George Albert's office, by various means betraying acute and apprehensive uneasiness. The Consul-General leaned slowly over his desk to address the girl who sat straight-backed before him with fingers nervously kneading a smart suede leather handbag held propped upon her knees.

"Think back, Miss Lawson," he begged. "Try to remember every last detail of what you heard and saw at the Three Moons. Are you sure, for instance, that Major Stoddard at no time gave even a hint of what he intended to do, or where he intended to go after this interview with North?"

Razib Albey, Chief of the Turkish Army Counter-Intelligence, shifted thin shoulders beneath a gray worsted jacket that could have only been cut by a sound British tailor, and fixed alert and liquid dark eyes upon that slender figure before Mr. Albert's desk. "Yes, Bayan, please, any small hint in that direction would be of the greatest assistance to me and my men."

His hand crept up to tug absently at a small and curving black mustache. "For an Army officer and an American, especially an important official, so completely to vanish is without parallel in my experience."

"Two men have disappeared and Major Stoddard was not

the more important, either. Let me see." Briefly, Jingles Lawson closed her eyes. "No, I believe I have told you every last, even the tiniest, detail that I can recall. I'm sure Ted made no mention of his intentions, and please recall that it's essential in my profession to observe and remember things." Hopelessly she turned to a thick-bodied figure seated to her left. "Tell me, Colonel McKenzie, haven't you really had any word of Major North?"

Slowly he shook his head. "For thirty-six hours now Colonel Razib, the secret police, our own Military Police and Intelligence agents have been raking every quarter of this city and following up anything that suggested a lead." He sighed, spread large hands flecked with brown splotches. "For all we have been able to ascertain, North and Stoddard might have gone to Mars. Otherwise, the last time we can be certain of their whereabouts was when you left them talking on that pier."

"You found no trace of them at the Three Moons?"

Razib Albey's lean dark face contracted. "Despite, er, urgent persuasion, that fellow Vasil denied that your men ever returned to his café. I fear that he is telling the truth."

The Lawson girl's slightly full lips flattened. "What may have happened is—is just too horrible for imagining. Can't anything further be done?"

"I wish there were," came Colonel McKenzie's grim comment. "His disappearance at this time is nothing short of disastrous."

Razib Albey's dark, carefully manicured hands described an arc eloquent of hopelessness. "Bayan, this matter has received my complete personal attention. Since Colonel McKenzie here," he half bowed towards the American Military Attaché, "informed me of Major Stoddard's disappearance, he and I have watched our best interrogators question those two so-curious Americans named Samuel Alberoni and Peter Kuzak."

Mr. Albert interrupted, "What about this Captain Larkin Miss Lawson has mentioned?"

It was Colonel McKenzie's turn to be embarrassed. "I'm afraid there's no lead in that direction."

"And why? What was he doing at a crummy joint like Vasil's?" the Consul-General wanted to know.

"It happens that Larkin is A-2 of our Military Mission," McKenzie explained steadily. "He was—er, on duty."

"I see. That let's him out, I suppose." Mr. Albert leaned back and nervously wiped tortoise-shell-rimmed spectacles. "Still I wonder. Are you very sure he's all right?"

"There is no doubt he had no part in this business," McKenzie explained. "He was seen on the Terstaneh ferry while, by Miss Lawson's own account, she and Stoddard were still at the Three Moons."

That his Excellency Colonel Alev Razib of the Turkish Counter-Intelligence was exceedingly troubled, and that he was considering his reputation at stake was patent.

"A most perplexing business this," he growled. *"Vellahi Ajaib!* This Balata Quarter is, and always has been, a spawning ground for trouble, a refuge for criminals, Communists, spies and rogues, therefore by custom I remain unusually well informed as to what transpires there. I confess myself mystified, gentlemen, that two officers of a most friendly Power should thus vanish without a trace."

The Lawson girl got up suddenly, walked over to a window and stood staring with miserable eyes at the magnificent sunlit panorama sweeping away into the distance. She took in nothing of the sparkling blue of the Bosphorus, of the famed Leander Tower standing on its islet in the distance. Not even the fascinating and compelling mosques and palaces adorning Seraglio Point could capture her attention any more successfully than could the graceful minarets and dome of the majestic Saleimaneh Mosque. She even failed to notice the slow progress up the Straits of a huge American airplane carrier and her attendant cruisers and destroyers.

"Poor Hugh," she was thinking. "If only we'd come out here together. Wonder what sort of rotten deal they gave you, darling, back in Washington? Oh, if only I knew where you are, my dearest, if only there were something I, or any of us, could do." It was difficult to fight down a series of sobs, to restrain the tears struggling to fill her eyes.

Colonel McKenzie sighed and slowly rubbed one hand across the back of its companion. "And I had hoped to have some good news for Mr. Spencer by the time he gets here."

Explained the Consul-General to Razib Albey, "The ultimate purpose of this meeting is to confer with our First Secretary. His Excellency, Ambassador Welton, is having Mr. Spencer flown over from Ankara. He should arrive at any minute." Again polishing his speckless glasses Albert appealed, "Mr. Spencer, I have been informed, will pose us—Colonel McKenzie and me, that is—some very critical questions. Isn't there any form of encouragement that I can give him? To say that both our State and Defense Departments are profoundly exercised and alarmed would be a gross understatement."

The Turkish officer arose, a small spare figure in gray, and took a quick turn down the office's gray-blue rug. "Please, Mr. Albert, be good enough to assure Mr. Spencer that, had His Excellency the President of this Republic suddenly become missing, nothing more could be done than has been done to find him."

Razib paused, first cast Colonel McKenzie a penetrating glance, then eyed the girl standing so motionless at the office window before he said, "Do not delude yourselves, gentlemen, that we of the Secret Police have failed to perceive the true and disastrous significance of these disappearances. How else can one estimate such events in the face of the so-grave present international disputes? Rest assured that our Foreign Office is no less alarmed than your State Department over the Soviet insolences of the past few days."

The speaker's light voice rang out, filling the Consul-General's comfortable ork-panelled office. "You have merely to consider that we, not you, will be the first to suffer in the event of a Red surprise attack! Therefore, as quickly as I receive intelligence—even the merest hint—as to the fate of these two unfortunate officers, you may rely upon it that you will hear instantly." Razib Albey drew himself up, clicked his heels to the two men and then bowed stiffly to the Lawson girl. "If I need to call upon you later, Bayan, where may I find you?"

"Either at the Trans-World Press office or at the Khamoun Apartments in the Rue Sakak," came the instant reply. "Of course, I'll do anything—*anything* to help you. Is there anything more, Mr. Albert?"

"No, Miss Lawson. Thank you for coming and—and try not to worry too much. Surely something will turn up before long."

Nodding farewells to the others she turned and hurried from the room, her neatly shod feet flickering briskly towards the door. "Try not to worry." The words rang like an evil chorus through her head. "Try not to worry," and right now Hugh North's weighted body might be lying in the slime at the bottom of the Golden Horn—a stretch of water that, during its long history, had received and concealed so many pitiful victims.

Colonel Razib was the next to take his departure amid an atmosphere of unrelieved gloom.

Once the door closed, the Consul-General reached over to select a perfecto from a box of cigars at his elbow, then over the flame of his lighter his smooth and rather plump American business man's features tautened as he treated Colonel McKenzie to a penetrating look. "Well, let's have it. What is the truth about Major North?"

McKenzie grunted and stared hard at the engraving of George Washington above Albert's semi-bald head. "I presume you've heard what's being said?"

"Yes. And not from just two or three sources, either. The diplomatic and military people here in Pera as well as Ankara believe that North has blown his top over something and has sent in his papers."

"In other words he's become fed up with our side?"

"Yes. Do you think that is true?"

"It begins to look like it," returned the Military Attaché after a momentary pause. The speaker settled deeper into his chair, pulled out a pipe and absently commenced to load it.

"D'you know, Mr. Albert, that girl's right. Stoddard is— or was, an excellent Intelligence officer, still his sort can, and will, be replaced. But the loss of Hugh North's services at this precise moment is, well, calamitous." As he spoke his eyelids lowered as if to inspect the match he had just ignited.

The Consul-General sat back in his upholstered swivel chair and his fingers tightened against its arms. "You've read the State Department's comments on the latest U.N. crisis?"

"Yes. There's no denying that the Reds are becoming unbearably truculent; possibly through duress."

"You mean their subject peoples have grown restless?"

"Yes. Stalin's régime just about now is finding out what they could have learned years ago through a study of unbiassed history."

"And that is?"

"That the Czechs and Poles, not to mention the Balts and Finns, are experts at the art of resistance. They know now that the Soviets have lied to them about the rich rewards bestowed by Communism; this is especially obvious when they take a look across their borders and see what's going on in Marshall Plan countries. You see, Mr. Albert

——" The Military Attaché broke off when the telephone jangled at the Consul-General's elbow.

"Yes, the Colonel is here," said he uneasily. "Please show Mr. Spencer right up."

Presently strode into the room a brisk, spare man of about forty in a black Homburg hat and a velvet-collared, black cloth coat, both of which he removed at once. On a rather short nose he wore a pair of rimless pince-nez; the violet-colored rosette of the French Palmes Académiques was in his buttonhole and a mechanical smile beneath his neatly-trimmed blond mustache.

"Ah, there, Colonel McKenzie, so glad you're already here. You're well, Mr. Albert?" From beneath the clamp afforded by his arm he removed a briefcase as he said in a crisp Harvard accent, "Well, gentlemen, I trust you have some good news for me, because I have none for you."

He studied the two a long moment then seated himself. "Um. I deduce that you haven't. That's bad, very bad, because during the past twelve hours the Secretary of Defense has been raising holy hell and, well, there is no telling what will happen in the next few days if——" His eyeglasses gleamed as he cast a quick look at McKenzie. "—Has Mr. Albert been fully briefed concerning the matter of the W missile drawings?"

A little stiffly the Military Attaché shook his head. "No, sir. I have not been authorized to go so far. But I have explained enough for him to appreciate the enormous significance of the matter in question, as well as the difficulties under which we labor. Personally, I believe that you should explain. Mr. Albert must be made to appreciate the utter gravity of this situation. Not since the fall of France has the World faced such critical days."

C. Poindexter Spencer nodded. "I concur, Colonel, but suppose you tell him. You know how much he already knows and I don't."

Puffing irritably at his pipe, Colonel McKenzie arose, tightened a belt over an ample abdomen and commenced slowly to walk back and forth under portraits of various renowned Presidents. "As you already have been informed, Mr. Albert, the W missiles are long-range projectiles having to do with bacteriological warfare, a form of warfare which has been developed to such a point that, if they're used, there won't be much left of either combatant."

"Yes, you've already told me that," the Consul-General said in a low voice. "I've been losing sleep ever since."

"Tell me, Mr. Albert, do you recall a member of the Soviet Supreme Command named Kravenko?"

"You mean that Air Marshal of theirs who got himself, er—liquidated about two months ago?"

"Yes. As usual there's more to the story than appeared in the A.P. report. Kravenko belonged to a clique on the Soviet Supreme Command who, realizing the real war potential of the Atlantic Pact nations, favored concluding an understanding with the West. Someone betrayed the clique, with the result that three marshals and I don't know how many generals were arrested and promptly executed by the MVD. All save Kravenko, that is."

Albert's pale eyes narrowed. "What happened to Kravenko?"

"He got away for a while because," the Military Attaché smiled a little, "G-2 was fortunate enough to plant a very able agent on the Air Marshal's staff back in '47; a chap called Walewski. As I said, our man Walewski managed to warn Kravenko, and together they tried to fly from Russia. Through sheer ill luck their plane became grounded in bad weather; the alarm was out and Kravenko was recognized, but they got away again and made for the Iranian border on foot." The room became a pool of silence broken only by the impatient honking of cars in the Avenue de Pera. "As Kravenko foresaw, he hadn't a chance of escaping so, just before the Secret Police grabbed him, the Marshal gave Walewski a microfilm of the varied-phase multi-jet mechanism drawings."

"Multi-jet mechanism?" quietly inquired the Consul-General. "What's it for?"

"The W-3b missile—one we have not yet been able to perfect to our own satisfaction," McKenzie explained absently, brushing pipe ashes from the lapel of his rather sloppy gray checked suit. "Anyhow, Walewski took the microfilms and by some miracle managed to get away. Being intelligent, he reversed the direction of his flight."

"How do you know?"

"Because, less than a week ago one of our agents in Greece picked up a faint signal from him. They spotted Walewski as being somewhere in Bulgaria—we've agents there, too, you know. Unfortunately, the message faded out towards the end so we're in the dark as to where he is or what he intends doing. Worse still, that was the last communication we have received from him."

Colonel McKenzie shot the impassive First Secretary a quick glance, and his hands, plump and splotched with brown freckles, tightened momentarily. "Now, perhaps, you can imagine just how disastrous North's degeneration and subsequent disappearance are? You see, he knew Walewski intimately—understood his ways of thinking, as well as his usual tactics under tension. It was said North could almost read his mind."

C. Poindexter Spencer drew long legs under him, straightened in the deep green leather upholstered chair.

"The loss of North is deplorable for yet another reason." He shot a penetrating glance at the Consul-General. "We are convinced in Ankara that our old enemy Gramont is directing Soviet espionage efforts here in Turkey, as well as in the Balkans."

The Consul-General's silvery brows rose a fraction of an inch. "Gramont? Who the devil is Gramont?"

"A very interesting social phenomenon—and a most menacing one, may I add." Precisely, the First Secretary seated himself, lifted the knees of his trousers in order that their knife-sharp creases might not become spoiled.

"Gramont, my dear Albert, is a little-known American traitor. I believe it to be no understatement when I say that this man is a king-pin in the Soviet Hate-America offensive."

"The hell you say! But why isn't he better known?"

"You'll learn in a minute," Spencer told him, and helped himself to a drink of water from a carafe on Mr. Albert's desk. He remained silent a moment, occupied by that same view which had attracted Jingles Lawson.

McKenzie's pink-lidded eyes blinked slowly like those of a large gray tomcat drowsing before a fire.

"Under what name or under what cover story Gramont now operates, we simply can't find out. You see, he's a highly intelligent and well-educated young fellow. Wish to God I could lay my hands on him; the bastard's caused our Near East Bureau more real grief than all the rest of the MVD lumped together."

"What about this traitor? Who is, or was he?"

C. Poindexter Spencer's eyes sought the engraving of George Washington and lingered on that sternly serene countenance.

"Our subject was born Benjamin A. Gramont—curiously enough, the A stands for Arnold—quite a coincidence, eh?"

Swift recognition entered the Consul-General's manner. "You mean Ben Gramont, the son of that Wall Street broker? The one who went parlor pink while still in college?"

"Yes, he's one and the same. Well, Ben was just about to graduate from one of the more famous Ivy League colleges," McKenzie cast a wry smile at C. Poindexter Spencer, "when World War II broke out. To everybody's surprise young Gramont immediately put in for the Army Air Force, giving out that he'd seen the light and was admitting, that although America wasn't perfect by a long shot, it remained, nevertheless, the best place on the earth to live.

"Since young Gramont once was supposed to have held a Communist Party card, we in the Counter-Intelligence Corps naturally kept a close eye on him, but couldn't find a thing to criticize. His record at the flying school in Miami was excellent and, proving himself a brilliant flyer, he led his class at graduation. Accordingly, he was given a clean bill and confirmed in a post requiring considerable responsibility."

That hoarse and long-drawn roar typical of passing jet pursuit ships momentarily checked McKenzie's discourse; all three men shifted uneasily in their chairs.

"Well," continued the Military Attaché, "Gramont was ordered to England for duty with the Eighth Air Force and, as a major, was placed in command of a squadron of B-17's. No one felt suspicious when, on almost his first mission—it was one of those shuttle jumps to bases in Russia—his B-17 disappeared. After the ship had remained unreported for the usual period and none of the crew were heard from, the bomber was presumed to have exploded in flight. Families were notified in due course, including old Mr. Joseph Gramont, who was heartbroken."

Nodding, Mr. Spencer delved into his briefcase, invited grimly, "Go on, Colonel."

"Purely by chance one of our C.I.C. lads recognized him in Paris, apparently on leave from Frankfort; I say by chance because he was using another name and apparently he'd been in a plane or a car crack-up for his face was so changed that only someone who had known him very well would have recognized him.

"As it was, Gramont calmly denied his identity, but one of our Intelligence lads obtained a set of his fingerprints and confirmed the identification. Since then he's been recognized, sometimes as a civilian, sometimes in American Army uniform, at a half a dozen trouble points such as Trieste, Iran, Vienna and Berlin. Always this deserter and traitor was equipped with perfectly forged AGO cards, travel orders, ration books, et cetera. Mr. Spencer can tell you how well the MVD tends to such details."

The First Secretary sighed. "—And we once imagined the Gestapo and Abwehr pretty clever! Well, Mr. Albert, the fact is that we have reason to believe that this fellow Gramont is here in Turkey, either in Ankara or Istanbul, doing his best, not only to sabotage the work of our Military Mission, but to obtain every bit of intelligence he can, while at the same time crippling the Turkish and our own Counter-Intelligence." Delicately he joined fingertips. "The only officer who possibly could have brought this traitor to account now has vanished—*spurlos versenkt,* as it were."

The Consul-General frowned, pulled at the lobe of his ear. "Suppose we manage somehow to contact North, can anything be done to win him back to duty? Surely you, Colonel McKenzie, who have known poor North all these years, could accomplish something?"

The Military Attaché shrugged and looked miserably unhappy. "I doubt it, sir. You see I happen to know that he was given a pretty raw deal by the War Department after V-J Day. They failed to approve his permanent promotion to colonel."

"Why?" burst out the Consul-General. "How could he have been treated so shabbily?"

"Possibly because, back in 1939, he made some unpopular predictions that came true and made certain Senators and an Assistant Secretary of War look like assorted kinds of lop-eared jackasses. After all, a West Pointer who graduated when he did, and especially one with his brilliant and extraordinarily successful record, should rate better consideration."

"God bless my soul! Why, why such ingratitude is incredible, unforgivable!" Albert burst out. "Didn't they at least award him some decorations?"

"Oh, the French and the British came though handsomely enough." A slow sigh escaped Colonel McKenzie and a slight plucking became evident at the corners of his mouth. "I believe we gave North something really magnificent—like the Bronze Star—while plenty of cooks and truck drivers were being decorated with the Legion of Merit. It was all too raw for words. So now if he's fed up who's to blame him?"

"No one," succinctly agreed C. Poindexter Spencer, "but that doesn't answer the Ambassador's question of how are we going to find Walewski and stop Gramont?"

"Isn't there some way of identifying Gramont?"

"Not without careful inspection. We've learned that since his residence in Moscow he's become a past master in the art of impersonation; in addition he speaks several languages without the trace of an accent. He's North's own equal about attention to detail. Despite everything Colonel Razib can do, his police agents, being too damned anxious to avoid any affront to our forces, are almost hopeless in coping with anyone wearing American uniform."

Spencer cut in, "What especially worries his Excellency is that Gramont's here to make sure Walewski fails in contacting Colonel McKenzie, or any of our agents for that matter. The logical points——"

A sharp, imperative jangle of the telephone caused all three men to start. Mr. Albert's hand shot out. "It's for you, Colonel."

"Yes? Who is this?" Pause. "Oh, never mind that. Yes. Go ahead." Pause. *"What!* You saw North in Galata? You're sure? My God, that—that's wonderful. Yes. Report to my office at once!"

CHAPTER 5

The Blue Villa below Bechic Tash

To MAJOR HUGH NORTH it seemed that a whole platoon of imps shod in red-hot shoes were executing close-order infantry drill across his cranium. Whether his translation from complete unconsciousness to semi-awareness required seconds or hours he had no way of determining, the lassitude upon him was so overpowering that a great effort seemed required even to part his eyelids. He reclosed them promptly because of strong sunlight which, slanting in through arabesque apertures in the wooden blinds, lent to his simple blue and white striped cotton bed cover a mottled effect. These bright spots were no more painfully brilliant than the little meteors whirling about in his eyeballs.

"God! How can a single head hurt so much?" he wondered, then tentatively flexed the fingers of his right hand.

He groaned because of that sharp pain which shot up his wrist and ascended into his shoulder. From further cautious experiments he deduced that sometime in the distant past he must have suffered a very thorough beating. At the drawing of each breath his whole right side ached dully, persistently, and this difficulty he was finding in opening his left eye was due to a huge swelling above its brow. Subconsciously he realized that only a series of kicks could have inflicted such damage. It proved terribly disconcerting to retain not the least impression of where he now found himself nor of how he had come here. Feebly at first, but then with increasing determination, he attempted to penetrate these mysteries.

"Judas in the foothills," he reflected, "if this kind of hell is what an alcoholic goes through it's a wonder there are so many of 'em."

After forcing himself to draw several deep breaths despite the anguish it caused his battered ribs, he felt a trifle more rational and a steadily increasing number of phenomena penetrated his consciousness.

For instance a steamer whistled surprisingly close by and, somewhere inside this house, a radio was playing an aria from "The Master of Clamecy" by Dimitri Kabalevsky. North became interested to note that the first of his senses to return to full efficiency was that of hearing; for instance he was able to recognize the distinctive lap-lapping sound of water beating against some vertical surface. Next he identified the crowing of a cock, the raucous cawing of a crow in high flight, the soft rushing of wind through many bare branches.

Next his olfactory senses commenced to contribute items of information gradually filling in that uneasy blank which, at the moment, represented his mind. For example, the pleasant aroma of boiling coffee mingled itself with suggestions of some female's delicate and faintly erotic perfume. On the other hand, the sharp reek of a disinfectant permeating the distinctive sweet-sickly odor of dried blood, too, proved even more noticeable to his nostrils.

"Um, an interesting combination—gives one to think."

At length the inert figure risked opening his eyes once more and found that he could see much more clearly. "So my ears weren't lying," he breathed when a shimmering reflection dancing on the ceiling attested that his present quarters lay indeed near water of some kind. "Must be in the afternoon," he thought, "so this room faces west."

Again the crowing of a rooster, so characteristic of all quarters of Istanbul, sounded off to right.

At the cost of no little effort North managed to raise his battered head and focus his eyesight enough to ascertain that the room he was occupying certainly could not have been that of a man. Frilly curtains of a gay red and white Anatolian peasant pattern modified the bad design of very tall and narrow windows, while a painfully *moderne* dressing table supported row on row of cosmetic bottles and jars, a box of cleansing tissues, toilet set, and a small facial vibrator equipped with a pair of rubber rollers. Across a chaise longue lay flung a pair of gunmetal-hued stockings, a black garter belt and a pair of decidedly frivolous black silk and lace panties. Next to a *moderne* armchair stood a small table supporting some magazines, a half-consumed box of nougats and a tray of red-smeared cigarette butts.

A cool wind beating in through the slightly open window further refreshed him and partially cleared his brain. Presently he was able, by a great effort, to raise himself on one elbow until he could catch his reflection among snapshots and invitations fringing the dressing table mirror.

"God above!" Incredulous, he stared at the black-haired, swollen-faced and bloated image of himself. "You'd frighten a werewolf and turn the Horror of Glamis green with envy."

Then he commenced softly and painfully to chuckle; a most gorgeous shiner was disfiguring his left eye and cheek and there was a ludicrous-looking lump rising at the middle of his short and normally straight nose. Then he made a significant discovery. Someone had washed his face and head—had brushed his hair into place beneath a wide bandage designed to secure a compress over his right ear. Um, from the way that organ ached it must have suffered a cut or at least a deep scratch.

By contrast, the objects supported by another table set by the head of his bed were starkly severe; upon it had been arranged with military neatness several rolls of bandage, some spools of adhesive tape, a pair of surgical scissors, a jar of compresses, some bottles of antiseptic; even a curved surgeon's needle threaded with silk lay ready for use in a glass container.

"Somebody," he assured himself, "has certainly gone to a hell of a lot of trouble over me. Why?"

By running his tongue about he was infinitely relieved to discover no evidence of broken or missing teeth; that *was* a comfort. All his life he had retained an almost pathological terror of losing teeth. For a spell he was forced to lie back, struggling to retain that tenuous grasp on consciousness.

Presently he roused to the sound of a door opening, then a strong feminine voice inquired, "Velvalee? You home yet?"

There came no reply but a cat meowed and, as that door down the hall closed, the sound was drowned out by the booming whistle of an ocean-going steamer. This time the signal sounded much louder than before.

North peered through one of the larger arabesques in the stout-appearing shutters and, to his amazement, discerned glimpses of a liner's superstructure, of masts and a towering gray and red funnel sliding by not two hundred yards distant! He was still trying to identify the probable location of this house when a patter of light feet along the corridor apprised him that he would not remain alone much longer.

Presently the door to his room creaked and, through nearly closed lids, North witnessed the entrance of a rangy, rather muscular young woman. Hatless, she was wearing a thick gray sweater over a tomato-red blouse. The day must have been cold and windy for the newcomer's rather pointed features glowed with color and her brown hair, short-bobbed though it was, lay tumbled all over her head.

"Hello," she greeted, pulling off fur-lined gloves, "so you've finished listening to the birdies? Well, it's about time."

After a brief disappearance she returned minus the sweater and wearing a business-like blue wash apron. For a long moment she lingered above the bed, dark blue eyes narrowed as in speculation, then plucked a clinical thermometer from a glass of disinfectant, shook it expertly, then warned, "Don't talk—yet."

North had just time to manage a caricature of a grin before, none too gently, this brisk young woman forced the thermometer into his mouth. Fingers yet retaining a chill from the out-of-doors closed over his pulse and she gazed steadily at a large, man-sized wrist watch.

Looking up, he received an impression of straight, rather domineering dark brows that almost merged, but didn't quite. The very dark blue eyes were small but fringed with some of the longest lashes North had ever beheld while the nose was straight, pointed and distinguished by thin, pinched-looking nostrils. His ministrant's mouth was triangular, smallish and a bit severe at its corners, an effect relieved by a perceptible dimple in the small, firmly rounded chin.

At length the young woman literally dropped his wrist onto the bed and, after reading the thermometer, remarked quite dispassionately, "You've sure got the constitution of a gorilla."

For the first time—in how long?—Hugh North spoke aloud, if quite weakly. "If it's you who has patched me up and cared for me—I—well, I can't begin to thank you. It was you?"

"It was," said his nurse, straightening the bed cover. "Guess I've done all right, too. Brother, you sure were a terrible sight when they lugged you in."

"They?" he mumbled. "Who brought me here?"

She shot him a quick and subtle searching look. "That for the moment is unimportant. I suppose you have a name? What shall I call you? A nickname will do for now."

"Why not 'Barleycorn'?" North suggested. "Please, can't you find me a highball somewhere? I'm drier than a temperance lecture and feel like death warmed over."

The girl's expression so hardened as to suggest menace. "Now get this, Mister, from now on you're going off the stuff, understand? For a good while, anyhow; for keeps, if you've the wits God gave a titmouse." Almost angrily she advanced to the bedside. "I suppose you don't yet realize that you came within an ace of kicking in through alcoholic poisoning? No, my fine fuzzy friend, you're going on the wagon and there'll be no jumping off to pick up the whip until you're really Hugh North again."

"Why did you ask my name just now?" he croaked and rallied every bit of wariness he could muster.

"To learn how far you'd recovered," she informed him evenly. "No, there's no mystery. You mentioned your name while you were playing tag with those lavender baboons and chartreuse tarantulas a while back."

"Oh." He smiled up at her as well as he could through cracked and swollen lips. "And what may I call you? Dea Hippocrata perhaps?"

"Don't try to be funny," she snapped, looking quickly aside. "We'll say that my name is Murfee, Miss Esmé Murfee to you."

"Yes, Miss Esmé Murfee, and what do you do?"

"I do Red Cross work at the U.S. Mission Infirmary—for fun—here in Istanbul—I study painting," she replied a shade too promptly and wiped off the thermometer before restoring it to its glass. "I live in this house with my friend, Velvalee Petrie—this is her room—and her brother, Stephen—they're Southerners."

North, finding need for quick reflection, was relieved when Miss Murfee announced, with that brisk authority of a trained nurse, "I'm going to prepare you a meal. You're not to thresh about, get up or get yourself excited. Although you've managed to escape any broken bones—God knows how—you've been a lot nearer death than you realize. What with that going-over you took and all that hooch in your system, you ought to be just a sad sweet memory to your friends."

"Please, Miss Murfee," North pleaded, touching his bandaged head, "I feel terrible. Won't you let me have just one, even a very little, shot of something?"

The tall severe figure paused in the doorway. "No. If you've the least gratitude for what Velvalee and I have done for you, you'll quit begging for liquor. You see, I know about you and the noisy nuisance you've made of yourself around town recently."

"Oh—oh. Excuse please. Hadn't realized my binge had been celebrated with neons. Did I make much of a fool of myself?"

Miss Murfee hesitated, looked hard at him. "Well, you said some mighty injudicious things for an American Intelligence officer. Now be quiet and rest, we'll talk later."

He felt really pleased to relax—by God, he really was pretty weak and on the verge of vertigo. The problem presented by Esmé Murfee needed cogitation all right. "So she is a Red Cross worker? Um. No wonder she applied bandages and dressing with such sureness. Red Cross worker perhaps, but, brother, if she's not a trained nurse too, I'm in worse shape than she thinks."

After a little he opened his eyes and stared blankly at this little room's rather gaudy wallpaper of cabbage-sized red roses on a canary background.

"How in hell did I get here?" he pondered. "Let's see how far back I can remember for sure. Um. It was at the Three Moons—Ted Stoddard and Jingles showed up. Wonder if I put on a convincing act?" The patient's powerful chest lifted to a quick sigh. "Poor Jingles. When she walked off she certainly looked as if she'd just had her wind knocked out." His swollen lips formed a sad smile. "Funny how I keep thinking of Jingles. Wonderful sort; game for anything, but with no nonsense about her. *Verdad, es muy mujer.*"

Odd, how readily he could visualize her, browned, her breath-taking lovely figure revealed in the Chevy Chase pool by a tight, white silk bathing suit; laughing and very striking in a yellow and black evening gown at the Brazilian ambassador's ball; smart in that black, tailored suit she'd worn to the Mayflower for their last lunch in Washington.

Somewhere in the depths of this house sounded a rattle of dishes and the occasional clank of a saucepan.

The pain induced by a deep sigh made him wince. "And to think you used to be pleased about the amount of liquor you could tuck away without getting silly or sick! 'Swelpme! It's going to require a bit of doing to keep up this act; even the smell of a drink would make me retch!"

Once the patient consumed a supper which proved at once tasty and nourishing, Miss Murfee considered the row of bottles at his bedside, selected some tablets from one, then dissolved them. "Drink this, please."

"I'm not going to," he announced, "not until I get a slug of whiskey. Damn it, as a trained nurse you should know that a drunk has to be eased onto the wagon. I—I'm—my stomach is simply afire."

Over this severe young woman's strongly modelled but definitely handsome features crept a curiously taut expression and her lips tightened until most of their color vanished. "Listen to me, Major, I'd hate to hurt a man when he's down," her voice was as sharp and unsympathetic as that of a drill sergeant, "but if you don't drink this solution I'm going to give that bruised side of yours such a jab that you'll scream. Do as I say. It's for your own good."

North actually downed one swallow, but allowed a second to remain in his mouth while making so artful a pretence of swallowing he effectively deceived his jailer, as he was beginning to think of Miss Murfee. The first instant she turned aside, North raised his pillow and spat out her bitter-tasting dose. Fervently, he prayed that the fluid might not penetrate the mattress.

After an interval of convincing duration he deepened and slowed his breathing and feigned an increasing drowsiness. Once he appeared to be unconscious, Esmé Murfee came to stand so close by his bed that he could identify her perfume as something banal like "Evening in Paris" or "Quelques Fleurs."

"Eight grains of seconal, my troublesome tall, dark and handsome souse, should knock you out for at least ten hours."

To the patient's disgust Esmé Murfee plucked the lingerie from the chaise longue then, selecting a newspaper, lit a cigarette and settled herself to a leisurely perusal of the *Orient News*.

Meanwhile sleep tugged so hard at North's eyelids that presently he dozed.

CHAPTER 6

Wind off the Black Sea

Noise caused by a poorly secured shutter tapping against its casement was the sound which at length roused Major Hugh North. Slowly at first, then with a rush, he regained consciousness, but the throbbing of his head and slow unremittent pains of his bruised body made his return to wakefulness a tedious affair. How long had he been dozing? The luminous hands of a clock on the dresser indicated the hour as ten-fifteen, nearly five hours!

He became aware then that a violent gale was rushing in the partially opened window, filling the bedroom with that biting chill and penetrating dampness which is peculiar to the Dardanelles region. To North's immense satisfaction he discovered that, during his sleep, a considerable amount of strength had returned to him—far more than he had any right to expect.

For instance, when he sat up he was delighted to find that his head no longer swam. To reassure himself that he was indeed no longer dreaming he passed his hand under the pillow. "Good enough!" That spot upon which he had spat out Esmé Murfee's potion was still damp. How fortunate that the enigmatic Miss Murfee hadn't exercised the basic precaution of making him speak after his second swallow.

While sitting on the edge of his bed and recruiting his strength he thought back. Last time he'd pulled that dodge had been years ago—back in Washington during his investigation of the Legation Murders. He thought briefly of

Vanessa Byrne—that lovely, copper-haired Irish girl who had clung so steadfastly to a corner of his heart until, at length, she had vanished during World War II. Odd, how much Jingles and Vanessa resembled one another. It bore out his deep-rooted conviction that men fall in love with a certain type and quality of woman rather than with the individual girl.

The air was so cold that, presently, he stood up, steadying himself by the cast-iron and brass footboard. The floor wavered beneath his bare feet a while, then steadied.

Like soldiers responding to a call-to-arms his faculties commenced to rally. The pajamas he was wearing must belong to—what *was* that name? Ah, yes, Stephen Petrie, Velvalee's brother. Velvalee! Lord what a saccharine, maudlin name to wish onto a defenseless infant!

This promised to prove as curious a ménage as he'd encountered in many a blue moon. Esmé Murfee? He frowned through the wind-filled darkness. If he were any judge, Esmé was American all right; her clothes, speech and manner left small room for doubt.

"Um. I'd surely like to meet the Petrie gal and her brother. Are they also Americans? Their family name, of course, is Scotch."

Odd, this having absolutely no understanding of those circumstances under which he now existed—not in the least a pleasing sensation.

He drew a deep breath and tried standing without support but was forced hurriedly to clutch at the bedstead.

Presently he wobbled across the room and closed the window, then pulled aside a shutter which admitted a measure of starlight. By marshalling Fact against Premonition he was able to gain something like confidence in the immediate future.

"After all," he reassured himself, "for all her frozen-faced

manner, this Murfee wench has done you nothing but
kindnesses—so far."

Now that the closed window had stopped that restless
wailing of the wind he felt better, more able to concentrate
on immediate problems.

The newspapers Miss Murfee had been reading lay beside
the chaise longue so, with the help of a match, he was able
to arrive at the date; November thirteenth. Great God! His
last recollection had been of Armistice Day, November
eleventh! So he'd been two and a half days completely out
of the picture? A sudden doubt seized him. Fifty-six hours
was a very long time for anyone to remain in an alcoholic
stupor. Had he really been passed out all this time—or had
someone given him soporific injections?

He sat down quite heavily on the chaise longue, absently
curling his toes away from contact with the chilling tiles of
the floor. In fifty-six hours so much could have happened!
Was this lapse of time disastrous, or had it been a wise and
supremely subtle investment? There could be no insight on
that point for some time.

For a long while he listened, but hearing nothing, struggled upright once more. The floor still rocked gently as,
very cautiously, he groped his way to that tall and narrow
window. The night was clear and cold; myriad stars were
shining and the wind was beginning to sigh through the
bare tops of a big tree standing in the center of a small garden which, apparently, was all that separated this dwelling
from a body of black, light-dotted water so wide that it must
be either the Bosphorus or the Golden Horn.

Ha! The distinctive two long and two short flashes of that
lighthouse located on Leander's Island informed the pa-
jamaed figure that this house stood on the Bosphorus, not on
the Golden Horn nor yet on the Sea of Marmora. Because
the light flashed far off to his right he deduced that at
present he could not be far from the Dolmah Baghcheh

Palace and in either the Top Hané or the Bechic Tash quarter of Istanbul. The sudden screeching wails of a pair of tomcats beginning to exchange insults directly beneath his window startled him, added to the granulations already engendered by the chill on his skin.

By thrusting his bandaged head far out of the window, he further oriented himself. The now familiar lights of Scutari over on the Asiatic shore and those of the ferry landing place at Kuzgunjuk afforded him a rough basis for triangulation by which he determined his whereabouts as on the Strait shore, below the Mejidieh Mosque and very near to the Cheragan Palace.

It proved comforting to have settled at least two important facts—the date and his approximate whereabouts. Next job was to determine whose guest he was, their purpose in bringing him here, and the *quid pro quo* for all this efficient, if not loving, attention.

All at once he fell to wondering what steps Stoddard might have taken. Poor Stoddard, how grimly shocked and disappointed he'd been during his final disillusionment. Yes. He certainly had been shaken by Ted's unwillingness to be convinced of his old mentor's downfall. Certainly a five-course dinner at the Semiramis, plus an impressive array of choice liquors, were the least he owed that loyal young friend.

Because a sudden nausea gripped at his throat he lingered a little longer, listening to the gradual acceleration of this bitter wind off the not-too-distant Black Sea. How had Alex McKenzie been making out these last two days? "Bet Washington's been riding him until he's on the edge of a nervous break-down. Must contact the poor devil at the first possible moment."

Teeth chattering gently he speculated on Walewski— what incredible courage, what chrome-steel nerves a fellow had to have, even to contemplate such an assignment in the heart of the Soviet regime. Was the agent still living? Did he still possess the microfilms? If so, in what direction would that amazing young genius at espionage be likely to head?

A burning impulse to get ahead with this assignment so stung North that, stealthily as a lynx on the prowl, he commenced a search for his clothes—if the rags he had been wearing could be thus dignified.

In the room's old-style wardrobe all he discovered were quantities of frilly dresses, gowns and suits—none of expensive quality—probably belonging to the unknown Velvalee. Come to think of it, why should he have been put to bed here, rather than in Stephen Petrie's quarters? Briefly, he pondered the point but could arrive at no explanation. Still he could hear no sounds from within this curious little villa.

" 'Twould seem further explanation is in order," he decided. Drawing a deep breath and with bare feet that shuddered at each contact with the icy floor tiles, North made his way to the bedroom door, which he was fervently thankful to find unlocked. Apparently Miss Murfee was reposing complete confidence in the efficacy of her dose of seconal.

Exercising infinite care, the shivering patient gradually eased over the knob until the door catch came free then, setting his shoulder firmly against it, he eased it open, inch by inch, and tried to fight down the dizzying effect of sharp stabs of pain in his side.

Presently he emerged in a short and very narrow hall that was indirectly illumined by light shining around the door of a room at its far end. By listening intently he now was able to catch the sound of voices, faint and unintelligible, as a sort of obbligato to the keening and booming of the wind.

Cautious investigation of the two doors immediately to the left of his own revealed that these opened into a bathroom and another bedroom. This villa, North decided, apparently had been constructed for some minor diplomat about the turn of the century but had been none-too-tastefully renovated not long since.

A glance out of a window to his right afforded view of a small courtyard in which stood a pair of inexpensive-appearing automobiles.

Treading warily, silently, and pressed flat against the hallway's inner wall, North continued towards his left until he became confronted by a staircase leading downwards. Heart pounding, he strained his hearing and found, though the voices were much more audible, that he could not yet distinguish either what was being said, or even the language employed in what seemed to be a basement room.

No alternative suggested itself to inching his way downstairs—a hollow-eyed, bandage-crowned figure in lurid green and white pajamas. A huge, smoke-gray Persian cat appeared from nowhere, considered him suspiciously then vanished towards the street level.

Once he found himself standing in a small over-furnished living room he became aware that the furniture was a wild conglomeration of Turkish and Occidental styles.

At the foot of the stairs he paused because someone—a woman—had begun to speak angrily. Was it imagination, or did the voice sound like that of Esmé Murfee?

"—That stupid greedy rat! You're positive Alberoni phoned the Consul's office?"

"Of course," came a faintly familiar masculine voice. "He admitted it."

"Why?—*Seemed* trustworthy." Due to the wind's roaring only an occasional word from below reached the anxious listener.

"—Wanted—chisel—dollars reward. Tried to get away with——"

"Dead? Where did——"

"—He's done double—never find the body——"

"That's good—won't tolerate another failure!"

Then for several minutes he could catch nothing; the cat reappeared and sat considering.

A man's unfamiliar voice suddenly grated. "Dammit, I tell you this bastard's lying to us, and by God, I intend to get the truth out of him."

The semi-recognizable voice snapped, "Get on with it, then."

"Oh—*non! Non! Je vous en prie! Je ne*——" The plea ended in a hair-lifting squeal of terror.

Gingerly, North opened the door to a second staircase which led below. What the devil was going on downstairs? The voices, he realized, sounded in some chamber located beneath the living room, a chamber which, because this villa was built into a hillside, apparently fronted onto the Bosphorus and that little, high-walled garden he had peered into from his bedroom. Like most such walls it had been effectively protected by a crown of spikes and broken glass.

There followed a sound as of several ringing slaps and a gasp of pain.

"I swear I'm not lying! I followed him a long way," babbled a voice in frightened French, "then I lose him, I admit. *Nom de Dieu!* I couldn't help it. I only know that he saw Skoularis——"

"—Which Skoularis?" cut in Esmé Murfee's metallic voice.

"The one who calls himself Phoebus."

"You lie! He's not here."

"I tell you I did see him and I lost him among the crowd on the Grand Rue de Galata. I'm sure he was making for the *cache* at——" North could have cursed because the place name became lost in the sudden rattling of a shutter.

Was it in any way possible to look into that lower-level room? It would be an ineffable advantage to see, and possibly to identify, the various actors in the scene being enacted. There were, he deduced, at least five persons down yonder. Esmé Murfee and some other woman who might, or might not, prove to be Velvalee Petrie, the man being questioned and at least two male inquisitors. He thought he would recognize their voices—years in Intelligence work having lent him that faculty—but he needed to hear more examples of their modes of speech.

The deep voice snapped, "All right, Nestor, since our friend Bernard insists on being stupid, we've no choice but to coax him more urgently."

A frightened squeal escaped the man called Bernard when he was ordered to rise.

"All right, Peter, take him into the work room," Esmé's voice was as trenchant as a well-sharpened scalpel when she added, "Remember, we're the ones who'll catch hell from Georgei if you don't get this Frog swine to tell us where Captain Larkin went."

There ensued the sounds of a small struggle then a door closed with a bang and, for a moment, only the whine of the wind and the roar of waves beating against the northern shore of the Bosphorus filled the house.

The second woman's voice inquired in liquid Spanish, "You are sure, Esmé, the patient is asleep?"

"Sure, he's out like a light. I dosed him with enough seconal to knock him cold for at least ten hours. Now what about——"

A scream, muffled but edged in agony, was barely audible in the lower regions of the villa but, because the "work" room must have been insulated, the cry barely penetrated to the listener.

His mind, North realized, once more was functioning as of custom—with the precision of a first-rate calculating machine. "Better get back to bed," he warned himself, "you're getting faint——"

But at the front door sounded the jingle of a key ring and an oily *cluck!* from its lock. A momentary paralysis of complete indecision gripped North, then he lunged across the living room, knocked over a chair and halted before a small portable bar. Lights flooded the villa's hallway and living room as the new arrival flipped over a switch. Swaying, black hair tumbling wildly above his diadem of bandages, North was up-ending a bottle of whiskey when, carrying a snub-nosed automatic of impressive calibre, there appeared from the hall a tall young man resembling nothing so much as the star half-back of some Middle Western college. He was noticeable chiefly because of his powerful build, crew hair-cut and a crooked scar that flashed across a stubborn-looking jaw like a streak of dull red lightning.

North hugged the bottle to himself, turned, greeted, "Howdy, friend, I was fixing a little drink. Had to."

The newcomer's dark brown eyes narrowed in the pink rectangle of his features as, under his dark blue topcoat, broad shoulders bunched themselves.

"So you're at it again?" he growled. "Put that bottle down, you goddam lush. Esmé? Esmé! Where in hell are you? Your bloody patient's loose."

When, once more, there arose that very faint screaming, North betrayed no indication whatsoever of having noticed it. "Don't need to act so snotty—I only wanted a single drink," he remarked, reluctantly replacing the bottle on the bar. "Who are you?"

"I'm Steve Petrie," announced the other, pocketing his weapon and stepping closer, a menacing twist in his lips. "Say Mister, just how long've you been down here?"

North swayed, managed a weak giggle. "Not long enough to get me a drink. Easy, friend—my head hurts like hell. For God's sake let me have just one little slug."

Furtively, North's hand had crept out towards the Scotch bottle. "Lay off, you." The young giant slapped North's hand aside. Surprisingly small brown eyes narrowed, Petrie then inspected the bottle's contents; he seemed to be satisfied.

"No. Get back to your room, don't let me catch you out of it again or you'll be nursing some more sore ribs." He paused, then eyed the tall, bandaged and pajama-clad figure pausing uncertainly beside a floor lamp. His manner relaxed. "Okay—I won't be rough on you—but you see we've got plans for you which we don't want spoiled by your getting cockeyed again. Now get!"

Switching off the lights, he followed North back to his room. "Now stay there, damn you." He paused then inquired, "Where are the others?" so quickly that North almost replied, "In the basement," but the Intelligence Officer caught himself in time and substituted, "I don't know, I haven't heard them, mebbe they're asleep or have gone out."

The door lock clucked ominously, then the man called Steve Petrie went striding off.

CHAPTER 7

Velvalee Petrie

IN A WAY it was a relief to be back in bed, decided Major
Hugh North. His whole body was dangerously chilled
while his various hurts ached with renewed poignancy, especially his lacerated left ear. One thing, he intended to find
out. Whom had he to thank for this beating? Retribution
was in order to those who'd so cruelly maul a helpless man.

All the same, this wasn't an especially pleasant interlude;
this shivering and listening to the gale scream across the
Bosphorus. What would happen when that hard-faced
wench, Miss Murfee, learned of his prowl below stairs?
Um. What was being done to the wretch called Bernard?
He wrote down on his mental slate every name he could recall, including that of Phoebus Skoularis, who very likely
must be a Greek.

What were his own chances of being hauled down to that
sinister little chamber beneath the living room? Thank
God, he'd had the presence of mind to go for a bottle. In
sudden panic he tested the damp spot beneath his pillow.
Although it was much drier, anybody could have detected
its presence. A measure of reassurance returned to him
when no one appeared. A little feverishly he tried to fit the
sum of his knowledge into a recognizable pattern.

The presence below of Kuzak, the accordion player, lifted
a veil of ignorance, that and the reference to Alberoni. The
latter, he judged, was no longer a factor—*had he succeeded
in reaching the Consulate?* This precious pair had been almost constantly at the Three Moons. Um. Had Stoddard

been shrewd enough to size up Vasil's filthy little establishment for what it really was?

What of Esmé Murfee? There was a rarely enigmatic personality for you. Undoubtedly she was American born and bred and had been a trained nurse—probably in the Army Medical Corps. Could she belong to that small group of Wacs, Red Cross workers and Army nurses who, for a variety of reasons, had refused to return home with the victorious American forces? The more he considered the possibility the more he felt convinced that this Murfee girl had much in common with certain disoriented and unhappy females of that ilk; one came across numbers of them around Paris, in London and, most frequently of all, in Italy.

The *click-clock* of a key turning in its lock roused him from a deepening lethargy. Well, here it came! What would it be like to be beaten with rubber knouts, to feel needles driven under his fingernails—if the questioners felt disposed to be gentle? A sour fluid invaded his mouth. Torture, psychologically, was something he wondered whether he could brave. Thus far, beyond a ghastly session in a cellar in Shanghai, he had escaped even the threat of torment. Distinctly, he recognized moisture breaking out on his palms, his face and his thighs. It would prove futile, of course, but he tried to postpone the inevitable by feigning sleep.

His ears told him, surprisingly enough, that but a single person had entered the room—a woman. After closing the door behind her she paused and must have been peering down at him. Was it Esmé? No telling because he kept his eyes tight shut and tried not to breathe too slowly—many a shammer had fallen into that error.

A light at the dressing table flashed on—a low lamp with a rose shade. Shadows darkened his eyelids as the intruder commenced moving about. Gently, he raised the lid of one eye a fraction of an inch and got the surprise of his life. Yonder, garbed in a simple gray tailored jacket and skirt, stood no threatening Amazon, but a very petite and shapely young woman whose back was turned as she commenced to unbutton a white silk blouse. The light, striking upwards, became entangled in candy-blonde hair trimmed into a shoulder-length, page boy bob.

Breathless, North watched this girl, now clad only in brassiere, stockings and some rather severe scanties, cross to a closet and from it select a peignoir of pale blue and yellow. Pink-white arms and thighs flashed when, securing the gown about her, she returned to the dresser and took out a nightgown. Suddenly she turned and cast him a searching look. He thought he got his eyes shut in time; apparently he had because, humming very softly, the girl he was certain now to be Velvalee Petrie seated herself and peeled stockings from limbs that would have delighted Billy Rose. How very tiny she was. Again the apparition arose and paused before the dressing table long enough to permit him to view (in silhouette) an erect figure stimulating to even so battered a creature as himself.

Once more the small, yellow-haired figure turned quickly and glanced in his direction then, to his surprise, she collected mules, her nightgown and a jar of cold cream. After turning out the light she left the room and locked its door.

"Well, I'm damned," breathed North. "No Esmé, no roughnecks; just what in hell is this?" He was still wondering when, perhaps half an hour later, he heard the door open once more and recognized the soft rustle of silk.

He sensed Velvalee draw near, caught a whiff of some rather sweet perfume, then a strand of hair brushed his cheek and a soft voice murmured in his ear. "Goodness, Major, what does a po' gal have to do to make you wake up?"

North took care that his simulated return to consciousness should be convincing. The sweet scent grew stronger then cool fingertips brushed his brow and the girl whispered, "Wake up, Major, but fo' God's sake, wake up quiet."

"Wha'—oh——" He stifled a groan.

"There, there, Sweetness—if you're not the most beaten-up boy Ah evah did see! Even so, Ah think you're awful sweet and the handsomest man evah. Please wake up, Big Boy, 'cause Ah've got you a little snack to eat—and, if you won't tell anyone—just the tiniest shot of bourbon."

That Southern accent was so deep that, for a little, North wondered, but it proved to be convincing and he recalled hearing such broad inflections among Alabama and Mississippi troops.

"Thanks. Ah, that's better!" A damp cloth was, with consummate delicacy, brushed over his lips, his eyes and then his forehead. He stirred, sighed, then opened his eyes to look up into large, dark-rimmed eyes the color of very clear old sherry.

"Ah've just come home from the Air Base. Ah'm a special secretary and night operator theah. Ah reckoned we might eat a bite together." She laughed a little. "You see Ah saw yo' eyes open a while back.

"There now." She switched on the dresser light again but dimmed it with a kerchief before bringing a small tray to his bedside. Sure enough, there were ponies of whiskey upon it as well as an assortment of sandwiches.

"Here's lookin' at you, Major." The girl held out her glass as he roused onto one elbow.

The liquor burnt furiously, but went far towards restoring him. North batted his eyes several times. "Thanks, Miss——"

"Miss Petrie—but yo' can call me Velvalee—if you want."

"Did I get awfully soused last night?"

"No, oh, no. You been, well—pretty sick fo' neahly three days. Ah felt evah so sorry fo' you." She nodded and her candy-blonde bob swayed above the powder-blue peignoir. "Yo' look lots bettah tonight. Reckon Esmé's been fixin' you up. She's a real fine nurse." All the while he was aware of Velvalee's unvarying attention. Her pretty, pointed features were so facile and expressive it became hard to believe that, at some time, she had not been in the theater.

Said he, "This food sure puts some bright colors back into life—and so do you." He smiled broadly and suddenly appeared years younger. "You're so very lovely I thought at first I was dreaming—or delirious."

"My, you're sho' recoverin'! But thanks, Ah haven't had such a nice compliment in evah so long, and," she actually reddened a little, "these foreigners are all right Ah reckon, but Ah declare Ah'm awful lonesome fo' a real American man."

Velvalee removed the tray then turned on him the devastating effect of singularly white, if slightly irregular, teeth, of softly bright lips. He realized now that she could stand a scant five feet and four inches. "Ah'm so glad yo' like me."

"You were sweet to give up your room to me."

"Oh, Ah didn't mind *a bit!* Really. There's a spare day-bed in Esmé's room." Reseating herself, Velvalee lit a pair of cigarettes and gave him one. When she did so the negligee slipped forward, briefly exposing small, but well-proportioned and rose pointed bosoms.

"That's a lot better," he sighed, sending a swirl of smoke ceilingwards. "Tell me about you and Miss Murfee."

"Now lean forward, Major, whilst Ah slip this pillow under yo' shoulders." Next she ran to fetch a comb. "Ah cain't bear to see that fascinatin' black hair of yours all messed up. If yo' don't mind, Ah'll fix it."

"So you're a lady barber who whacked off my beard?"

A fleeting tautness evinced itself at the corners of Velvalee's bud-like mouth. "No. That was Esmé."

"Three deep bows to Sister Esmé. I must have looked like Boxcar Willie himself."

"Well, Major, you certainly look a heap bettah right now —except for all those ugly bandages." Cigarette poised, Velvalee sat back, smiling at the patient's strong, rather Indian-like, features now sharply outlined against the pillowcase. "Yes, Major, that mouse ovah yo' eye's still bad, but mah goodness, yo' should have seen how yo' looked when," she hesitated, "well, when Steve, Sam and his friend Pete lugged you in. Glory! What kind of a toot were you on to get yo'self all beat up?"

Hastily, North noted the names against the fact of his arrival here. His gaze rose to the pretty, piquant and somewhat vacuous features attractively gilded by the lamp. "Can't imagine why you're so nice to me, Miss Petrie. I guess I must have looked unattractive—and silly."

The negligee swayed open—not unattractively—as she bent towards him and the tawny eyes half lidded themselves. "How do yo' mean 'silly'?"

"Oh, running out of control and getting so goddam cockeyed."

"Well, Ah *was* wonderin'," Velvalee admitted while grinding out her cigarette, "how come a real American and a gentleman should trifle around such riff-raff as Pete Kuzak," she wrinkled her somewhat retroussé nose, "and Dirty Sam Alberoni."

North expelled a great lungful of smoke and lowered his gaze. "Guess I sound pretty absurd but—I, well—I don't expect you to understand, but there was something I simply had to get off my chest."

"What do you mean, Major? Were you in trouble? Tell me about it, Ah'm evah so interested." Amid a swirl of the yellow-blue negligee skirts the girl called Velvalee dropped onto a cushion on the floor beside his bed. "Ah declah you sound like Mister Mystery himself. This, this thing yo' wanted to get rid of—was it a—a broken heart? Po' boy." Her fingers closed gently over his. " 'Co'se Ah cain't imagine any girl resistin' that simply bewitchin' wave in yo' hair and the *adorable,* distinguished-lookin' patches of silver above yo' ears." She smiled a smile that at once managed to convey sympathy, curiosity and a hint of envy.

Gently to return the pressure of her fingers seemed not only genteel but wise, and he muttered, "Sorry to disappoint you, my dear, but it wasn't love that prompted my downfall."

A look of severity sketched a quick V between Velvalee's well-groomed eyebrows. "Now don't tell me you got to gamblin' or—or in trouble—Ah mean, yo' aren't runnin' from the po-lice?" She gave his hand an encouraging pat. "If you are—Ah won't tell anybody. 'Deed Ah won't!"

North frowned at the small twin peaks formed by the outline of his toes beneath the red and white coverlet, wondered, "Where does all this sweet sympathy stuff fit in on the same program with Esmé Murfee and the gentle Steve?"

Aloud he replied, "I guess I just got fed up. You see, for more years than I like to count, I've been an officer in the United States Army, but——" He broke off, then continued, "They gave me a real run-around—one too many."

"Oh, Honey Bun—how perfectly awful! Ah guess Uncle Sam doesn't always treat his soldiers right, does he?"

"I presume sometimes the old Gent with the Whiskers does play square—so maybe I guess I oughtn't to say anything?"

"Here, Honey, how's about anothah cig?"

The bourbon was still warming to his stomach and, all at once, he felt infinitely stronger and clear-headed. Sitting up a little higher he smiled at her and the Indian-like aspects of his features became more pronounced than ever; his mustache, usually close-trimmed, now was scraggly and uneven.

"Hope I never recover because you're certainly one of the loveliest girls I've seen in a month of Sundays. Believe me, I really do appreciate your being so kind; especially since life—and some roughnecks unknown—have been kicking me around lately."

Her lips parted in sympathetic smile. "You po' boy! Won't you tell me about it? Maybe Ah can help."

"As the French say, with the Army 'I've got my shoulders loaded.'"

"What was wrong?"

Craftily, he begged, "Couldn't you sneak me another little drink?"

"Not right now, Honey. Esmé is dead-set against your drinkin' any more. An' now how was that nasty ol' Wah Department mean to you?" Beneath well-simulated casualness, he could detect her vibrant impatience.

"As I've told you, I've served in our Army a long while, and not always without a certain distinction. To be honest, I suppose I've risked my life at least a dozen times in order to secure or preserve for the United States secrets that might otherwise have been lost." He shrugged, drew hard on his cigarette. "I suppose I've missed a lot of good things to do this—I've never had a home of my own, for instance. Instead, on occasion, I've damned near frozen to death, been drowned or otherwise made pretty miserable."

"Really, Honey Bun, Ah don't see how they *could* treat you so mean." She looked really as pretty as a calendar girl, and, just as skillfully, revealed feminine fascinations not usually in evidence.

"Don't get me wrong, Velvalee. I wouldn't have minded any of it if others, who hadn't accomplished half so much, hadn't been promoted and put above me." He injected a cold rage into his tone. "All that most of those fat cats did was to loaf comfortably on their butts about the Pentagon, and what did they get but promotions, decorations and degrees from publicity-hungry fresh water colleges? *I* got what the boy shot at."

She caught up his hand, pressed it briefly to her cheek.

"Oh, Honey Bun, that's simply outrageous. But Ah know what you mean. Take my Uncle Cartuh, he was a Regular, but he said you got to expect that in our Army." The great sherry-brown eyes, very round and luminous, swung to meet his. "Sho'ly you wouldn't think of, well, quittin'? Not that Ah'd blame you one bit if you did."

The back of his forefinger brushed at one of the bright locks framing her face. "I'm glad you said so because that's just what I've decided to do as soon as my leave is up. Yes, my dear, the United States Army can shinny right to the top of the pole and sit on it."

Once more the Intelligence Officer's voice grew flat, harsh. "What a fine grateful country to slave for. Why, the U.S. is so goddam self-satisfied, rich and blind it's riding for one damned disastrous fall. I suppose they think it's fair to reward long and faithful service with reprimands and slights. Well, here I am pretty near broke, and not getting any younger, and what have I got to show? Nothing. A major's rank and a lieutenant-colonel's pay with some fogies thrown in; which the dear old income tax takes care of *muy pronto*. Well," his fingers gripped the edge of the blankets and he glowered at his reflection in the mirror, "I've had a belly-ful."

Gently she stroked his cheek and lowered her face to within a few inches of his. He sensed that her suppressed excitement was reaching a climax. Her voice, however, was cool and quiet, level as she murmured, "Honey Bun, please don't say such awful, such wicked things about Home. After all, you and I are Americans. Of co'se there are bound to be injustices everywhere. Please, Hugh, tell me you're not goin' to let a silly little ol' grudge come between you and yo' duty?"

The violence of his mirthless laughter made the bedframe creak and, were anyone listening on a microphone, they must have flinched.

"Grudge, hell! It's more than a 'little ol' grudge as you call it. I'm fed up, disgusted and mad clear through. How'd you like being saddled and rowelled by superiors who didn't know a cipher from a cryptogram? Well, Uncle Sam can take this whole raw deal and stuff it where the monkey put the nut."

A tremulous quiver came to her lips and her eyes grew very round; Velvalee recoiled a few inches. "Oh, deah, do yo' *really* mean that? Aren't you bein' hasty?—just think about Home. Ah know plenty of people criticize it, but Ah believe America is the very best place on earth."

"Do you—really?" He shot her a shrewd glance.

"Why, of co'se. Ah love mah country."

"So did I, and for a damned long while," he admitted bitterly. "But that's done with, besides, I can spot a losing outfit further than most people. Me, I've always wanted to play on a team that knows what it's about; that backs their people up and rewards their services."

The girl arose and stood looking down at him. Was she entirely unconscious that the lamplight left little to be imagined concerning the exact proportions of her figure?

"Hugh," she cried, "Ah think yo' are still out of yo' haid. Isn't there—anythin' can make you change yo' mind?"

"I've never been more clear-headed and in earnest than right now. I feel that I've more than discharged my duty to America; from now in I'm going to work for one Hugh North, and for whoever will pay best for my services. Incidentally, they will be making a damned good deal."

Velvalee suddenly seated herself on the side of his bed. "Honey Bun, do you think Ah'm really cute?"

North's wasted features relaxed, but not his wariness. "As they'd say down where you come from 'you look sweet enough to eat without butterin'.'" He took her hand, marvelled at its softness a little, then burst out, "Look, dear, I've still some money left, enough to last until I can land a—a

new connection. Why shouldn't we have a bit of fun together?"

"Why Ah'd admire to, really Ah would. You cain't do
much whoop-de-doo on a switchboa'd and special secretary's
pay." Suddenly she demanded, "But what will the newspaper gal you been playing around with say?"

"Nothing. Why should she?"

"Folks say she came ovah heah just to be neah you." A
suggestion of a pout appeared on Velvalee's tiny mouth.

"You mean Jingles? Old stuff; sure, we had some fun together back in Washington. She's a good kid but, hell! Career girls are too damned self-centered to stay interesting.
Incidentally, how come you know so much about her?"

She treated him to a wide-eyed stare and spoke slowly.
"Why Pete Kuzak, well, he 'llowed she came ovah to Balata
and made an almighty fuss ovah yo' bein' so stinko. Golly,
Hugh, the whole American colony knows she's crazy over
you."

"That's something else again. I tell you Miss Lawson
means nothing to me—she's part of the past I'm cutting
loose from."

"Well, that's good." Velvalee ran fingertips over his brow
just below the bandage. "Honey Bun, yo' do think Ah'm attractive, kind of pretty?"

"More than I can express."

"Well, then, Ah reckon we could—" Velvalee's naturally
soft voice sounded richer than ever, "—have fun, Ah mean
a lot of fun—but on just one condition."

"Well?" Then he got one of the major surprises of his
career.

"Promise me, that no mattah what happens, you'll not
evah sell our country down the river? Honey Bun, Ah'm
no saint but me, Ah've no use whatevah for turncoats and
traitors."

For several moments stillness persisted in Velvalee's bedroom, a silence broken only by the shrill crowing of a cockerel in some neighboring chicken run.

"Velvalee, if I hadn't already made up my mind, you would be the one person who might have made me change it. You see, I suspect it was you, not Miss Murfee, who's been caring for me. But," desperation mingled with anger became injected into his voice, "I'm through serving the United States; please don't think I reached this decision easily."

"Oh!" The girl leaped up, glared at him from tawny and furious eyes. "Oh, you're simply hateful and contemptible! You're no bettah at all than Benedict Arnold, Best, Farnsworth and the rest of those—those miserable traitors." She paused at the door, her cheeks flushed. "I shuah hope you get a relapse and—and die!"

"Just a minute—tell me one thing. Were you ever on the stage?"

"Suh, you are no gentleman and you can go straight to hell!"

The shutters bumped to her slamming of the door.

CHAPTER 8

Party Line

NEVER, decided Major Hugh North, had he more appreciated the wearing of clean garments, the familiar luxury of finding his body once more cleanly and his face freshly shaven. It was fine, too, to discover that his stomach no longer felt as if it had been digesting sulphuric acid and broken glass. He and Stephen Petrie, it turned out, were so nearly of a height and size that a suit of that young man's by no means new gray flannel trousers and tweed coat fitted satisfactorily.

Despite his untroubled mien, Anxiety's talons were clawing at his peace of mind. What had been behind Velvalee's curious nocturnal visit? What had become of the man called Bernard? How was this inexorable flight of time affecting the main problem? Come what might he must, at all costs, and quickly, get in touch with Colonel McKenzie. Maybe that worthy had received a further signal from Walewski. Or as seemed all too likely had not the MVD already pounced upon that heroic, if unrecognized, patriot and had regained possession of those priceless microfilms of the variphase multi-jet mechanism?

Whether or not he had been justified in pursuing this course and in gambling more than a week of precious, unforgiving time, remained to be decided. Thoughtfully the dark-haired Intelligence Officer lit a pipe purchased for him by young Stephen Petrie who, to all intents and purposes, seemed to be no more than a senior clerk at local purchasing offices serving the United States Military Mission to Turkey. Was his name really Petrie?

A blind man could have told by a dozen indications including speech, bearing and physique, that Steve was no more Velvalee's brother than her grandfather. What a consummate actress that doll-pretty little female had proved herself. A cold rain drumming on the window panes attracted his attention, and he crossed to the window to look out on serried ranks of whitecaps pursuing themselves along the slate-colored Bosphorus. Done in gray, white and brown, the Asiatic shore suggested the sea coast of Limbo.

At Velvalee's dressing table he re-examined himself in the mirror and grimaced at the reflection; his features still looked haggard, bruised and swollen from the effects of that long debauch, but the bandages were gone and his deep-set eyes had recovered their clear gray-blue, while the swelling above his left eye had all-but subsided. On testing his lacerated ear, he found that organ to be still extremely sensitive.

Through the threshing, leafless branches of a fig tree he noticed a small stone jetty projecting from beyond that glass-crowned garden wall he previously had noted. About it the tide was licking so hungrily that a sudden possibility suggested itself.

Could he who had screamed downstairs last night eventually have been launched into yonder furious current and the silencing waters below? If so, there was ample precedent; curious to ponder on how many thousands of human beings had disappeared into these waters since that day when, in the 657th year before Christ, Byzas Megara had founded Byzantium. Who could count the number of heroes, viziers, villains, princesses, courtesans and lesser folk whose lives had ended beneath that grim gray current? And here he was removed, by a scant hundred yards, from those waters upon which a fresh series of rain squalls now were commencing to sketch silvery designs suggestive of scale armor.

"Hope you like our view." Only North's well-trained re-
flexes prevented his whirling about to see the door swing
open. "It's considered a superior one."

The speaker was Esmé Murfee, but over her shoulder
loomed the flat, reddish features of Pete Kuzak, the accordion player.

"Hi, Doc!" greeted the latter, as he swung in, tightly
curling blond hair gleaming. He offered his hand. "Feelin'
better? Boy, you sure was a sad sight when I picked you up
near the ferry. Who handed you that Triple A shellackin'?"

"I'd give a lot to know," North replied in all sincerity.

"How does it feel to be sober?" demanded the Murfee
girl.

North grinned. "Pretty good. Believe it or not, I don't
often get ossified like that."

Esmé inquired, "Still want a drink?"

North thought fast. "No," he said. "I'm not usually a
heavy drinker. That binge was sort of a catharsis."

"Huh?" demanded Kuzak.

"I just had to, well, drown out a lot of bitterness and
sort of find a new page to write on I suppose."

Without seeming to, he became fully aware of an intent
inspection by the Murfee girl's hard, dark blue eyes. Otherwise, she looked neat, if not smart, in a golden-brown jersey
dress relieved by a belt of scarlet leather and a small gold
lapel watch.

"I believe you," she observed cheerfully. "Well, Major,
I hardly recognize you from two days ago. So Steve's things
fit all right?"

"Sure do." North smiled. "Thanks a lot for the nursing;
you did a wonderful job. Hope to pay you back sometime
soon."

"Maybe you can," the Murfee girl said quietly. "Let's all

go downstairs, Major. I hear you went exploring there last night."

"Last night?" North acted convincingly vague. "Did I? Must have been dopey—out on my feet. All I remember is hunting for a drink and somebody leading me back to bed." He wondered whether to mention his intriguing little séance with Velvalee; decided against it and asked instead, "Say, Miss Murfee, what was that sedative you gave me, anyhow?"

"Seconal, and not enough, it appears," came the wry rejoinder.

In the oddly furnished living room the three seated themselves.

"Pete," Esmé said, "there's a kettle boiling in the kitchen. Let's have some tea since," she cast the Intelligence Officer a faintly derisive glance, "it's not yet cocktail time."

On a wide ottoman covered with a handsome shawl Esmé Murfee seated herself, crossed sturdy legs. She reached for a cigarette, an oversized Turkish affair equipped with a long paper filter. North rekindled his pipe.

"I hear my friend Velvalee—er—dropped in on you when she came in," she remarked over a spiteful spatter of rain against the window panes behind her.

Here it came. Over his match flame he studied his hostess a moment.

"She did. Incidentally, she's quite something to look at— the way I saw her."

"Velvalee's a swell friend, a little devil and a sentimental fool to boot. What did you make—maybe I shouldn't use that term—think of her?"

"I don't know what gives around here," he evaded, "but, well, she seems one American girl who, well, still hasn't rid herself of some solid red, white and blue convictions."

"Have you?"

"Yes, about five weeks ago." North got up and groaned a little as he did so.

"What happened?"

"One double-cross too many from the Top Brass." Briefly, almost sullenly, he repeated his reasons for wrath at the complacent stupidity of the State and Defense Departments, lack of recognition, fatigue, the necessity of a financial hedge against old age.

To it all Esmé Murfee listened intently, her unblinking gaze fixed on the speaker's long, high-cheekboned features. "I am beginning to believe," said she, "that you're quite as smart as I've been informed."

"Smart enough at least to call quits on the raw deal I've been getting. Like yourself, for instance."

The cold blue eyes narrowed. "You interest me, Major. What makes you think that I, too, have had a raw deal?"

"It shows both in your face and in your manner. In fact, I'll bet a pretty penny that somewhere along the line dear old Uncle Sam dealt you a swift kick in the vicinity of your panties." He decided on bolder tactics. "Incidentally, Miss Murfee, if you want us to get along, please don't try to kid me. I'm sober now and not the dumbest hombre in your vicinity."

"So what?" Sullen lines marred her expression. "What are you driving at?"

"You were an Army trained nurse?"

Esmé sat straight, defiantly flicked the ash from her cigarette. "Sure, but my name was different then."

"What went wrong?"

"Some drugs disappeared from the American base hospital at Liège. I was blamed for it. They court-martialled me and gave me a D.D." Angrily, she continued, "Okay, so I took them to give to the Russians, our Allies, who hadn't any."

"You got paid for those drugs?"

Esmé bit her lip. "Only the cost price. I tell you I felt really sorry for those poor Russkies. Some of their officers

were awfully helpful during my trial. Of course reports
of the scandal got back home and my fiancé broke off our
engagement; next, my folks wrote that if they never saw
me again that would be soon enough." The color ebbed
from Esmé Murfee's cheeks. " 'To hell with them, the Army
and the whole damn' United States,' that's what I said to
myself." She broke off, a trifle disconcerted. "Say, I thought
it was you we were going to talk about. What's your opinion of the Berlin situation?"

"The continued occupation of our Sectors serves as an excuse to keep the munitions barons busy; a dodge to earn fat
dividends on Wall Street," he declared. "No crisis means no
big Army, Navy or Air Force. Simple, isn't it?"

The profound interest in Esmé's manner was inescapable.
She leaned forward, lipstick-stained cigarette poised. "So
you really believe that the Berlin air-lift business was merely
a Capitalist excuse for precipitating another war?"

"Sure." North sent a furious cloud of gray-blue smoke
whirling up to the ceiling. A draft caught the fumes,
whisked them towards a pair of bright blue, red and brown
Trabzon hangings masking a door to the dining room.
"Look, my dear Miss Murfee, I know what I'm talking
about. Haven't I been, well, on the inside of this? I know
plenty; for instance, that it was England and America, not
the Soviets, who first violated the Yalta Agreements, who
tried to maneuver control of the Danube—and lots more besides."

In the girl's handsomely severe features color was mounting. "Why doesn't the World know these things—I suppose
the corrupt press of the Western Powers sees to it. How can
the World be expected to believe America when everyone
knows we—they, are rearming all Europe—aside from building air bases for jet bombers in Iceland, England, France,
Germany and now right here in Turkey—a neutral country
that had no part in the war."

Her voice grew stronger. "Let me tell you something, North, the North Atlantic Pact is the last gasp of the decadent West! But the Soviet Union realizes that it's a dangerous last gasp." Beneath the brown jersey the outlines of large but well-formed breasts commenced to rise more quickly.

"Quite correct," North agreed, "and making a pile of money at it, too!"

"You sound washed up with that stinking, rotten thing known as American democracy."

"If I weren't I wouldn't have chucked in my hand." He spoke slowly, distinctly. "Listen, every time I watch England and the U.S. use the United Nations as a pressure group to preserve their corrupt, undemocratic and decadent civilization I see red."

Down the corridor could be heard the hissing of a samovar, the clink of cups and the noise of a kitchen grate being shaken.

Esmé's eyes were shining and her words seemed to explode from her lips. "Is it any wonder that Russia has to take counter-measures when a United States Expeditionary Force—alias a Military Mission to Turkey—is poised to strike not only at the Ukraine, Russia's bread basket, but also at Baku, the only important oil fields in the U.S.S.R.? As if America and the British already don't control the oil of Indonesia, the Near East and both Americas."

"No, it's no wonder. In fact it's amazing that the Soviets have been so calm."

A brief silence ensued during which North frowned at Steve Petrie's scuffed brown house slippers, so far the only footgear allowed him.

"For a fact," continued the Intelligence Officer, "I can't see how the North Atlantic Powers are going to be stopped."

"Don't you?" Esmé flung the stub of her cigarette into a

small fire burning sullenly in a grate. "Well, don't be too concerned over that. I—I am—well, I understand the Soviet Supreme Staff has some surprises in store—some terrific surprises. They aren't asleep in the Commissariat of Defense."

She arose, smoothed her skirt and commenced to clear a tea table with a hammered brass top. "I know this is so because to complement these new weapons the MVD is searching for new, shrewd and clever operatives, persons who understand intelligence work at the highest level."

North nodded. "I expect that's true. After a while first-class governments get wise to their rivals' methods—and personnel."

Passionately Esmé Murfee broke out, "Why can't the World realize Russia wants peace; that it's the corrupt and predatory Plutocracies who want war, who right now are arming great armies of Japs and Germans against the U.S.S.R.?" Suddenly she faced him. "Major North, would you be willing to join in the fight for peace?"

That long-limbed figure in the rather inadequate-appearing *moderne* armchair leaned forward, elbows on knees. "You mayn't believe, Miss Murfee, but all my life I've fought for peace—by trying to cripple and thwart aggressors. For a long while I believed the United States to be, morally at least, the greatest force for peace. Now I've reasons to change my opinion. Between you and me, Esmé, I no longer believe in anything so wicked and archaic as nationalities. I, well, I want a peaceful world—so much so I don't care a hoot in hell what country, race or religion brings it about. Wendell Willkie, maybe, had the right idea, although he thought of his One World as American sponsored."

"Tell me," tensely demanded the Murfee girl, "would you be willing to work for peace—*even* through the U.S.S.R.?"

North's voice lowered itself for down the corridor came the sound of Kuzak's returning footsteps. "Why not? I may act crazy now and then, but I'm not fool enough not to realize that the whole world's going Communist. Central Europe, the Balkans, Malaya, North China and Korea already have joined up. Unless I miss my guess, Japan and Central America will go Communist before the year is out!"

A quick smile flitted across Esmé's squarish mouth. "You're certainly up on what's coming. Ah, Pete, just in time, I'm about starved. And Major—maybe you might think over what we were talking about."

"My dear, when I make up my mind on a decision as important as this one I don't change. However, it will be a pleasure," he smiled, "to reflect on a quarter hour spent in such wholly fascinating company."

After lighting a fresh cigarette, Esmé Murfee crossed the room, hesitated by the door. "Pete, you know how to work the samovar and how I like my tea. Major, I recommend the caviar, it's really fresh. See you in a minute."

At the prospect of husky-looking sandwiches, caviar and Russian brick tea North felt cheered; his stomach still felt as though an army of Mexicans had camped in it.

Pete Kuzak grinned. "How do you and the Ironpants Kid get on?"

"Well enough, Pete. You known her long?"

The curly-headed young fellow crumbled tea into the samovar. "Long enough. She's a smart dame is Sister Esmé, but sometimes I'd like to figger out what she keeps under her bra in place of a heart."

They had consumed a bowl of tea and a couple of roseleaf and honey preserve sandwiches before Esmé reappeared carrying a document which she promptly passed North. She did this swiftly but not so rapidly but that he sensed a glance pass between Esmé and Pete Kuzak.

"Do you think this is a forgery?" she invited while selecting a piece of lemon. "They tell me you're something of an expert on such matters."

Purposely Hugh North finished his grated onion, caviar and toast before unfolding the sheet of paper. The letter-head proved to be disturbing. Beneath a surcharge stamped in purple TOP SECRET he read, "Military Mission of the United States to the Turkish Republic." His eyes at once sought the signature. Fortunately years of experience steeled him against the shock he then experienced; the communication was signed "David H. Larkin, Captain, USAF."

CHAPTER 9

Tests

From the Intelligence Officer's wooden expression no one could have guessed that he was conducting a rapid re-estimation of the problem confronting him. He merely inspected the document as if it held no more than passing interest. Esmé, tea cup poised, went to look over North's shoulder. "Read it," she directed, "go ahead, read it and see what you think of U.S. security in these parts."

TOP SECRET

From: A-2, Hadji Field, Turkey

To: CO, A-2, Embassy of the U.S., Ankara, Turkey

Subject:	Report on material arrived, November 10 per U.S.S. Carrier Lingayen Gulf.
Item I.	8 P-38 Pursuit Ships
Item II.	9 Instructor Pilots
Item III.	500 Drums Jet Fuel
Comment:	Probably foreign intelligence agents are aware of arrival of this shipment but not of its nature or amount.
Recommendation:	More effective security measures must be adopted at once. Estimate the number of counter-intelligence agents on duty at Hadji Field and at Haidi Pasha Terskaneh Unloading Area should be doubled and those already on duty thoroughly screened. Immediate action recommended.

(*Signed*) DAVID LARKIN
Capt. USAF
A-2 Hadji Field

TOP SECRET

Kuzak was the first to speak. "Well, Doc, what d'you make of that?"

North refolded the paper, gave it back to Esmé. "If I were still with the Army I'd court-martial said David Larkin for an inexcusable breach of security."

Esmé dabbed a lock of dark hair back into place. "What I'd like to know is—first, is this letter genuine, and second, has it been tampered with?"

During that period he had been reading, North's mind had been rushing about like a cat with its fur afire. Why would this frozen-faced young woman thus disclose so vital, so damning a piece of evidence? How should he react to this revelation? With gratifying promptness Experience erected a series of finger posts.

"I'd say offhand that this document appears quite genuine." He walked over to the window and exposed it to rapidly fading daylight. "Yes; the paper, at least, is correctly watermarked and genuine U.S. Army stock. The genuineness of the signature, of course, I can't vouch for—not without a microscope."

"Suppose," Kuzak said softly, "I was to say this here letter really did come from Hadji Field? Can you tell us whether the dope in it is phony or the McCoy?"

"You mean can I tell whether the letter's been doctored? Sure, let's take a look at it." While he reread the text North's hand rose to test his injured ear; it kept tickling, a reassuring sign that it must be healing. If only his battered ribs would stop aching. He looked at Esmé over the letter. "First off, the phraseology is officially correct; but any T5 stenographer could imitate it."

"That ain't what we're talking about," grunted the big fair-haired accordionist. "What we want to know is whether this here letter was rigged with false information, say by someone in the Counter-Intelligence——"

"Shut up!" Esmé's voice struck out like a quirt. She arose,

heavy-breasted figure looming tall above North's seated figure. "Pete's already said what he means; has the letter been tampered with?"

North blinked, hesitated. "Not at first glance."

He wondered at the searching quality of the gaze Esmé fixed on him. "Major, I'd like you to make a thorough examination. Under normal conditions what's the first thing you'd do?"

"Head straight for a police laboratory."

"Well, there isn't any laboratory available," the girl announced coldly. "Can't you improvise, get somewhere without one? I'm told you're celebrated for ingenuity and resourcefulness." Her voice hardened. "Come on, show your stuff. I've got to know right away whether this letter's been doctored or not."

North thought a minute. The threat in her manner was as evident as was her anxiety. "Does this—er—borrowed letter have to be returned in an undamaged condition?"

"Yes, and before sun-up."

"Too bad. This eliminates the surest tests such as various reagents, red lead or an iodine bath. Um. Let me think." Catching his breath he got stiffly to his feet, commenced to limp about the little living room. Abruptly he halted. "Have you a radio?"

"Yes."

"Some small-gauge insulated wire?"

"How about that, Pete?"

Kuzak's curly blond head jerked a nod. "You want I should fetch it?"

"It's no good where it is."

Very well North was aware that everything depended on what he said, and did, during the next half hour. Possibly the trail he had sought so long and at such cost might open before him the way leading to Josef Walewski and the essential microfilms.

"Um, since I mustn't injure this letter I'll have to go Rube Goldberg." Momentarily he fingered his jaw, making a little crackling noise on the bristles once more beginning to darken it. "I noticed on the dressing table in Velvalee's room one of those facial massage vibrators. Now if you'll fetch it and a—well let's say a 8″ x 10″ picture frame which will have to be of metal, I'll see what I can learn."

All the while watched by Kuzak—who undoubtedly was carrying an automatic under his left arm—North cleared a table and then arranged upon it the empty picture frame to which the letter in question had been secured, very taut, by strips of carefully applied scotch tape. Into the space where the glass should have been he introduced a piece of blotter carefully cut to size then, praying that his improvisation might succeed, he grounded wires from the radio's loud-speaker to the picture—the radio had previously been tuned to a neutral wave length—and bridged them by the picture frame. The vibrator was plugged in separately, in such a way that no actual current could pass between it and the radio which, in effect, had become merely an amplifier.

Selecting an appliance of the vibrator consisting of a tiny rubber cup designed for massage of the gums, North removed the cup, retaining only a ball-pointed metal spindle. Straight black brows merged in concentration, he then arranged the framed letter horizontally upon four books of uniform size.

"Pretty smart, by Jesus," Kuzak commented. "They wasn't lyin' about our pal here, was they?"

"Don't get your hopes up," came Esmé's caustic advice. "This arrangement's pretty damn' crude and may not work."

North treated her to a taut smile. "How right you are, Sister."

The instant he flicked the switch on the vibrator and applied the spindle to a blank space on the letter paper he was enormously relieved to hear the radio's loud-speaker set up a steady, high-pitched hum. When, deliberately, he moved the spindle point across the paper the even whine continued.

"What's the idea, Doc?" Kuzak blurted out. "I don't get it."

North, his battered hands guiding the vibrator with delicate precision, glanced up. "This paper, my friend, is of an even thickness, so the vibrations set up by this massage motor retain a level pitch until the thickness of the paper varies." He glanced up at Esmé who stood, arms folded, frowning in concentration. "Now you will please notice what happens when I pass the spindle's tip over typewritten areas." He did so and immediately the buzzing in the loud-speaker rose higher, interrupted itself. "You see the pitch changes slightly because the resistance of the ink and the imprint of the type alter the paper's thickness, resulting in differing sound waves which, of course, register on the loud-speaker."

Thinking hard, he returned his gaze to the rectangle of paper. "If on Captain Larkin's letter there have been erasures or washing out of ink with chemical, the normal thickness of the paper will have been altered and should register on the amplifier. Now please observe as I pass the indicator over the body of this letter."

Esmé Murfee bent so low over the table that a strand of her short bobbed, black hair brushed his cheek.

The key pitch of the radio remained level, uninterrupted, until the guiding rod arrived at the first paragraph which read, "8 P-38 Pursuit Ships." When the rod paused to rest above that blank space which immediately preceded the figure "8", the radio squeaked like a trapped mouse; on continuing to the figure "8" North's instrument resumed the key normal for a typed area. Again the amplifier

squeaked over both the "3" and the "8" following the identification letter "P."

"This would suggest," North informed his utterly rapt
companions, "that the original text mentioned more than
the eight pursuit ships now listed, and that these were of
another type."

"What type?" Esmé demanded breathlessly.

North straightened, rubbed the bruised spot on his nose.
"There's no telling—without using an iodine bath—broken
fibres in the paper probably would materialize. As it is, one
can only guess as to the number of planes received; it could
be ninety-eight just as well as eighteen."

And Kuzak looked his admiration. "Say, Doc, what was
that you said about the designation of them pursuit ship
types?"

North replied without the slightest hesitation. "Obviously
the ships received were not P-38's, which are obsolete. Some
other and newer model actually was shipped."

"Wonderful! Wonderful!" Esmé's small dark blue eyes
shone. "Go on. Where else has this letter been altered?"

Again North resumed his patient examination and dem-
onstrated that the number of instructors caused a protest
from the loud-speaker; also the quantity of drums of jet
fuel.

"You're a smart apple, Doc," Kuzak commented, then
added unexpectedly, "So that bastard was trying to kid——"

"*Will* you shut up?" instantly put in the Murfee girl. "Or
must I send you for a little talk with Eric?"

"Oh no! I'm sorry——" the accordionist cried hurriedly.
"Please forget I said anything."

Larkin? Where did the A-2 fit on this increasingly disturbing picture? North felt tempted to put an indirect question on the subject but restrained himself.

"Well, there you are," he said and switched off the vibrator. "Of course, as I've said, it's quite possible to develop

the actual numbers that were erased, but I'd have to spoil the letter. That's up to you, Esmé."

Esmé had resumed her seat and was staring fixedly at North's gaunt and battered countenance. "Apparently you don't feel concerned over having exposed a fellow officer's very clever attempt to double-cross us?"

"Hell, no." He might have added that, from the start, he had been convinced this whole episode of Larkin's letter primarily was an attempt to gauge the sincerity of his apostasy. Now, however, he was becoming alarmed over the apparent authenticity of that TOP SECRET communication. How had this letter reached this enigmatic young woman? Could Velvalee Petrie, who typed as well as operated the switchboard at Hadji Field, have explained it?

"I'm grateful for your care and nursing—have I evened the account?"

"Well, almost." Esmé smiled and North's respect for the girl's acumen soared. "We'll call it even if you'll go ahead and develop the erased words and numbers."

"Okay, but what will you do then about returning this report to where it belongs and undamaged?" His question was most casual.

Outside a dog began howling mournfully, but Esmé's bright lips curved. "Why, we've got all the Army paper we need and Velvalee can type a copy. Steve can forge that signature so well that Larkin himself couldn't tell the difference."

At Esmé's direction Kuzak went to a deep bookcase and removed two rows of books; concealed behind them stood a frighteningly complete assortment of chemical reagents, brushes, red lead, lampblack and a powerful transverse microscope.

As a result of lampblack delicately brushed over the erased areas by means of a camel's hair brush, the minute fibres impressed or broken by the impact of a typewriter's

keys cut the smudge particles and resumed a faint outline
"5," thus "8" pursuit ships became "58" and the type serial
number to be "P-80A" rather than "38." As for the number
of newly arrived instructors, "19" actually had arrived in
place of "9" and 1500 drums of jet fuel had been delivered
in place of 500.

Um. So Kuzak was figuring that Captain Larkin had
double-crossed or otherwise deceived him? What was the
dark-faced A-2 up to?

Otherwise, many things now became explicable—Esmé's
work at the Army infirmary, Larkin at Hadji, Velvalee's
job at Hadji Field and, perhaps most dangerous of all,
Stephen Petrie's high post with the Purchasing Commis-
sions. Um. Odd, to reflect that not one of that group, which
also included Kuzak and Alberoni, although Communists
to the hilt—with the possible exception of Velvalee—were
Russian, but born and bred Americans. It stood to reason
that presently he would encounter others of this dangerous
group.

How appalling to realize that the MVD's slimy tentacles
had stretched so skillfully and so far into the Military Mission's affairs. Grimly, the Intelligence officer yearned for an
immediate interview with Captain Larkin, A-2 of Hadji
Field, Turkey.

CHAPTER 10

The Recruit

WHILE disconnecting the apparatus, Major Hugh North looked up pleasantly and suggested, "Now that we've had our fun, what about something to eat? Right now I could lunch my way clean through a middle-sized cattle ranch."

"I could tie on the feed bag, too," Kuzak grinned. "Come on, Doc, and let's fry us a big steak."

"Sounds like heaven." North straightened his shoulders under Petrie's gray sweater; it was of a type he particularly abhorred, one boasting pearl buttons all the way down its front. They were heading for the hangings when Esmé held up a muscular but not badly formed hand.

"Hold on, Major, we'll let Pete go ahead and start supper. Velvalee and Steve ought to be in before long. You'll find plenty of mushrooms and rice in the pantry."

When the musician had disappeared Esmé Murfee offered a box of cigarettes. "Comrade, I'm beginning to think you'll do. I'm pretty nearly convinced you meant what you said a while back."

"You may as well believe me." North offered a match for her cigarette. "Reward me reasonably, and you'll get the full benefit of my not valueless services. The United States didn't reward me," he reminded bitterly, "so they have lost them. Were the British or the French to make a satisfactory offer I'd work for them just as readily, provided they're out for world peace."

"Surely you're well aware they're much too decadent and too broke to fuss with," Esmé observed smoothing the top of her brown jersey dress. "Still, I understand your saying so."

"Why?"

"You're either too smart to try to kid me, or too wary. I don't believe you understand much about the Party Line, the basic principles of Communism, practically nothing, in fact, of the true goals of our World Revolution, but Comrade Eric and I will do our best to sell you our, the winning side's, viewpoint."

"Who is this Comrade Eric?"

"You'll meet him before very long," was all she would say.

North felt a measure of self-confidence returning. So, he had been wise in failing to express any sudden deep affection for the Communist idea, or to present himself in the role of a too-willing mercenary.

"Esmé," gently he placed his hand on hers, "do you mind if I tell you that I think you're just as clever as you are pretty—and that's saying plenty."

"Whatever makes you think that?" She was looking inordinately pleased and couldn't disguise the fact.

He went over to seat himself on a big green and white striped leather hassock—his legs still felt a trifle uncertain. "First off, you're aware I must know plenty about United States Intelligence work, and that in my own racket I'm tops. Moreover, you were smart enough to approach me at a moment when I was wide open to persuasion. Right?"

Esmé hesitated and her carmined lower lip crept in between strong but uneven teeth. "Perhaps. Tell me, Hugh, when you were in Washington did you ever come across a man in G-2 named Edmonds, Luther Edmonds?"

North shook his head and looked serious. "I'm glad you've brought up a point which I consider all-important. If I did know this fellow Edmonds, I wouldn't admit it—not now, at least. We may as well get one point straight right now: I don't intend to go back on, or betray, my former associates. Facts pertaining to my previous career aren't available—but work predicated on the future is wide open." He sensed that this big young woman was disappointed, but not unduly so. Possibly because of this she was even more firmly convinced of his sincerity. "In other words I feel that my skills are my own property, so what you are hiring in me is a technician, pure and simple." He smiled. "To be sure, I don't know whether I qualify under either of those adjectives."

"You mean you refuse to pass on knowledge concerning the operation of American Intelligence?"

A smile widened his still somewhat swollen lips. "Would you trust me if I did?"

"No, I expect I wouldn't. We've noticed that men of your type and ability take a lot of convincing before they become true Proletarians. For the present then, if Eric approves, we'll think of you as a mercenary, honest and expert about Intelligence operations."

"Then I expect we can work out some kind of a deal—if you'll meet my price."

"I must say, Hugh, you're a rarely logical cuss," Esmé remarked after a momentary deliberation. "And I believe Eric will take to you a lot easier on this basis than on sudden conversion to the Party's political ideas. We have plenty of loyal workers who lack theoretical background—like Velvalee, for instance." Esmé smoothed a stocking well above her kneecap, and quite unconcernedly refastened her garter catch; he didn't deem attractive the way she allowed her cigarette to remain dangling from her lip. "What are you thinking? You look so damned sad."

"How much I want a drink."

"You'll get one later, after Eric shows up. Incidentally," she laughed a little, "don't think me such a fool as to set you down for an habitual drunk. I know better. You went on a pretty famous toot, by all accounts, but there were reasons for it," stated this amazing young woman. "Me, I'm all set to believe that you can and will go back to drinking in moderation."

"Thanks. That puts another star on the gold frame I am beginning to see you through. Do we get a cocktail before supper, or shall we say dinner?"

Esmé ground out the end of her cigarette. "I suppose the bourgeois would call it dinner. What would you like?"

"You, my chick."

"Look, Major," she snapped, "you're not talking to Velvalee. And remember this; if we do hire you, you'll be taking your orders from me and I don't permit familiarities from my subordinates."

North permitted himself to look somewhat startled, then he laughed. "Very well. I like it better that way, and so long as you are asking, I want an even sixty thousand a year for my services."

"How crazy can you get? Twenty-five grand is tops."

He smiled and went over to the window to watch the slender, blue-gray minarets of the Valideh Mosque blend with the twilight. "Miss Murfee, you seem to forget that the bargain basements lie over on Third Avenue. Let's have no more of this. I say sixty thousand and that's what I intend to get if I go to work for you. Hell, even the poor broke British could match that! The French, too——"

"How do you want the money paid?"

"To the Havana Branch of the National City Bank under a name I'll give you when the deal is closed. Incidentally, before I lift another finger in your service I'll want to handle a cabled receipt. *Comprenez?*"

"What's that mean?"

"Do you understand?"

She considered him in reluctant admiration. "For a rumbum you've certainly pulled yourself together in one hell of a hurry, but let me remind you that, if your terms are met, you'll be completely, one hundred per cent, under the order of me and my superiors. Also, at the first hint of deviation from duty you'll find yourself liquidated and nobody will have the least notion of what became of the once-famous Major Hugh North."

"I'd be an idiot to expect anything else, Miss Murfee. Wouldn't I now?" Silently, he added, "First, you'll have to catch your 'possum."

News within News

THE STORM so abated with nightfall that, by the time the trio sat down to enjoy the promised cocktails, no wind noises troubled the Blue Villa. Kuzak, thanks to a pair of murderously strong martinis, was in good spirits, while North, having sipped a single cocktail, began to feel more like his old self than he had in nearly a fortnight. Esmé drank nothing save a glass of anemic-appearing Turkish beer.

Esmé Murfee however, after having talked at length on the telephone, reappeared, abstracted of manner, although otherwise pleasant enough. Everyone looked up when a key rattled in the front door and in came Velvalee together with her tall and athletic *soi-disant* brother. On beholding North, so amicably partaking of refreshment, they pulled up short.

"Come on in," Esmé invited. "There's plenty left in the shaker. Cold out?"

"Yes, it's damned raw," Steve Petrie replied stripping off a topcoat, "but the stars are out. Any vodka? I've been 'way out to hell and gone——" He checked himself.

Esmé smiled. "You can speak freely. We've a new member to our cell. Eric and I have just contracted for the services of the eminent Major Hugh North."

Narrowly North studied the reaction on Velvalee's lively pink and white features; he learned little, her grimace might have expressed either disillusionment or surprised satisfaction. "Well, isn't that *some*thing? Sho' now, Steve, Ah lose my bet, don't Ah?"

Steve offered his hand. "Well, it's swell knowing we're going to work together—great stuff. Comrade Esmé is pretty hard to convince."

"What are you so excited about, Steve?"

"This. I found it at our letter drop in the Rue Iskander."

What he held out, North perceived, was nothing more unusual than a copy of *La République,* the local French-language newspaper.

Velvalee burst out, "And Ah found another copy at my li'l ole brass beater's shop."

"Both are from Yusuf." Steve appeared greatly agitated. "He's been in contact with Phoebus Skoularis."

Esmé uttered a small incredulous gasp. "You're positive?"

"Sure. They're pin-pointed with Yusuf's mark." His broad, tobacco-browned forefinger indicated the apex of the letter "A" in the newspaper's title.

North, although manifesting only a mild interest, was made aware of three tiny holes puncturing the newsprint. He experienced a feeling of suspicion mingled with disappointment. Surely the mighty MVD's agents would not employ so archaic a means of communication as the ancient and highly vulnerable perforation code?

Without waiting to do more than to shed their outer garments the new arrivals hurried over to the desk.

"Well, Esmé," Petrie challenged, "let's see what your expert makes of these newspapers."

"Don't bother me with such kindergarten nonsense," North snapped. "One will get you ten that those newspapers are speckled with pin-point perforations. Go ahead and read the messages yourselves, you know how." His manner was so natural that Esmé seated herself, pulled forward a student lamp and tilted upwards its glowing green glass shade until light flooded her firm, squarish face and cast the silhouette of her head upon the ceiling.

As North had predicted, the moment Esmé held a sheet of the single fold copy over the light tiny bright points glowed through the punctured newsprint. He watched Velvalee's pencil commence to take down the letters immediately above those tiny holes as Esmé read off: "E K S J B——"

Kuzak objected suddenly. "Say, you're doin' it wrong. That don't make no sense at all."

North chuckled at the evident embarrassment of his hosts. "Of course not. Even in a Banana Republic the Intelligence wouldn't be childish enough to use pin point in clear."

"Well!" Kuzak flushed angrily when a check-back proved the accuracy of Esmé's observations. "What the hell's wrong?"

Steve scratched his crisp, brown-topped head; resembling nothing so much as some football hero faced with a stiff exam, he drawled, "Well, Major, what d'you make of this?"

The room became a well of stillness until North grinned. "Obviously, Esmé or some one of you knows the key word. Of course, I don't."

It puzzled him that for some moments Esmé sat biting nervously at her lower lip and staring at the jumbled line of letters. "There is only one thing wrong," she spoke as to herself. "Yusuf hasn't been given any code word other than Beria. Should we try that?"

North was immensely amused. Incredible that these renegades should really be stumped. Or were they? He attempted a calculated risk.

"Looks like it might be ye olde reliable Playfair construction. What do you think, Steve?"

Petrie hesitated, then blurted, "Here, let me see if I can get it."

"Meanwhile," the Intelligence Officer begged plaintively, "Pete, don't let that dinner scorch, will you?"

"Jeeze—I clean forgot," and he bolted out to the kitchen.

The student lamp created melodramatic high lights about the cheeks and eyes of the witnesses. Velvalee, still rubbing plump small hands against the chill of the outdoors, almost hungrily fixed her huge, sherry-tinted eyes on North's lean features. "That man's sho'ly improved his looks," she thought. "Laws, he don't look a bit like that hunk of dog-meat Steve and Pete fetched in."

On a sheet of ruled paper Petrie was drawing a grid with four horizontal spaces and six vertical ones. Soon the square was filled in to Petrie's satisfaction.

E	K	S	IJ	B	A
C	D	F	G	H	L
M	N	O	P	Q	R
T	U	V	W	X	YZ

"Now, Esmé," Petrie directed, "read off the letters above the punctures in the newspaper, will you?"

North, having retreated to the background, smiled to himself and poured off the dregs of the cocktail shaker; he felt the need of reinforcement, he was that ravenous.

Esmé read off the message. Dutifully, Petrie called off the letter to the right of the one corresponding on the chart. Presently he threw down his pencil and glared at the sweater-clad figure in the background. "Whatever's the answer, it's obvious that we're not using the correct key word."

"Sho'ly seems like we-all are goin' at this problem all

cock-eyed. Maybe we should invite Hugh, who seems to be havin' such a good time, to take ovah?"

Velvalee swung her panelled gown across the room, sank into an armchair so deep that her position exposed a length of definitely stimulating hosiery and two crescents of pale under thigh.

"If you'll stop working me before I'm either fed or paid, I'll make a suggestion that we examine that second newspaper." He cast the discomfited Murfee girl a patronizing glance.

The ensuing repast was memorable. The others, save Esmé, seemed all too glad to postpone a study of the newspaper until the last of the beef, onions, *borek* and concluding *kadingoğsü* had been consumed. Turkish coffee, thick as maple syrup and nearly as sweet, having been consumed, North arose, deliberately surveyed his companions, and winked at Velvalee. Half the battle with this species of humanity, he knew, was to refuse to become impressed beyond a point.

"All right, *amigos,* suppose we take a look at that second copy of *La République.*"

"What about it?" Esmé wanted to learn.

"Don't know yet. Let's hold it to your light."

Very quickly he found that no punctures whatever had been made in the second newspaper dated Tuesday, November 14, beyond those three holes in the letter A which constituted the unknown Yusuf's identification mark. "Um. This first is for Monday, the second's for Tuesday. Why should your lad Yusuf leave two newspapers at the two different drops on the same day?"

Kuzak slowly massaged his big jaw with powerful fingers. "Mebbe he used a chemical, huh, Doc?"

"No," came Stephen Petrie's instant objection. "It's next to impossible to use chemical ink on newsprint; there's too much acid in it already."

North did not agree but only continued to scan Tuesday's paper until, all at once, he noted a very tiny puncture through all the extreme corners of both sheets. "What's this?" He thought a moment, aware of an intense regard from four pairs of eyes. "I'm not sure, but maybe I've a lead. Have you a linoleum-covered table—or is there some linoleum flooring anywhere?"

Esmé said, "Why yes, there's linoleum on the kitchen table, but what do you want with it?"

Thoughtfully North fingered the obnoxious pearl buttons on his sweater. "I want to test a theory—that these two newspapers complement one another. After all, they were deposited by the same agent, weren't they?"

"How might they combine?" Velvalee demanded in round-eyed suspicion.

"You'll learn, Sugar Child."

A few moments later the entire group found itself bent above the kitchen table.

"Pete, draw a tight circle around each puncture mark you find in Monday's paper. And someone fetch me some thumb tacks."

Presently, by means of tacks affixed at each corner, North arranged the Monday paper precisely above the Tuesday edition of *La République*. Once the papers were pinned one above the other, North's movements quickened. He was fully aware of Petrie's and Esmé's half-suspicious, half-hopeful manner; Kuzak and Velvalee looked more at ease. "Now, Velvalee, Honey, suppose you run and dig me up a large darning needle."

When Velvalee returned she was looking remarkably sultry and alluring for having repaired her make-up and exchanged her blouse for a pale blue pullover that did ample justice to her bust. North poised the shining little strip of steel, selected the first puncture, then pushed the needle's point through the tiny circle Petrie had drawn.

North exercised great delicacy in raising the upper sheet. To Esmé he directed, "Take down these letters," then bent to see where the puncture appeared in Tuesday's paper. "Letter's a 'P.'"

"Check," Esmé said. "Go on."

The Intelligence Officer continued to puncture the journal beneath apertures in the newspaper above. Eventually he straightened.

"Well, there it is. Who sent it?" he asked so casually that Steve replied without hesitation. "Phoebus Skoularis, an agent of ours working in Bulgaria. Okay, Esmé, read off the whole message."

"Phoebus. *Walewski vu mais perdu a Umur Fakih.*"

"Come again," Kuzak invited. "That's French, ain't it?"

"Correct. You're a bright boy, Pete. Phoebus is saying that someone called Walewski was seen but lost at Umur Fakih."

Walewski! North felt his heart give a surge mighty as the rush of a comber up a shelving beach. By God, then Josef Walewski *must still be alive!*—or had been not long ago. Where Umir Fakih might be he had no idea, but that ignorance could be repaired.

"Get on with the translation of that letter." Esmé's voice was that of a virago.

"Can't you read French?" North appeared dumbfounded.

"No, even though I do speak Serb, Czech and some other languages."

"'Walewski seen but lost at Umur Fakih,'" North repeated. "MVD is reported closing in on Walewski, but you must alert all agents along frontier."

What frontier? It was infinitely exasperating not to know. Kuzak's breath came in with a soft, hissing noise. Petrie was looking questioningly at Esmé, but Velvalee was quite calmly lighting a cigarette.

Esmé hesitated, then almost ran over to a telephone in the hallway. Unfortunately, she dialled so rapidly that

North could not count those clicks which might have be-trayed the number called.

"Eric? Yes, this is Esmé. I've news—yes, concerning the matter we talked about this morning.—Of course, I'm sure."

Velvalee drawled, "Whyn't you tell him it was the Majuh——"

She fell silent, pouted at the Murfee girl's furious look. Esmé listened over a long interval.

"Okay—I'll hurry right over. What's that? Oh, swell, glad you took care of that." She turned, beaming. "Eric is de-lighted over your—your wonderful work, Hugh. This is really a great day for all of us." She smiled. "I'll give you the cable receipt for your salary as soon as the office is open in the morning."

Petrie looked as annoyed and jealous as a football star unexpectedly pulled out of a big game to be replaced by a promising substitute. "What else did Eric say?"

"Why, he thinks it'd be a good idea if you, Hugh, can get yourself and Velvalee invited to Melek Effendi's dinner dance."

"Maybe, when is it?"

"Tomorrow night."

"I'll need plenty of money—that's a pretty closed corpo-ration crowd." No one would have suspected that behind his impassive expression North was calculating as shrewdly as ever he had. "God knows if I can reduce these bruises—and I'll have to cook up a yarn about my thick ear, but I imagine I can wangle an invitation."

Invitation! Sometime, a long while back, he seemed to re-call having promised Jingles Lawson to escort her. Jingles? How was she taking all this? Suddenly he yearned for the sound of her voice and the play of those fascinating gray-blue eyes.

"What do you want me to do at Melek Effendi's party?"

"You'll get Velvalee an invite, too?" Esmé returned to the point.

"Yes. Will she be my partner?"

He experienced a modest shock when, vigorously, Esmé shook her close-cropped black head and said, "No. Honey Chile here is going, but not with you. You'd be surprised how she can sweet-talk useful information out of those wet-behind-the-ears hot pilots. You weren't on the stage for nothing, were you?"

Velvalee manufactured a smile as artificial as a paper rose. "Ah was considered a real fine actress by——"

"Sure I know, we all know who. Major, you will arrange an invite for her."

"I'll do my best if I get the promise of at least two dances with our lovely comrade," declared he with such seriousness that Esmé frowned. "Right now I need some shoes, an overcoat, a hat and some money. Pray God the hotel hasn't sold my luggage for room rent."

When, an hour later, Hugh North in company with Kuzak had disappeared in search of a cab, Velvalee Petrie stretched with feline grace and commenced to get ready for bed. While unhooking her brassiere she demanded suddenly, "Tell me somethin'?"

"What?" The Murfee girl's query was muffled by the jersey dress at the moment half over her head.

"You fixin' to trust him—Hugh—all the way?"

Esmé turned. "I expect so. You couldn't shake him, could you? I know I couldn't."

"No, and Ah sho'ly gave him the works," Velvalee admitted, "but, Honey, he's smart like a barnful of owls. Ah, well——" She seated herself and commenced to undo her garter catches. "Ah cain't say why, but Ah'm not sure about this heah change in him. Maybe it's because Ah've found nobody Ah could trust," she sighed, "since Ah left home."

"Steve doesn't agree, and neither do I." Sharply Esmé considered her companion's slight figure. "No. If he had fallen for the Party Line arguments, or pretended to cotton to our ideas of World Revolution, I'd have said you're right. But he didn't, so, Velvalee, I'm certain—sure he's fed up and ready to look out for Number One."

"Whatever he is, he's sho'ly mah idea of Mister Dreamboat. Hasn't he the grandest manners? So polite and pretty talkin'?"

"I suppose so," Esmé agreed, "but don't think we're not keeping him watched day and night."

The blonde young woman hesitated. "Suppose he was to try a two-time?"

Esmé's teeth glinted. "He'll get exactly what Alberoni, Bernard, Stoddard and the rest got." The taller girl hesitated in the act of removing her slip. "Of course it doesn't pay to be too sure, so suppose, Honey Chile, you use your best bitchery to win him back to duty with dear old God-damned United States?"

CHAPTER 12

The Khamoun Apartments

IN THE BEDROOM of her modest apartment on the Rue Sakak Miss Haïdi Lawson gazed with an unusual lack of enthusiasm upon that slight and sprightly girdle which had arrived so recently the air of New York still clung to it. Lips pursed, she slipped the peach and white contrivance from its cardboard cylinder and tossed it onto the bed, then returned to her dressing table, and dolefully commenced the routine of applying "Cinderella's Pumpkin" to long and narrow fingernails.

If tears would not undoubtedly have swelled her eyelids and turned her nose a baby's bottom pink, she most probably would have yielded to an all-but overwhelming impulse to fling herself down for a good long cry.

Weren't men the absolute zero? Damn Hugh North anyway! When she learned that he was still alive and about town somewhere her heart had been lifted up among the planets.

"Damn him for not even phoning," she muttered and blew savagely at her fingernails to harden the enamel. Mechanically she inspected her image in the mirror. Her Kelly green negligee fringed by ostrich trim two shades lighter went not at all badly with her tanned complexion and light brown, shoulder-length hair; but she never noticed it.

"Whatever in the world could have upset an eminently sane Joe like Hugh North to send him running wild like this?" Jingles glanced at her travelling clock. "Lordy! Eight-fifteen already?"

She was barely able to smile at her doleful expression on reflecting that if Hugh hadn't gone haywire he would be calling for her within the next fifteen minutes. And to think that for days she'd been anticipating Melek Effendi's party! How wonderful it would be to come sailing serenely into the budding season's most brilliant affair on the arm of the famous Major Hugh North. There was something about his bearing that attracted, almost demanded, attention whenever he entered a room—not that he ever could be accused of posing or play-acting.

In spite of everything her eyes filled and she had to dab hurriedly at them with a bit of cleansing tissue.

Why was he, after all these years, still only a major? True, back in Washington there were those who claimed that he had refused promotion time and again saying that higher rank almost certainly would chain him to a desk in the Pentagon. She could understand his revolt at such a fate. The living death of those who worked in the artificially lighted, poorly ventilated catacombs of that strategic monstrosity generally proved too much for a person of either sensitivity or imagination.

Jingles arose, let fall the negligee, and on mules of green satin crossed to her bureau.

A small but imaginative array of lingerie confronted her. Should she wear the yellow panties with white lace, or that frivolous dark blue and ecru job which only a Parisian couturière could have devised? What the hell did it matter? In tempo with her mood she decided on a severely tailored affair of eggshell white. At the same moment the doorbell shrilled.

"*Ne istiyorsunuz?* What do you want?" she called, resuming the green negligee.

"*Tun aydun, Bayan,* good evening, Miss." A uniformed

Turkish lad whose dark eyes were as eloquent as a Southern Democrat's electioneering, bowed profoundly while offering a square pasteboard box that could only have contained flowers.

Puzzled, she smiled. "Wait a minute, *Tesekkur ederim,*" and returned with a ten-piastre note. The boy's triple row of silver tunic buttons twinkled to the profundity of his bow.

"Who in the world? It couldn't—*no!*"

Fingers quivering, Jingles ripped open the envelope to an attached card and read:

Hope that these insignificant flowers will remind you that we have a date for tonight. If you haven't made other arrangements, please meet me at the Peacock Bar and we'll go on to Melek's shindig from there. I'll wait until nine.

The initials "NH" were entirely superfluous.

"Oh, oh! Hugh, you sweet and infuriating bastard!"

For several moments Jingles remained before the dressing table mirror and now, in spite of everything, she wept just a little in her overwhelming relief.

The corsage proved original and exquisite, of white and scarlet orchids as tiny as her little fingernail.

Yielding to a rapturous change of heart she discarded the severely tailored number and, without an instant's hesitation, buttoned on that frivolous Parisian confection. Merely to make assurance doubly sure, she phoned the Peacock Bar and instructed the bell captain to inform Major North that she would appear within half an hour. Actually, nearly an hour would elapse before she'd put in an appearance; after all these dreary hours he'd caused he had a chastening wait due him.

"Talk of last-minute miracles!" she thought, then became aware of an inexplicable sense of disquiet. It ruined her peace of mind, like the threat of a ragged fingernail which could ruin an expensive pair of stockings.

"Well, my dear, I guess you'll do," she laughed as, radiant and groomed to the last detail, she paused before the full-length mirror on her way to the door.

Even before she appeared at the rendezvous she guessed her ensemble to be more than adequately successful. A young French captain of Spahis, very handsome in his pale blue tunic, brave with scarlet trimming and silver buttons, treated her to such a frankly appraising stare that she flushed, and a Turkish naval officer smiled, raised his eyes to Heaven and, bowing just a trifle, placed a hand above his heart.

Like a prima ballerina advancing upstage Jingles sailed into the bar's foyer and tried not to run when she recognized that familiar straight wide-shouldered figure standing near some jeweler's showcase.

Lord! Could this decorous and distinguished gentleman wearing a sparkling row of miniature decorations on the left lapel of his dress suit be one with that ghastly creature she had last beheld at the Three Moons?

"Hugh! Oh—my dear." He spun about and the familiar wide smile flickered beneath his close-clipped black mustache.

"Jingles!" She read, beyond risk of mistake, a swift up-rush of joy in that gaunt and unaccustomedly pallid countenance as he strode forward. He halted two strides short of her, and stood quite still peering from under straight black brows.

How very lovely she was, this supple and alert young woman, with the shining gray-blue eyes and soft brown hair a-gleam in the foyer's lights. The little orchids seemed to hover over, rather than be affixed to, her evening purse of silver and pastel blue brocade. Her strapless evening gown was of silvered lamé and cut so low that—as he told her later—he was afraid to look for fear she might sneeze, and again afraid not to for fear of missing the result. At the moment Jingles' smooth and somewhat squarish shoulders were concealed by a dark blue velvet stole trimmed with chinchilla. She halted, summoned an uncertain smile.

"All right, I'll stop so's you 'can drink me in,' though I expect you'd prefer a cocktail. I know I would."

"If it didn't suggest a horrible pun—I'd say you look like a nectar special." He evoked a magnificent look of envy from the Captain of Spahis by bussing her soundly on the lips and thus acquiring enough lip rouge to have interested even a Rumanian colonel. "—And how's my favorite ink slinger been making out?"

"As if a certain king-sized louse named North ever gave it a thought," Jingles reproached. "Darling, do we have to head straight for Melek Effendi's little clambake?"

"I suppose we should be on our way right now, but to the Devil with it. Do you still go for stingers?"

"Just you wait and see, you great infuriating oaf."

Many heads, feminine as well as masculine, followed the progress of the pair across the foyer and all the way into the cocktail lounge. Once they had settled into comfortable armchairs and North had ordered their stingers, his expression sobered. A quick but not obvious inspection of their near neighbors reassured him sufficiently to ask quietly, "Jingles dear, will you please forgive and pretend that I've just arrived in Istanbul? I know you think I've acted like a damned fool—maybe so. I only ask you to believe that I've had some excuse——"

"Oh Hugh, of course. I'm not even going to be curious. You see—" her hand darted out and closed over his, "I'm so—so unspeakably relieved. Really," her teeth gleamed in the generous width of her smile, "I won't give the past two weeks a thought, cross my heart and hope to die. When are you going to return to duty?"

Mechanically North considered the entrance of a very lovely young Turkish girl chiefly noteworthy because of dark, brown velvet eyes and hair so black it gave off blue highlights. With her strode a gangling and hawk-faced Scotch brigadier out of the Argyll and Sutherlands. The red tabs on his lapels and the highly polished buttons wrought an effective contrast to the sombre dinner coats and dress suits beyond him.

Other uniforms were in evidence, several American and British naval officers, a few Turkish field officers in gray-green, two French airline pilots wearing herbaceous borders of decoration ribbons, and a Greek major-general in a threadbare uniform. Of course there were plenty of American Air Force pilots tilting their hands in explanatory maneuvers and bending elbows between times.

The Lawson girl accepted a cigarette. North missed her massive bracelet and its innumerable tinkling charms and said so.

Smiling, he settled back and ordered a second set of stingers. "You know, Jingles, I forget you're the product of a celebrated educator and a Turkish princess until you get all dolled up? Your mother must have been a brave young woman to marry a professor and keep house in the Near East, especially after World War One."

Her eyes crinkled at their corners. "Why? Don't money and brains make a satisfactory combination? Just think— with your money and my brains what a paragon we'd produce!"

When at length their chuckles had subsided, North inquired, "How goes your assignment?"

There was a momentary hesitation. "Been wanting to discuss it with you, Hugh. You'll recall that T.W.P. sent me out here to do a series on the modern Turkish woman and her place in the community?"

"I suppose your foreign desk had no one else who speaks

Near East lingoes." He grinned but detected a certain undercurrent of seriousness. "Well, so what?"

"I've pretty near covered the subject." She placed slim fingers on his wrist. "Hugh, have you talked to the Embassy?"

"No," said he quickly, "and I don't intend to. But it's you we were talking about, as I recall."

"Well," she told him in a lowered voice, "I'm free-lancing now. Having been raised in these parts I figure I can dig up some pretty hot stuff on Commie infiltration into Turkey."

It was amazing how imperceptibly, yet definitely, his easy manner departed. "Look, Jingles, that's dynamite, more than you suspect. For God's sake don't start mixing in a mess like that."

Her chin went up a little and she stared curiously at him. "I don't understand what you're driving at, Hugh; maybe I don't want to, but already I've got some pretty damn' promising leads."

"For instance?" North invited over his cocktail glass.

Jingles continued, "Tell me, have you ever heard tell of a wench calling herself Esmé Murfee?"

He offered her a very long Turkish cigarette. "Can't say as I have. What's that lady's claim to distinction?"

"She ain't no lady," Jingles corrected bitterly. "I recognized her on the Rue Djent Yami two days ago and I wasn't mistaken because I covered her court-martial in Liège back in '46. Incidentally, her right name's Sheridan, Patricia Sheridan."

"Yes? What was she tried for?"

"Stealing. The gal was an Army nurse who shacked up after V-E Day with one of our gallant Russian allies and got caught at it—along with the theft of ten thousand c.c.'s of penicillin which she sold to her boy friend, Colonel Zalezeski."

North's sudden inspiration that the elusive Ben Gramont

was about to be identified died aborning. Jingles kept her voice low and ran her eye over nearby tables while speaking. "Well, as I said, la Sheridan got court-martialled, was convicted and sentenced to serve five years, but she escaped into the Russian Zone."

"—Sounds like a fascinating gal. What d'you figure she's doing in these latitudes?" North demanded and, leaning forward, picked up a microscopic coffee cup.

They both hesitated because a dance orchestra in the adjoining lounge suddenly commenced a rendition of "Time on My Hands" as loud as it was weird. North considered the implications of Jingles' recent revelations and found them replete with possibilities. Over the hysterical braying of a trombone he caught her voice.

"I made some inquiries and learned this much. La Murfee poses as an art student. This dear little Commie baggage has been here for nearly a year and lives out beyond the Valideh Mosque somewhere."

Very casually North inquired, "What makes you think she's active for the Commies?"

"Think?" Jingles flared. "On account of her conviction she hates America, and how! At the end of her trial I myself heard her rail and curse the United States until the M.P.'s shut her up."

North signalled for the check. "Clearly a fascinating bitch, as they'd say in Shanghai; why worry over her?"

"Because," she bent forward, "she's got herself a Red Cross job in our Military Mission's infirmary. She's sweet as pie there and, my God, does she get around!"

The Intelligence Officer quite mechanically straightened his white tie. "Could be she's up to mischief but, Jingles, it's a damned dangerous business you are proposing to meddle with. Besides the C.I.C. is here and on the job. That's what they're paid for." He shifted to the edge of his seat. "How's about shoving off?"

"In a minute, Hugh. I wish you'd take me seriously, I'm not fooling." A slim diamond bracelet on the Lawson girl's wrist flickered when she raised her cocktail glass. She made no motion to drink, however. "Listen, dear, there's not only the Murfee wench to think about, but I've noticed quite a few of weird and wonderful Americans hereabout."

"Nothing strange about that," North pointed out. "Ever notice that most Americans who live abroad—by choice, I mean—are usually as queer as a nine-dollar bill? Your true expatriate generally can't, or for some odd reason doesn't want to, live in the U.S."

"Yes, generally I suppose they haven't made good at home, but still that doesn't mean they're anti-American."

The dance music swelled and the two for a moment watched dancers in the lounge.

"A fine evening, no?" The speaker was a short flat-faced fellow in a baggy dinner coat and wearing a gold pince-nez. He went on in some Slavic language North could not identify, but which Jingles answered fluently and gave him a nod of dismissal.

"Simpich of the Bulgarian Consulate," she explained. "He's forever trying to pump me for news. Are you still staying at the Pera Palace?" Jingles inquired, rearranging the orchids on her purse.

"Yes. Praise God, the manager didn't sell my luggage. By the bye," he was at pains to appear casual, "where in Turkey is a place called Umur Fakih?"

"Umur Fakih?" Jingles' lovely gray-blue eyes widened, swung sharply in his direction. "Why, that isn't in Turkey at all. Umur Fakih is a town in Bulgaria very close to where the Greek, Turkish and Bulgarian borders converge." She treated him to an unflinching regard. "Hugh, what the devil! Are you trying to put over a fast one?"

"Of course not, why?" Momentarily, he visualized that kitchen in the Blue Villa with Esmé, Velvalee, Petrie and

Kuzak bending above those brilliantly illumined copies of
La République.

"It's about the hottest espionage center in the Near East.
Now will you tell me why you're interested?"

"I've become a profound student of geography, darling."
North smiled.

Jingles gave her strapless gown a reassuring upward
twitch. "I ketch—as Dwight Fiske's Colonel Butlerpants
used to say, 'It's none of your damned business,' but I'll linger in your hair until you have promised you'll see Colonel
McKenzie."

He was at once fascinated and alarmed, and while holding her stole demanded, "Why should I?"

The Lawson girl, noticing that nearby couples were entirely self-absorbed, whispered, "I'm not asking where
you've been but—but don't you know all the World is holding its breath?"

The peculiarly stimulating fragrance of her person eddied
about him as he helped her into the evening wrap. "Oh,
Hugh, I don't exactly know what's up, but—well—I've been
in the newspaper racket long enough to develop a sort of
sixth sense. Why should the Soviets suddenly get so damned
bold at the U.N.? Why should security measures at Military
Mission Headquarters and the Embassy become stringent
all in a week? Why should the censor clamp down so hard
on our dispatches?"

North glanced once about the dimly lit bar and its useful
pale blue mirrors before evading, "Damn it, Jingles, I'm no
busman, and I'm still on my holiday. What say you, my
poppet, to hailing us a taxi from the street, painted and oh
so fair, and then on to our excellent Turkish host and his
party?"

CHAPTER 13

Melek Effendi Entertains

THE dinner dance given by Haroun Melek Effendi in honor of General Hasan Rechad Pasha, Chief of Staff to the Army of the Turkish Republic, proved to be quite the most lavish and brilliant of recent years. Not a few foreign diplomats, Cabinet ministers, and even an ambassador or two, somehow, had found it imperative to be in Istanbul on that date, even at the price of a rough aerial voyage down from Ankara. Melek Effendi's residence, formerly the Imperial German Embassy, had been brilliantly and tastefully refurbished affording a flattering background for the vari-colored uniforms of the Consular Corps, military, air and naval attachés and various officials of the Turkish government; campaign ribbons and decorations gaily challenged the glitter of old-fashioned crystal chandeliers which still supported candles. These last shed a rarely warm light on the vari-colored gowns and plentiful jewelry of ladies whirling and gliding to dance tunes rendered by Michelle Mahoney and her Merry Men.

A small chill invaded North's being on watching Peter Kuzak happily and expertly playing his accordion among them.

If their music did not quite reflect the trend current in New York, it remained, nonetheless, a most satisfactory facsimile thereof. Despite a chill wind beating down the Boulevard Avas Pasha, the former Embassy's ballroom grew so warm that more and more guests sought cooling drinks and entertainment of other sorts in Melek Effendi's salon, or in his well-tended conservatory. Others in search of even less noise wandered into the library or retired to the billiard room.

Hugh North still was attempting to digest a trifling eight-course dinner including such hors d'oeuvres and appetizers as *balslava* and *simits, tavouk geresh,* a delicious dish of powdered chicken breast cooked in milk, *inam bayildi* and sheeps' ear consommé. Regretfully he avoided a huge buffet designed to satisfy the hunger of such guests as had arrived near midnight, and after the dinner itself. Upon it lay a heap of luscious-appearing kadingoğsü, that sweet pastry which Turks call "breast of woman."

He was finding it equally trying to ignore the presence of Velvalee Petrie—radiant in a bouffant gown of rose taffeta, and of Colonel Alexander McKenzie, West Point classmate and lifelong friend. Alex, he perceived, must be laboring under tension; not in years had the lines of worry been so deeply etched on the Military Attaché's craggy features. He noticed also that, as the night wore on and guests commenced to take their leave, McKenzie kept disappearing into the library.

North deduced that Melek Effendi's private study must lie beyond it. Thus far they had exchanged only the most fleeting glances, yet North became aware that he must see McKenzie and wondered why he had all but imperceptibly warned against a rather handsome young fellow in a commendably tailored dinner coat; this Levantine, quite possibly by coincidence, had remained in the background ever since he and Jingles had quitted the Peacock Bar.

A slim panatela between his fingers, North wandered back into the ballroom and, after taking possession of a cocktail, lingered on the edge of a stag line watching Velvalee undulate amid a circle of admiring young pilots. How crisp, sunburned and naïve they looked in their new slate-blue uniforms. The diminutive secretary's candy-blonde hair for the occasion had been trained into a glistening crown, the make-up was effective, and her flowing, old-fashioned gown of rose taffeta could not have been more flattering.

"Wonder what the comrades back on Lubliana Street would think of such Western decadence. Hope to God those young heroes button their lips—there's nothing like a girl from home."

In search of Jingles he sauntered into the humid atmosphere of the greenhouse. She wasn't there, though quite a few enamored couples were making good use of screening palm fronds and other greenery.

He discovered her at length dancing with a young man in a faultlessly cut dinner coat. He had trained his reddish mustache Coldstream Guardee fashion, flat, thick and flaring upwards as if to divert attention from a faint white cicatrice sketching a demi-lune across his chin.

All at once North wondered why Ted Stoddard wasn't on hand. Certainly an M.I. officer should have attended such an occasion.

Among the guests were represented nearly every Intelligence Corps in Europe and the Americas. Several of them he recognized instantly. He started to address C. Poindexter Spencer, First Secretary of the Embassy, yet checked himself because that individual stared as if he had been a complete stranger. Even less assuring was it to behold Velvalee chatting first with Michelle Mahoney and then with Kuzak.

Like a siren commencing to attain full pitch and volume, alarms sounded at the back of Hugh North's mind and, for the first time in months he found himself wishing that, instead of a heavy silver and gold cigarette case, he were carrying that compact .32 Colt automatic. Praise God, he seldom had found use for it, but tonight, he was beginning to decide, might prove an exception which proved the rule.

"Can't wait much longer. Must talk to McKenzie," he ad-

vised himself. "Something seems about ready to break, and
Alex should hear about Walewski's having been seen."

An English footman, impeccable in livery, striped waist-
coat and white gloves, approached him bearing a loaded
tray.

Having selected a glass of champagne, North made his
way to that spot where his host lingered in company with
the guest of honor. General Rechad noticed North's approach, took a step forward and greeted in heavily-accented
French: "What a pleasure, *mon cher Commandant,* thus to
renew our acquaintanceship of Smyrna days. *Dieu!* How
the years fly by, is that not so, Melek Effendi?"

The big-nosed tobacco dealer nodded. "Madame Melek
and I were in despair that you could not attend our little
fête." Still smiling he added softly, "It is most urgent that
you come to my study before three o'clock—and how did
you leave our friends in Washington?" he continued in a
normal tone.

"—Hoping for your return, my dear sir. Your hospitality
is still talked of among the hostesses of Washington," he
stated a little louder than was necessary for, from the corner
of his eye, he glimpsed Jingles approaching on the arm of
her tall, red-blond dancing partner.

"Ah, Miss Lawson," smiled the grizzled Chief of Staff,
"we were hoping you would not dance all night. Eh, Haroun? And I am sure Major North is consumed by jeal-
ousy."

"Naturally—but I've learned to try to be not too selfish.
Right?" He smiled widely at Jingles.

"Really, General, when there's so well-stocked a bar about,
I've learned not to worry over Major North's pining." She
turned to her partner. "Eric, I wish to present you. General
Rechad," the Turk's aquiline features broke into a broad
and friendly smile, "this is Wing-Commander Brecon-
Fyffe."

"I'm only an ex-wing-commander, sir," smilingly corrected the tall young man in clipped British accents. "Only an airline officer these days, you know."

"And this," Jingles continued, "is my companion in crime —Major Hugh North."

"A pleasure," North said and, as the two men shook hands, made a swift appraisal. Eric, after all, was neither a common name nor an uncommon one.

"You two really must know each other better," Jingles declared lightly. "Eric plays a very sound game of poker and when it comes to limericks!"

All three nodded as Melek Effendi and the Chief of Staff excused themselves and moved off in the direction of the library.

"Sounds like the start of a beautiful friendship, Commander," North observed, "as I'm on leave, I'd dearly love a game of draw or five-card stud. Perish those confounded poker perversions which call for wild cards or spits-in-the-ocean!"

"Hear! Hear!" Brecon-Fyffe's ruddy features lit. "I say, Miss Lawson, won't you please bring your friend around for a drink and a quiet game—say Thursday next?"

"Why not?" She slid her arm through North's. "Eric is engineering plans for a British International Airways depot to be built here next spring."

"Sounds like quite a job."

Brecon-Fyffe nodded. "It's all of that. Perhaps you'll look in on our efforts out to Ayazeyeh."

"I will if I learn how to spell it."

"AYAZEYEH."

"Did you say the fourth letter was 'zee' or 'dee'?"

"Zee," Brecon-Fyffe returned. "What say we catch the top of a fresh bottle of Mumm's Cordon Rouge? Next to Moët & Chandon, that's my favorite."

The music struck up for the benefit of a diminished

crowd and Brecon-Fyffe turned with a broad smile. "I'm quite aware that Miss Lawson is your partner, Major, but I'm having such a wonderful time I'm wondering if I might bribe you for a second dance by introducing you to a very charming young lady."

"You place the request so very diplomatically," North smiled, "you leave me no choice—provided Miss Lawson doesn't object." He gave her arm a little squeeze that pled for understanding. "Come along, Jingles, let's see who you might get swapped for."

"Commander Brecon-Fyffe is a divine dancer, so I'll let you go." Then in an undertone she breathed, "Hugh! Let's leave at the first opportunity. I've learned something you must know—it's—it's critically important."

Firmly, almost rudely, Commander Brecon-Fyffe shouldered his way through a group of young flyers until he reached Velvalee at the core of the circle. The former actress' eyes were sparkling and her candy-blonde hair shone like a glistening aureole.

The Englishman bowed rather awkwardly. "Miss Petrie, I've been wanting you to meet a compatriot. Major North here has recently arrived in town and knows very few people so I trust you'll be kind while I embezzle his partner for this one dance."

Nothing could have appeared more genuine than Velvalee's delighted, "Why, Commandeh, aren't you the nicest man?" she fluttered, smoothing her full, old-rose skirt. "All evenin' Ah've been wonderin' who this perfectly stunnin' stranger might be. Did you say, suh, yo' name is No'th?"

Certainly she was proving a far better actress than North had estimated her. Not by even a tremor of her full, brilliantly tinted lips did Velvalee indicate that she and North had met previously, almost intimately, one might say.

The Intelligence Officer bowed over her hand. "If my surname won't prejudice you against me, Miss Petrie, shall we dance?"

North directed a thoughtful glance after the couple which had preceded them onto the dance floor. Eric Brecon-Fyffe? Whoever he really might be, he certainly had mastered his British inflection to a T; and yet, how could he have been so incredibly careless as to betray himself by a recent and egregious error of speech.

Brecon-Fyffe was about to lead Jingles' slim, silver lamé figure onto the dance floor when he paused to acknowledge the nod of a U.S. Air Force captain. Savagely, North goaded his memory. Damnation! Where before had he seen that rather swarthy fellow? To part certain veils drawn over the past two weeks by alcohol was not proving easy.

Ha! He remembered, or thought he did. The fellow had been one of that weird and unsavory clientèle which patronized the Blue Moon. Name was Larkin? God! This then was the traitor—or criminally careless oaf—who'd managed to compromise that top secret report. Fervently, he wished he could make up his mind about Captain Larkin.

Velvalee naturally proved a most excellent partner and drifted over the parquet floor like a winged seed. North cast the flyer another look and found him over-decorated for good taste and anything but handsome. The A-2's eyes were very small and intensely black, his complexion darker than that of many Turks.

"My, isn't this a real whing-ding?" Velvalee demanded. "An' it's simply wondahful to be among so many home folks. At least Ah think so." Velvalee's great sherry-hued eyes lifted inquiringly. "How d'you feel bein' back among these—these decadent plutocrats?"

He wrinkled his still slightly bruised nose at her. "Why not help the poor devils enjoy life while they can? Who's that young Air Force captain with the chestful of ribbons?"

"Ah expect you must mean Dave Larkin," she replied

while expertly he spun her out of the path of a juggernaut-like Scandinavian couple. "Dave's just about the sweetest boy evah, a very special friend of mine. Want to meet him?" Had she, while cuddling close to his cheek, forgotten about that letter? For the life of him he couldn't make up his mind whether Velvalee could be as inept as she appeared.

"Later on, I'd like to."

"Hi, there, you two! How are you getting on?" For the first time North became aware of Stephen Petrie's presence. How he had gained admittance, and why he had arrived so late were matters for future contemplation. The fact was that he stood there to all outward appearances an American college man so recently graduated that physical fitness still clung to him.

The openness of Petrie's expression was marred by a chill gleam in those wide-set, light brown eyes of his. "Hullo, Major, mind if I have my duty dance with Sis?" His tone suggested a command rather than a request.

"I do mind," came North's affable observation, "but I suppose a girl's brother does have some rights in that direction."

North's smile faded when they went spinning off among the diminished number of dancers. Almost immediately Steve began whispering some urgent message into Velvalee's small pink ear. Increasingly ill at ease and alert for nuances, the Intelligence Officer sought the buffet and there accepted another glass of Melek Effendi's excellent champagne.

During a leisurely progress towards his host's library he found time to wonder over where Melek Effendi might have discovered this better-than-average orchestra. Clearly, Michelle Mahoney must once have ranked as a first-class café chanteuse—her voice was rich and her solos character-ized by a provocative lilt very reminiscent of Ginny Simms or Dorothy Shay. Furthermore, the singer's gown had once been the last word and still looked smart, despite certain transparent efforts at modernizing it. The Merry Men consisted of two Negroes and three whites—one of whom was Pete Kuzak.

Damn! There were too many representatives of the Blue Villa present—Velvalee, Kuzak and now Petrie—and that did not include the possibilities presented by either Major Larkin or the languid Commander Brecon-Fyffe.

How to get that interview with Alex McKenzie without arousing the suspicion of the Petries and the rest? It was in no way reassuring that Jingles excused herself and left Brecon-Fyffe free to circulate.

The presence of a discreetly plain door of Circassian walnut at the library's far end indicated the presence of a lavatory, especially when there emerged several gentlemen who had not previously been present in the library. Obviously said chamber, or whatever it might be, was equipped with a second entrance.

Brecon-Fyffe came drifting along, oh, so casually, just as he tried the heavy bronze handle to what proved, sure enough, to be a wash room. Entering, North immediately shot the bolt and found another door to this mirror-lined room.

Taking care first to start water running strongly into the hand basin, he tried the second portal. Though the time wasn't yet three o'clock by five minutes, his sense of impending disaster was so compelling that the Intelligence Officer stepped boldly into what undoubtedly must be Melek Effendi's private study, for in it stood McKenzie, the hawk-faced Chief of Staff together with another officer wearing the uniform of a Turkish police Colonel—or Albey.

"Speak quickly," he warned McKenzie. "I'm being shadowed and I've only a moment before there'll be suspicions aroused."

The American Military Attaché cast him one sharp glance

then indicated the stranger, a tall, red-gray-haired individual with a short, bright auburn mustache. "This is Razib Albey, Chief of the National Secret Service. Go ahead and talk."

"Has Walewski contacted G-2; recently, I mean?"

"Not in ten days, damn it!" growled McKenzie. "And the Department of Defense is scared sick over it. Hardly six hours go by but we get some frantic query. If we don't——"

North lifted his hand in a peremptory gesture. "Well, I have," he announced hurriedly. "Maybe you already know it, but here in Istanbul there's an extremely well-selected and organized Communist Intelligence cell."

"Names please?" rasped Razib Albey, fumbling into his dark green and silver tunic for a notebook.

"I'm sure of two women, one is named Esmé Murfee, the other Velvalee Petrie. Then there's Velvalee's so-called brother Stephen——"

"—Petrie's *a Communist?*" Colonel McKenzie stiffened as if jabbed by an invisible stiletto. "Are you sure?"

"Yes. And then there's a hoodlum musician going about as Kuzak; like all the rest, he's American born. Right now he's playing the accordion in the orchestra outside——"

An impatient knocking could be heard at the lavatory's further door.

All three of his listeners tensed when North continued.

"Walewski was seen at a place called Umur Fakih about five days ago, I judge."

The two Turks exchanged anxious glances. General Rechad growled, "That is a danger spot."

"Just a minute!" North called through the wash room then hurried on. "The MVD is closing in on Walewski, but here at least they don't know where he went from Umur Fakih." He eyed the Turkish officers. "Perhaps you can figure where our man might attempt to cross from Bulgaria into Greece or Turkey?"

"We will do our best," promised the Chief of Secret Police. "Shall I cause the traitors to be arrested?"

"Not yet, but have them watched. Alex, where can I reach you?" he demanded when that anxious rapping recommenced.

The Military Attaché mentioned a phone number which immediately became registered in North's memory. "Watch out," he warned. "Something I don't understand is afoot here."

An instant later he was slapping water onto his face, then, employing a towel, he crossed to unlock the door. To his surprise not Brecon-Fyffe but a weedy young man wearing a dress suit half a size too big came bursting in.

"Pardon, Monsieur, so sorry to hurry you," he apologized in French marked by a strong Greek accent, "but my stomach she is upset. I must to take my medicine." He pulled out a flat silver case, selected a lozenge and tossed it off with a glass of water. "Hah! *Ça va mieux.*"

All very plausible, but why could this Franco-Greek not have taken his tablet outside? One did not need to patronize a lavatory for such a purpose.

"Lovely party?" suggested North and, in no great hurry, returned to the library where he found Jingles. Quite as if his mind were not humming like an overworked dynamo, he relaxed in Jingle's supple and fragrant proximity and a rumba so expertly performed that other couples halted to admire.

Lips brushing his ear, Jingles suddenly begged, "Hugh, darling, you've got to, you simply must, return to duty! I can't tell you why in this place, but I've picked up the hottest lead since the fall of Chiang Kai-shek. You will help me, won't you? Please come up to my room at the Khamoun after pretending to leave me."

North made no reply, only guided Jingles into the conservatory. Here it was comparatively quiet with only a few smoldering cigarette butts and deserted champagne glasses to attest the memory of bright moments enjoyed in dark corners.

"Well?" She looked curiously at him. "I don't often invite gentlemen to drop in around four A.M."

"I know. Forgive me." He squeezed her hand. "Only, only you're so damn' incredibly lovely like this I simply can't think too straight. Of course I'll meet you, but you'd better come to my rooms at the Pera Palace. Less chance of scandal. Meantime will you do something for me?"

She lifted the warm oval of her face and whispered softly, "You've only to ask—you ungallant dog!"

Quite without warning his arms went about her and, in the lee of a clump of coyol palms, he kissed her so thoroughly that the weedy young Greek now lingering about the conservatory's entrance had sufficient tact to look aside.

"I've been thinking about this all evening—wish I'd been able to give it my undivided attention. As it is—what's happened to your friend Brecon-Fyffe?"

"I've no idea. He must have left. I've not seen him in some time. Why?"

"Never mind for the moment," he whispered. "There's something else—will you be a nice lamé-covered angel and intrigue yonder character you'll notice hovering about the entrance to this conservatory? Ask him to fetch you a drink, flirt with him, hint anything you think might work, but for God's sake keep that bastard off my neck during the next half hour."

Her expression became radiant. "Oh Hugh! Hugh my darling—then you have returned to duty! Just watch me."

There wasn't time, but he lingered long enough to admire the skill with which Jingles undertook her mission.

CHAPTER 14

Mata Hari Redivivus

AT HALF PAST THREE, the old German Imperial Embassy was still peopled by a gay but diminished throng. Some inner instinct directed North into the nearly deserted library, there to converse on trivialities with C. Poindexter Spencer, now inexplicably cordial. It was not by chance that, from where he sat, North was able to observe the orchestra and Michelle Mahoney singing a slightly sleepy rendition of Gladys Davis', "I Don't Care Any More About You." Most of the musicians were absent but Kuzak had remained, playing Michelle's accompaniment for the benefit of a mere handful of guests.

Both Poindexter and his companion noticed the appearance of a footman who bent to whisper something into the ear of Razib Albey. Of Turkish North knew nothing, yet he was positive he had overheard the words, "Umur Fakih."

Before the footman could straighten up there shuffled into the room, from the direction of the service quarters, a grimy and badly frightened individual wearing a threadbare brown coat. Between hands that certainly had not been washed in a very long time he was crushing an old-fashioned and shapeless golf cap. Grayish bristles of at least three days' growth stood out all over his narrow and deeply cloven chin.

The footman was at once outraged and apologetic, and tried to hustle out the intruder who struggled fiercely. "Where, please, is Razib Albey?" he panted. *"Vallahi!* It is of extreme urgency I see him at once."

"Here," stated the officer.

From the corner of his eye North glimpsed a movement so quick that instinct touched off a whole carillon of alarm bells. Although Michelle Mahoney continued to sing the accordion slipped, almost fell, off Kuzak's lap so rapidly did he arise. Like a snake into its hole the musician's hand disappeared into his jacket front.

"Ne istiyorsunuz? What do you want?" The Turkish Secret Police Commandant heaved himself to his feet, then said, "Come with me."

"Watch out!" North wanted to shout but, during that last split second which distinguishes the expert from the average, he remembered his role; no easy matter, he could see Kuzak drawing an automatic of business-like calibre. Had North himself possessed a weapon he probably would have risked a shot at Kuzak—gambling that this seedy stranger was that element he had been anticipating all evening.

Even as the intruder wheeled to follow Razib Albey from the library, Kuzak crouched, held his weapon rigidly with both hands at arm's length—no doubt as he had once been so taught by the O.S.S.—then fired once, twice. For once in his long career North remained indecisive, so many courses of action lay open. Now, of all times, he must commit no error.

The pistol's reports crashed loud as a field piece in this confined space and somewhere sounded a brittle jangle of shattered glass.

"Block the exits!" shouted Razib Albey when, to a resounding crash, Kuzak hurled himself bodily through a French door at his back.

Pandemonium shattered a brief, unbelievable stillness.

"Halt him! Halt that man!" shouted Colonel McKenzie rushing out of the now familiar wash room.

"Arretez-les!" bellowed Melek Effendi, charging in from the salon. "What passes? A thief?"

Brain buzzing with speculation, North ran over to that sordid figure now writhing feebly on the library's rose and gray Aubusson rug. Razib Albey's gold epaulettes glittered when he also bent over the stricken stranger.

A swift glance told North that, whatever Pete Kuzak's shortcomings, he was an excellent snap shot. The malodorous unknown had been shot through the lungs near the heart.

Over a rising uproar the Intelligence Officer heard the stricken man gasp, "Mata Hari," of all things, and then something like "Vaisal," just before his vital spark became extinguished by a gush of bright arterial blood.

Screams, raised in various keys by ladies who had not been restrained from crowding into the library, became stilled because outside the brilliantly lit former Embassy sounded two, three staccato reports. Viciously, they reverberated among adjoining buildings and down the Boulevard Avas Pasha.

CHAPTER 15

Perfect Confidence

"MATA HARI." "Vaisal." "Mata Hari?" "Vaisal?" Repeatedly those three words reverberated in Hugh North like the intoning of a Greek chorus. He remembered to arise and stand back which was just as well because first Stephen Petrie came running in then, of all people, Captain Larkin, his swarthy features an unattractive mask of anxiety mingled with alarm. The A-2 hesitated not a second but stemmed the inrush of guests by slamming the library door in their faces. North glimpsed his concern at watching Colonel Mc-Kenzie and the Turkish Chief of Staff appear gray-faced and hard-eyed from the lavatory.

Never in his experience had Hugh North been called to act his present role. Normally, he would have taken charge, directed the course of events. Not so, now. Stephen Petrie already was pushing forward. "Let me help him. I was in the Medical Corps," he announced. "Maybe I——"

"No, Monsieur, you will stay back!" Razib Albey's voice sounded succinct as the snap of a drover's lash. "There is nothing to do."

General Rechad meanwhile opened a side door leading to the salon and issued a series of orders in his native language. Beneath the library's bronze and crystal sconces stood only a handful of people, so prompt had been Captain Larkin's action. These remained almost motionless—suggestive of mannequins in a department store display.

"Mata Hari? Vaisal?" What in God's name did those words mean? Vaisal would be easier to interpret—but poor

Marguerite Zelle had been dead nearly thirty years now. Lost in speculation, North remained aloof with unseeing eyes watching a brilliant pool of blood gradually enlarge itself from beneath the murdered messenger's shabby coat. He lay on his back, with tobacco-yellowed fingers curved in agony above his chest like the claws of a stricken bird; deep-set eyes now had rolled back into their sockets and long greasy hair streamed over the old French carpet like an untidy kitchen mop.

Razib Albey's piercing blue eyes flickered from North, standing crisp, tall and completely calm beside a Louis XIV chair, to the plump and over-bejewelled wife of an Egyptian diplomat, crouching stricken on a sofa, her brown face gone greenish. Thence his gaze sought Stephen Petrie resembling a football god more than ever because a lock of his curly blond hair had tumbled low over his eyes.

Colonel McKenzie, like North, remained motionless, but his thick body was poised and his piercing blue eyes riveted on Petrie. Razib Albey, Chief of Secret Police, bent low over the fallen figure, but rose to one knee when a gendarme sergeant, big-nosed face red with cold, burst in. North noticed a fine sprinkling of new snow flecking his gray military-cut overcoat.

"Well, Razib," rasped General Rechad, "what has happened? Has the assassin escaped?"

Razib raised a face so gray and drawn that his red mustache seemed very bright. "No, Excellency, the murderer was shot dead. One anticipates the gravest difficulties, however."

"Why?"

"This man's identification papers and passport are American."

"And so," North reflected, "Pete Kuzak has rendered his last service to the Kremlin."

A delicate moment this; everything depended on whether

Stephen Petrie had arrived in time to see him bending above the dying man. Covertly, he inspected his left arm, the one with which he had raised the messenger's head; a slight smear of blood on his sleeve warned him against any attempt at evasion. Who was this unknown? Yusuf of the enigmatic newspapers? Phoebus Skoularis who had reported seeing Walewski? WHO?

Mata Hari! How the shade of that wretched, beautiful and overrated spy must be grinning. Mata Hari? What could she—or her memory—have to do with this critical phase in World history?

Hurriedly, he reviewed her history hoping for a clue; born a Dutch colonial, an unhappy wife, then actress, courtesan and finally a pitiful pawn attempting to cozen both the *Chambre Noire* and the Imperial German Secret Service. Why indeed should this spectacular failure's name become interjected into a problem infinitely more significant than any with which she, herself, had ever been involved?

Beyond the library's doors could be heard all manner of activity, people hurrying about, demanding in a dozen languages to learn what had chanced. How was Velvalee conducting herself—if indeed she had learned of Kuzak's death? What of Jingles and the Greek with whom she had been dancing?

Razib Albey stood up, straightened his handsome green and gold tunic, and spoke in French. "Messieurs, Mesdames, one regrets infinitely that an investigation must be undertaken, therefore those of you who actually witnessed this most deplorable of incidents will please furnish this sergeant with names and addresses."

Stiffly, he bowed to the various silent figures grouped around him, for all the world like waxwork dummies about a dime museum. "Soon you will be released to return to your homes, but, until you are summoned to an inquest, I must strictly require you, in the name of my government, to make no comment on this affair either to the press or to anyone."

Only fleetingly did the gaunt Chief of Secret Police's gaze seek McKenzie and then North before he motioned aside a quartet of burly gendarmes guarding the library doors.

For the first time Razib Albey betrayed his otherwise well-controlled excitement by lapsing into an Imperial Turkish official's mode of dismissal:

"You have our permission to depart," said he.

CHAPTER 16

The Pera Palace

STEPHEN PETRIE and the Greek gentleman were waiting beneath the gilded wrought-iron and glass porte-cochère of Melek Effendi's residence when Hugh North emerged.

"Hello, Major. In case you don't know it, that correspondent gal friend of yours has already left. My car's around the corner and since there aren't any taxis I'll be glad to give you a lift to the Pera Palace."

Of course there could be no refusing Petrie's invitation so, suffering various qualms, North presently entered a handsome coupé of American manufacture. Was this the start of a "ride"?

Tight-lipped, Petrie guided his car down from the heights of Pera and, very slowly, passed the mouth of an alley, across which was flung a cordon of flat-capped gendarmes. Further down its length lights wavered, picked out light snow lying beneath old-fashioned hareem balconies from which ladies of old Constantinople once had viewed the street through screens of elaborately carved cedar. Down there must be lying the bullet-riddled corpse of Peter Kuzak, late of San Diego, California.

"Well, Mister, just what did that bum say while he was checking out?"

North felt miserably uncertain as to how he should reply. The Greek in the badly fitting dress suit undoubtedly was handling a pistol beneath his old-style opera cloak.

"I know it sounds ridiculous, Steve, but all that stumble-bum said was, 'Mata Hari.'"

"Okay, I heard that," Petrie agreed. "What else?"

"—That was all."

"—Like hell it was!" The menace in Petrie's manner was unmistakable. "He said one other word. What was it? Speak up, or my friend, Nestor, might get trigger happy."

"Come to think of it," North admitted, "he *did* mutter something, but I wasn't sure whether it was a word or just a sound——"

"Goddam you!" Petrie snarled. "What was it?"

"I'm sure I don't know. It was something like 'Vaisal.'"

"You're sure on that?"

"Of course not. He was choking on his blood." Hopefully, North tried for corroboration. "How did it sound to you?"

"Dunno—I wasn't close enough. Well, you and Esmé will have to figure out what the hell he tried to tell."

The coupé swayed, bumped over a series of roads especially treacherous because of the thin film of snow which with each passing moment was thickening.

That ride downhill through sleeping Istanbul to the Pera Palace remained for many years a scene graven in North's memory with the clarity of an etching. Seated beside Stephen Petrie, for once completely silent and thoughtful, and before the threat presented by Nestor, he returned to those three infuriating and puzzling words.

What, he wondered suddenly, what about Jingles? For her to call tonight was unthinkable, impossible; inevitably such a visit would expose her to serious danger and compromise her usefulness beyond hope. God alone knew what these two intended.

Mata Hari, Fact One. Obviously, the slain messenger had been a member, however humble, of the Turkish Intelligence. Obviously, again, Kuzak, Petrie and the rest had been alerted to expect, and to silence, this miserable little fellow before he could talk.

Vaisal? What did those two half-choked syllables mean? Was that someone's proper name or was it a code word? What? *What?* WHAT?

Petrie slowed his coupé and steered under the dimmed lights of the Pera Palace's marquee.

"Lucky for you you didn't try lying," sighed Petrie, when he halted the car and North prepared to alight. "Funny part is I really didn't catch those first two words," he infuriated North by confessng. "Although I distinctly heard the third."

"I'm glad of that," North countered, "because I wasn't sure about it. Mata Hari Vaisal? Sounds like a third-rate actress' stage name."

"No," Nestor supplied unexpectedly. "Vaisal ees naming of Turkish village—near Edirne——"

"Shut up," snarled Petrie. "Keep your goddam trap closed. You're not on 'Information Please.' "

Once he stood on the hotel driveway, North inquired quietly, "By the bye, Steve, how much longer do you intend to shadow me? I'm really quite hurt that you'd waste Nestor's valuable time like that."

"Okay," Petrie said, suddenly cordial. "I'll call him off. I guess Esmé's right. I didn't think you really were on the level." Just before he ground up the gray coupé's window he added, "See you at the Blue Villa come seven-thirty this morning."

"God above," groaned North. "It's four-thirty now and I'm dead for sleep."

"Seven-thirty," Petrie insisted, "and you'd better be on time. Hell will be popping any time."

Hugh North was far too experienced with MVD methods to doubt that surveillance over him would be maintained, but exactly how thorough that watch would be was a matter for discovery. How without danger of detection could he get through to McKenzie? Could that worthy fill in some blanks concerning the identity of the murdered messenger?

"Dear old MVD, they trust everybody all the time," sighed North when, on entering an elevator, he observed a porter abruptly lay down his mop and go shuffling off across the foyer towards the service entrance.

"What a fine clean-cut gang of playmates," he reflected, and marvelled that any espionage system could function on a basis of unrelieved suspicion and mistrust.

Yawning, fumbling at his keys, North was nearing his door when the alarming fact that a light was burning in his chambers made itself apparent. Certainly he had extinguished them all on leaving ages ago, it seemed, to meet Jingles Lawson. Good God, she had kept the rendezvous in spite of everything!

His breath quickened on inserting his key into that keyhole glowing like a tiny bright eye in the corridor's gloom. Simultaneously footsteps halted somewhere around a nearby corner.

He took care to hum a bar of "I Don't Care Any More About You," while turning the key, then swung the door slowly, steadily open.

CHAPTER 17

Assignation

THE expressive gray-blue eyes of Jingles Lawson swung apprehensibly to his low but wrathful, "Exactly what the hell d'you think you're doing here?"

The silver lamé shimmered and the strapless bodice again threatened revelations as she jumped up and extended arms adorned by slim platinum and diamond bracelets. "Why, Hugh, I—I thought you'd be glad to see me."

"Like an attack of acute indigestion!" His alarm was very real. "Whatever made you come here after that mess at Melek's?"

Her smile faded. "I figured I *had* to see you. I knew you'd rid yourself of that nasty Greek and the others keeping the deady-deady on you." She caught her breath slowly. "I'm sorry you're displeased, but I *had* to talk——" Her speech faded before his frantic signals for silence.

Aware that, during his absence, the suite might have become thoroughly microphoned, he summoned a bleak smile and went over to turn on the radio. Then he wheeled, eyes steely gray.

"Are you trying to ruin your own reputation—and get me in hot water?"

Her easy manner vanished like a chalk mark under an eraser. "I thought you understood me better," she told him under the babble of the radio. "Are we being watched?"

"Almost certainly," he groaned. "My God, if *only* you'd stayed where you belonged."

"Don't look so miserable. What's so terrible about my

coming here? You know damned well I go where I please and when, and I've yet to get in a jam."

Worse than the plague he hated to break security to anyone not subject to the rigorous control of the Central Intelligence Agency. Right now, however, he seemed to be offered no alternative.

"Do you think anybody saw you come in?"

Jingles reflected briefly. "I don't believe so. The corridor was empty."

Angrily, he tuned up the radio until an eavesdropper would certainly have difficulty in distinguishing their voices. The worst of it was, he'd not the least idea of who might be occupying the adjoining suite; there'd been no time to investigate. He did recall, however, that a balcony encircled this storey and that the old-fashioned wooden shutters of his chambers were sprung and by no means secure.

"Jingles, listen carefully." He drew near and like any careful swain first took her hands in his. "Right now a most tremendous event is on the fire and by having you here my usefulness is in the balance. I know you'd the best of intentions, but my only chance of staying in the show is for you to pretend, to act as if you came here for exactly what most people would imagine."

Jingles summoned a tremulous smile. "You mean for an assignation, as they say in the melodrammers?"

He drew her closer and tentatively stroked her shoulder-length light brown hair. "Jingles, we've got to give a convincing imitation of—well—a snappy shacking up."

"You terrify me," she sighed, "and I just hate acting."

"Too bad. One of the MVD's bright boys has just reached the balcony outside that window."

"Don't sound so grim about it," Jingles protested, resting her head on his shoulder. "Will making love to me prove terribly uphill work?"

"There are times, my dear," he murmured into her ear,

"when I could snap your swan-like neck for all I—I'm so damned fond of you." He held her closer before the long French windows and gave her a kiss which even Charles Boyer might have studied to advantage.

"Oh-h. You're right. I s-see him—he cut a crack just now—light from the street lamp." Gently Jingles' slim figure commenced to tremble within his embrace. "W-what are we going to do?"

"Pretend we're clandestine lovers. Don't be frightened," he soothed. "They're not likely to move right now unless we give some cause. And now, dearest, let's have one of your special A Number One kisses—Rough racket this Intelligence work."

After a little they lit cigarettes and sought a divan and switched on a fairly strong bridge lamp. North's arm slid around her waist, drew her closer. It seemed more than slightly absurd thus to fondle so lovely a young creature while at the same time to be plotting never more intently. The radio continued to blare a version of "I Miss My Swiss——"

"Why did you want to come here?"

Jingles smiled lazily, settled back among the divan's cushions before her hand crept up and her fingers stroked his cheek. "Colonel McKenzie sent me——"

"McKenzie!"

"Yes. He was afraid you might not be able to contact him tonight. Apparently he figured that one correctly."

"But why *you?*" North demanded stroking her lustrous brown hair.

"Other side knows I'm a foreign correspondent—not an Intelligence agent."

Playfully he blew a curl away from her ear then kissed it, thereby provoking a perfectly genuine squeak of protest. "Stop it, you, you Torquemada." Quite without change of her languorous expression she continued. "The Colonel wants to know exactly what that shabby man said while dying."

" 'Mata Hari Vaisal.' That's all."

Jingles started a little. "Mata Hari? Good God, she's been dead a long time. What do you make of that?"

"As yet, nothing at all," North admitted. He arose, crossed to a sideboard and there poured out two liqueur glasses of warmly golden Cordial Campari. The radio played more softly now and, in poor French, threatened to go off the air within a quarter of an hour. There were now at least two men eavesdropping from that accursed balcony. While bending in search of a tray he was certain he had glimpsed a second shadow move beyond an inch-wide crack within the room's weather-beaten shutters.

Eyes heavy-lidded and hair just distractingly disarranged, Jingles lay back among the cushions with one shapely silver-shod leg bewitchingly exposed to its stocking top. Lazily, she repowdered her nose. By the flattering yellow-gold light she presented a vision well calculated to charm a modern Ulysses off his course.

While setting down the drinks North forced himself again to consider possible interpretations of the murdered man's last words. What about Mata Hari, the original one? He gave his reclining companion her glass and again riffled over his recollections of that *cause célèbre*. Marguerite Zelle had been Dutch, married to a brute of an officer in the Dutch Colonial Army. She had deserted him after a maltreated servant had poisoned their child, and then had drifted into dancing—dancing nude in a curious interpretation of the Javanese dances she had so often beheld.

Dutch East Indies? Java? Mata Hari? In Javanese the name held some meaning. Damn! A translation wriggled through his groping mental fingers like a small and slippery fish.

He reseated himself after bestowing an exceedingly convincing caress which left Jingles' hair more rumpled than ever, murmured, "Remember what Mata Hari means in Javanese?"

"Yes. It means 'Eye of the Morning.' "

"Thanks. I'll work on that."

"After we've done with this bird-in-a-gilded-cage act, what's next?"

"When you reach McKenzie," North blinked a little in the strong light from the bridge lamp, "say I want him to send two of his best operatives to Vaisal, and *muy pronto.*"

Giving an absent-minded upward twitch to the strapless gown, Jingles murmured, "What about the Turkish Secret Police? Want to call on them, too?"

"They'll be on deck," he predicted. "Razib Albey also heard those three words."

Her empty liqueur glass safely deposited, the girl took North's face between both hands and kissed his eyes. "Tell me, darling, truly, you have been working for G-2 ever since you reached Turkey?"

"Of course."

"And that silly business over at the Blue Moon was just part of the act?" His nod sent her arms slipping about his neck. "Bless you dear, you'll never know how it hurt me to see you drinking with that dreadful-looking woman."

"Part of the act," he repeated.

"Oh, Hugh! Hugh! I don't think that, deep down, I really ever doubted, but—you sure looked like Luke Lushwell himself!" The series of hugs she gave him left nothing to be desired as to genuineness.

"Presently the radio's going to sign off—just before I'm going to switch out the light for about twenty minutes. That'll leave our brave lads out on the balcony free to let their imaginations canter through the realms of fantasy—and envy. So listen carefully and tell McKenzie that although I'm tailed every second, I'm certain I've convinced

Petrie, Murfee and the other Commies that I'm on the level about transferring my allegiance. Oh, yes—I think Mc-Kenzie ought to check up on that phony Englishman called Brecon-Fyffe."

Jingles caught her breath. "What! Eric isn't English?"

"No more than you or I. He says 'zee' instead of 'zed.' Bottoms up, now."

He half reclined beside her, gazing with a rapturous intensity into the girl's darkish features, and at the fragrance of her person and perfume fought to maintain self-control. "As soon as—and if—I penetrate the true meaning of 'Mata Hari' I'll leave an empty, bright-blue envelope addressed, *poste restante,* to Leopold Maxim at the Central Post Office."

The music faded and the announcer's bored accents informed that the program would be resumed at eight o'clock.

"Well, brace yourself, my dear, for in the interests of science I'm about to attempt to make Valentino, Errol Flynn and John Barrymore seem like arthritic old men." His amorous advances accelerated until suddenly he reached up and flicked out the light.

Their heads now lay so close together that not even a microphone could pick up their whispers.

"You're a mighty convincing actor, Major," sighed Jingles. "Even better than I'd dreamed."

"You're either a beginner or a shameless flatterer," he objected lightly. "Believe it or not, my mind really isn't on your charms. I'm trying to foresee friend Petrie's next move. Incidentally, this Commie's headquarters is at number 135 Rue Top Hané. Ask Razib Albey to keep the place under observation, but not to start any round-up till I learn what gives in Vaisal."

"Can do. Anything else?" Her soft whisper came out of the gloom.

"One last thing—do you know anything about Captain David Larkin; he's A-2 at our Military Mission?"

"Did you know he was at the Three Moons?"

"Yes. Trouble is I can't figure out just where, or how, he fits in this problem. The Commies definitely are in contact with him; if he isn't deliberately betraying secrets, then he's being damned indiscreet. Get ready, I'm turning on the light in a minute."

When he snapped on the illumination Jingles Lawson was engaged in pretending to re-secure a garter catch; otherwise, her lamé gown looked interestingly wrinkled and she presented a vision of dishevelled loveliness. North arose, commenced to do up the tie he had just jerked loose. Then when she departed to the bathroom he smiled like Casanova fresh from another conquest and moodily ran fingers through his crisp black hair.

"Darling," smiled he, when she returned with hair smoothed and make-up replaced, "this has been sheer heaven."

"It *has* been wonderful, Hugh dear. When can we get together again?"

"In a day or so," he replied loud enough for the eavesdroppers to overhear. "I may be away for a few days. I can't tell where I'll be, but I'll be thinking of you every minute, and I'll call the instant I return."

Just inside the hall door they embraced in the lingering intensity of parting lovers, then North made a fine show of determining whether the coast was clear. Giving any listener in the hall a clear field, North fumbled with the lock, peered out and then beckoned. Bestowing a quick kiss, the girl, gathering her evening wrap about her, departed quietly into the hallway's amber-tinted gloom.

CHAPTER 18

Night Express to Edirne

AT NINE O'CLOCK the Edirne Express rolled out of Demur Kapu station, chuffed through the suburbs and left Istanbul behind. At this hour the former capital of the Ottoman Empire suggested a gigantic heap of coals stirred and scattered across several low hills. Once the car tracks had set up their rhythmic *clack-clack*, Major Hugh North thrust long legs out before him, rested his feet on the seat opposite, and commenced a perusal of French and English newspapers purchased at a book stall.

As was to be expected this first-class car was both aged and chilly and its seats, stained by the usage of years, harder than they should have been.

Nevertheless, the dark-haired passenger in Compartment Six was supremely content—anything to be shut of the Blue Villa and the distrust prevailing within its walls. No one there had seemed completely unsuspicious of anyone else.

That events of profound importance were in their inception, an observer far less astute than Hugh North would have sensed. The further he advanced into this jungle of intrigue, the surer he became he was engaged in measuring wits, courage and determination with the most dangerous opponents he had encountered since those hectic pre-war days down in Rio.

To just what conclusions had the events of Melek Effendi's now famous entertainment led Esmé Murfee and Stephen Petrie? More fiercely than ever he was lamenting his inability to read or to speak Turkish; these local English

and French newspapers had published only the most
guarded and non-speculative accounts of that assassination
in the former German Embassy.

La République alone ventured to suggest that Communist
influences had been at work. When, demanded the editor,
would the Soviet overlords of Eastern Europe learn that
they must respect the integrity of their neighbors' territory?

That which at once seized North's attention was an account in the *Orient News* of a plenary session of the Security
Council of the United Nations. On the preceding day the
Soviet emissaries, it was reported, still had acted truculent,
but it was felt that their fire breathing had been less intense than a few days previous. Could this diminution of
hostility be attributed to the fact that a certain Josef Walewski still was eluding the clutches of the MVD and its equally
sinister sister organizations operating in Bulgaria and Rumania?

The faint shadow of a tenable theory crossed North's
mind. Suppose that the arrival of that shabby little man
meant that Walewski was still alive and at large? Just suppose that the unknown Phoebus Skoularis was a double
agent and had sent the messenger to Razib Albey? Would
this not account for all that consternation in the Blue Villa,
and the presence of so many loyal comrades at the dinner-
dance? Naturally they had to kill the man presumed to be
bringing word of Walewski's whereabouts.

Vaisal, he had ascertained further, lay situated but a brief
two kilometers below one of the most rigorously guarded
frontiers in the World. Could Josef Walewski actually have
won his way across it? *If only he had,* how many hundreds
of millions of unsuspecting people ought to rejoice, and
to date time from that event.

Over the top of his newspaper North attempted to estimate the state of Stephen Petrie's mind—it must be far from
tranquil, were one to judge by the thoughtful scowl on that

young giant's ruddy features. He looked at once angry, worried and frightened, too.

When well out into the country, the express continued to gather speed, boring into a light snow storm behind its Cyclopean eye of glaring yellow and only confessing uneasiness through continued shrill whistlings.

North commenced to review the most recent events in this problem. He had been roused from his bed at the hotel by Stephen Petrie, looking very grim and tight about the mouth.

"Okay, Major, hit the deck," he'd directed. "You're to check out of here right away——"

"Where are we going?"

"You'll find out. Haven't got a gun, have you?"

"No. I don't carry artillery when I'm on leave."

Even so, Petrie hadn't accepted his word and had insisted on searching the whole suite. A single bag packed for cold weather would have to suffice, the renegade had stated; the rest of North's luggage could be checked at the Pera Palace.

Within the Blue Villa he'd found consternation heavy as a London fog. Passionately Esmé Murfee had denied that as far as she was aware Mata Hari held any secondary meaning.

"Don't you think I'd admit it if it did—or any of the rest of us?" she had raged, her small and dark blue eyes hard as agates. "Come on, Major. Think—think what he meant. A dying man doesn't mutter inconsequentials."

Lights from an auto waiting at a crossing briefly illumined the otherwise untenanted compartment, and like a theatrical spotlight picked out Stephen Petrie's handsome profile.

North had been curious to learn what could have warped this young fellow's mental processes until his mind was effectively poisoned against that country which had given him the very best of everything—except a name of his own —until, in a fit of anger, Velvalee had vouchsafed this bit of information. Stephen's father, she further had elucidated, was an Oregon politician of no mean stature.

"You'd best watch out for this lug," North warned himself. "Petrie's the violent type—and not too clever—a bad combination.

"Mata Hari means the 'Eye of the Morning,' " he reflected after taking a pull at a silver flask of cognac—the compartment was growing colder. "Let's explore secondary explanations. Maybe morning should be spelt 'mourning'? Mourning—that might mean black, or perhaps the opposite since white is the mourning color for the Chinese. Is there some agent named White or Black who figures in this?"

The *contrôleur* and his assistant appeared, briefly considered the two solemn figures within the compartment, then politely touched the brim of his képi and asked for their tickets. When they had departed Petrie arose and went over to pull down the shades and then to lock the compartment's door. "Let's keep our privacy."

"It's always welcome," North lied pleasantly. "Are Esmé and Nestor with that quaint Englishman, or are they on this train?"

"They left by auto this afternoon," came his companion's unusually frank reply, "but Velvalee's two cars back." When the big young fellow resumed his place on the stained upholstery North became aware that his right-hand coat pocket sagged in so unmistakable a manner that Petrie might just as well have removed the pistol it contained and laid it on the seat beside him. Um. He must have shifted that weapon from the shoulder holster in which he habitually carried it.

"What's biting my little pal?" North wondered. "Have I tipped my hand somewhere?"

North lit a cigarette, briefly considered what measures he'd have to take if he were to reach Edirne, alive and in good health. Idly he collected his newspapers, arranged them the one over the other, then folded and placed the resultant square of newsprint on his lap. Presently, as if lost in thought, he again folded the papers into first a large triangle, and then over once more into a smaller and harder one.

"You've had plenty of opportunity to use those high-priced brains of yours," Petrie remarked as the lights of a village whirled by and the black and snow-shrouded landscape continued to roll along. "What's about this Mata Hari business?"

"You still know as much as I."

"The hell you preach." Petrie's manner was anything but affable. "We hired you to figure out this sort of problem, and in our league we don't overlook inefficiency."

"Don't blame you," came the Intelligence Officer's calm agreement. "If a subordinate of mine flops I feel it's my fault, but they don't often fall down." By now he had decided that, in a slugging match, he wouldn't stand much chance against this brawny young traitor in the gray flannel trousers and brown tweed coat.

Petrie leaned forward a little, small eyes riveted on North's deep-set gray-blue ones. "Just what did you do last night after I dropped you at your hotel?"

"I went to my room."

"What did you do there?"

North hesitated. "Why, I went to bed. It was late."

"What happened before you went to bed?" insisted Petrie, his manner even more menacing. "Stop trying to kid me. I don't like it."

"Well, I entertained someone."

"Who?"

"It's none of your damn' business, Petrie," snapped North. "Sure, I'm in Miss Murfee's employ, but not during off hours."

"You have no off hours, and don't try getting nasty. That was quite an act you put on."

"Act? What do you mean?"

"It was a good job of romancing, and convincing"—he drew a deep breath and let his hand drop into the side pocket—"to someone *who couldn't read lips!*"

North felt like a man who, on boarding a train, remembers that he has left his ticket on the dresser. Here was an element he'd overlooked—a critical oversight, all right. Skill at lip reading formed one of the prime requirements in every Intelligence school among the major Powers—like learning to read upside down.

"What did the Lawson babe tell you about Colonel Mc-Kenzie?"

Now that the gloom beyond the railroad compartment's grimy windows was unrelieved by lights, the tension increased. Just how much had the eavesdroppers been able to distinguish? Of course Jingles and he necessarily must have turned away from the windows quite often during their little tête-à-tête.

"Miss Lawson merely mentioned him in connection with the party," North replied equably.

Petrie's big figure tightened. "You're a goddam liar! I learned enough from what you two said to make me wonder whether you aren't a poor risk, after all. Steady, Mac, you'd better not make any quick moves." Petrie pulled out and levelled that same Walther automatic North first had seen at the Blue Villa.

North chuckled, settled back on his seat, still fingering the folded newspapers. "Well, well, so we're going to indulge in real ten-twenty-thirty stuff. Tonight's headline, 'College Boy Plays at Espionage.' Tut! Tut! Waving guns about is kid stuff. D'you know, Steve, that in twenty years of Intelligence work I've seldom produced the artillery, and have been so inept as to shoot exactly two men?"

"Shut up! And lay off the lecture." There remained not the least doubt that Petrie had decided to kill him.

"You're like so many knuckle-headed operatives," North continued amiably. "When you get stymied in the brains department you want to start shooting. I'd figured you were smarter than that, Steve, so for Christ's sake take your finger off that trigger because, if you shoot me, you and Esmé will lose your last chance of doing a good job in Vaisal."

The click of the rails and the rattling of a loose window suddenly sounded very loud in Compartment Number Six.

Petrie demanded sullenly, "What are you driving at?"

"I now know, or at least I've a damned shrewd suspicion about what was meant by the name Mata Hari."

"Oh, so you're going to give out after all?"

"You'll learn, Steve, that I choose my own time about talking on such points—what's more, I intend to continue to do so."

He experienced an infinite relief on seeing the Walther's muzzle lowered. "Well, what about Mata Hari?" Suspicion was still hardening Petrie's expression.

"The key lies in the translation of Mata Hari's name— 'Eye of the Morning.'" On purpose he lowered his voice, forcing the other to bend forward, listening over the monotonous clatter of the rail. "At first I figured that it must be the code nickname of some female agent, but got nowhere."

Imperceptibly, while making brief explanatory motions with his left hand, North gathered and inched his feet further under him. "So I mulled over the word 'morning,' later considering the meaning as of mourning for a dead person. Still no dice. So I turned back to mythology. Does that suggest anything to you?"

Petrie relaxed a trifle and after a momentary hesitation asked, "Did the Greeks have a god of the morning?"

"Surely that diploma mill you adorned out West taught you that?"

"Lay off the comedy," Petrie snapped.

"Why should I? You disappoint and depress me, Steve, indeed you do. Now the morning is created by what?"

"The sun?"

"Right. Now to the Romans Apollo was their sun god. Do you happen to know his equivalent in Grecian mythology?"

"No."

"It's Phoebus," North said quietly. "Do you recall receiving a message from someone named Phoebus? I do."

"Phoebus Skoularis, by God!" Petrie burst out and lowered his automatic a little further. "That's it! And that's all I need to know."

North lunged forward with the speed of an expert fencer, the full weight of his body concentrated behind the hard point presented by that triangle of newspapers. The blunt point impacted with terrific force against Stephen Petrie's sternum—otherwise known as the solar plexus—with the result that he dropped the pistol and doubled up convulsively. Two hard chopping blows delivered by the side of North's hand ruptured the renegade's carotid nerve and tumbled him limp upon the compartment's floor. He lay quite still, as a man must when his neck has been broken.

Sixty seconds after he had mentioned Phoebus Skoularis' name North was alone in Compartment Six. The temperature had grown colder still because a door to a moving railway carriage cannot be opened, even briefly, without admitting considerable fresh air.

When, ten minutes later, the train groaned to a halt and a guard glanced in, he observed only a lean, dark-haired individual smoking a panatela and peacefully perusing a somewhat wrinkled copy of the *Oriental News*.

CHAPTER 19

Edirne

HAD Velvalee Petrie and her late supposed brother made any arrangement to communicate while on the train, or were they to pretend complete independence? Quickly he determined on his story should that sultry young Southerner appear, then set about re-arranging various items of definite information into a useful pattern. He found it immensely exciting to reflect that each turn of the locomotive's wheels undoubtedly was bringing him closer to Walewski—and those inexpressibly vital microfilms. What chiefly worried him was lack of knowledge concerning the sum of Esmé's information covering his now famous séance with Jingles.

Phoebus Skoularis, the double agent—there could be no doubt now that he had communicated with the Soviet agents in Istanbul while also attempting to contact Colonel McKenzie—might yet remain alive, probably in or near Vaisal. Pray God that he was.

The more he considered this thesis, the more North liked it; that shabby fellow, shot so promptly by Pete Kuzak, also must have been a double spy; how else would Kuzak have known enough to shoot him practically on sight?

North sighed, absently re-arranged in his side pocket that business-like Walther which had come so near to terminating his own career.

How must he set about finding Phoebus? Presumably, after the messenger's death, Alexander McKenzie must have taken appropriate measures and without waiting for suggestions from himself via Jingles Lawson. The question now confronting him was simply this: Could he, by preserving his hard-won Soviet connections, reach Phoebus —and presumably Walewski—quicker than by cutting loose and turning his suspects over to the tender mercies of the Turkish Secret Police?

Absently he massaged the edge of his right hand, still sore from that second terrific blow with which he had broken Stephen Petrie's neck. Praise God, so far his hand had failed to become discolored; moreover, Velvalee was aware that, when he'd boarded the train, he'd been unarmed.

Would he be able to convince her and those others awaiting him in Edirne—now not half an hour distant—that Stephen Petrie had left the train of his own free will? Would they credit his theory that the Turkish Counter-Intelligence had picked him off when he'd alighted to buy cigarettes during a pause during which the train had watered and refuelled at Burgas?

Briefly he deliberated then, after glancing out into the corridor, he crossed quickly to the window. Venting a regretful sigh he pitched Petrie's automatic far out into the night. A real blizzard must be making up, if those chill and furiously whirling flakes suddenly gilded by the compartment's lights meant anything.

How long before Petrie's body might be discovered? Maybe days, maybe only a few hours; he'd not the least conception of whether the traitor's body had fallen into a snow-filled gully or had come to rest in some peasant's barnyard. "Uncertainty of this sort, my lad," he reminded himself grimly, "is one of the quaint joys peculiar to Intelligence work."

Where, oh where, might those precious turbo-jet microfilms be at this moment?

Who and what was Phoebus Skoularis? Strange, he'd so

far not the least intimation of the fellow's appearance, although Velvalee once had described him as uncommonly handsome, vain and given to weird sartorial effects. From his name he should be of Greek origin, although in the Balkans that constituted no guarantee at all.

On sober reflection he decided that his best chance of success lay in continuing within the Soviet organization. Thus he would be forewarned of any sudden démarche on its part—and he entertained a wholesome respect for the guile and foresight of that bitter young woman known as Esmé Murfee. Again he would be in a position to instigate a most effective round-up should the happy day ever dawn when Josef Walewski arrived safely behind the Turkish frontier.

Passengers in Russian-style chapkas of lambskin or astrakhan, well-to-do merchants wearing black cloth coats lined in brown fur appeared in the corridor but occasionally; the Edirne express was indeed less than half full. Twenty minutes before the express was due at its destination—once designated by the more familiar name of Adrianople—Hugh North got to his feet and progressed, swaying slightly, along the corridor to the second coach rear. In its third compartment he glimpsed Velvalee's candy-blonde hair shimmering under dim, red-yellow electric lights. She also was alone and had apparently been passing the time by manicuring herself and consuming a tin box of nougats.

"Is Steve with you?" was North's first question.

"Why, no." The girl's large sherry-hued eyes grew round. "Ah was wonderin' where he was. He said he'd fetch me a little drink and a cigarette after we left Burgas. My, it's gettin' cold and Ah simply *hate* cold weathah. Down where Ah come from we nevah get anythin' like this." She smiled, straightened her skirt and put away her manicure set. "Where do you suppose Steve can have got to?"

"Maybe he's bumped into some friend in the wagon-restaurant. Suppose we take a look-see."

They peered into compartment after compartment, and ranged the length of the restaurant car but, of course, found no sign of Petrie. Momentarily Velvalee's agitation mounted.

"Ah declah, this is the strangest thing. Hugh, Honey, when was it you last saw him?"

"When we stopped at Burgas, Steve left our compartment to buy some cigarettes. When he didn't come back I naturally figured he had stopped in to visit with you."

"Oh, Hugh! What can have happened?" The pretty, heart-shaped features stiffened. "Something terrible has gone wrong."

"Looks like it." Firmly he directed her into his compartment. "You wait here and I'll go fetch your luggage. You'll be safer this way."

Upon his return he found Velvalee looking very small and curvaceous in a rather tight black gabardine suit and busily examining the compartment as if in search of some sign of violence.

"It's a cinch Steve is no longer on this train." North offered his cigarette case. She accepted one and, with tremulous fingers, held it to his lighter. "Have you by any chance noticed any Turkish counter-agents aboard, or at the station in Istanbul?"

"Why, why yes." He was infinitely relieved to hear the girl's wholly unexpected reply. "Come to think of it, two of them were standing near the gate watching the passengers go aboard. Steve mentioned it."

"Why the hell didn't he tell me?" came North's plaintive complaint. "Well, Velvalee, suppose we take a drink and try to figure out our next move."

"Oh, Major, Ah—Ah'm so frightened! Maybe you've got somethin' there."

North produced his flask of cognac, unscrewed the cap

and poured a generous measure of Monnet into its silver cup.

"Here's to us"—he smiled encouragingly—"and whatever part of the South you hail from."

Deeply flushed, she looked at him slowly over the tiny cup and her brilliant little mouth quivered. "Oh, how Ah wish Ah were back there right now!" she burst out. "Oh, my soul, how Ah do."

North pretended not to notice this last. "Well, to look on the cheerful side, they don't make such good cognac back home. You must have had a wonderfully exciting time over here in Europe."

A single gulp disposed of Velvalee's tiny cupful of cognac, then nervously she gathered her coat about her.

"Of co'se. After you've lived all yo' life in a stinky poverty po' town 'way down in Mississippi, 'most any change is excitin', 'specially——"

"Especially?" he prompted, refilling the cup she suddenly held towards him.

" 'Specially if you been through a war and, well if some, some sweet-talkin', no 'count dog deceives a gal, gets—gets her in trouble and then goes away." Velvalee looked fixedly into the amber liquor. " 'Twasn't as if Hubert had been a Yankee—you wouldn't expect anything different from them, but Hubert was a Texan and a gentleman."

"It must have been a great shock—very difficult for you."

" 'Deed it was. Ah just didn't know what to do aftah Ah couldn't dance with the U.S.O. any more." Her carefully blued eyelids lowered themselves. "Why did Ah have to get big so quick?"

Gravely North raised his cup. "It must be very painful for you to recall such things."

"Painful!" Velvalee's small body swayed as the train lurched around a bend. "You cain't imagine what it is to—

to—well to be nice to anybody who'd buy me a meal. Imagine me with a little baby and no husband? 'Co'se Ah kept hopin' Hubie'd turn up but he didn't, and Ah simply couldn't go back home."

"I suppose not," North agreed. "A little cognac?"

"Down our way people are so awfully narrow-minded. You see why Ah just couldn't go back to America," she straightened, raised her rounded chin a little, "and have people say 'po' Velvalee.' Well, like Uncle said, "If you take a licking in one place, fall back and fight on somewheres else.' So Ah did and—and Ah took up with a fine Russian colonel." Her flush deepened. "Everybody thought we were married and he was really good to little Hubie. Ah don't suppose you can forgive what Ah did, Major, can you?"

"Of course I can. You did the smart thing," North assured. "Especially by switching to the winning side. What happened to little Hubie?"

"Ah left him with a gal friend of mine," Velvalee explained. "It wasn't the South's fault we lost. We fought like a stack of black cats, but there just weren't enough of us."

"Granted," North mollified. "I presume there weren't enough people—like you and me—down in Mississippi to make your—er—error in judgment understandable?" He was careful about his phraseology. "After all we have the broad—the Continental viewpoint. Over here bastards are to be expected."

Velvalee shivered and her breath went out in a silver-gray cloud before she drew hard on her cigarette. "In some ways Ah think you are the most hatefullest man evah." Her full lips curved slowly. "But in some ways, Major, you're the," she fumbled, "most excitin' and the nicest. Do you really like me? Honest?"

In silence he refilled that little silver cup for a third time. "More than I can say—you're so very American in spite of all that's happened. Most girls would have grown hard and bitter like——"

"Like Esmé, you mean?"

"I didn't say that. Esmé's all right in her way."

"Hugh, what can have happened to Steve?"

"Did he mean a lot to you?"

"Laws no! Ah couldn't stand him. Always acted so suspicious and superior. Wish you could see my real brother—he's something!"

Ordinarily Velvalee must have been less susceptible to a little alcoholic pressure, he estimated, but obviously the unexplained disappearance of her so-called brother had thrown her defense mechanism out of gear.

"Tell me what is it like in Leningrad?" he invited.

"Sho'ly you must have been there."

"Once," he admitted, "but that was 'way back in Czarist times when I was only a small boy. Only then it was called Saint Petersburg."

She produced a handkerchief, dried a brow that suddenly had become spangled with sweat, glanced out into the dark where, here and there, a few scattered lights warned that the express was reaching the environs of Edirne. "Please, don't use that decadent name."

Sighing, Velvalee settled back on the stained and threadbare upholstery, careless that her black travelling suit was commencing to show various unsightly wrinkles. "If only Hubie hadn't left me like that—there'd never have been all this trouble."

"I suppose you met that Russian colonel in Berlin?"

"Yes, just after Ah quit the U.S.O. That was where Ah met Ben Gra——" She broke off, flicked the ash from her cigarette. "Well, Ah met a very interestin', cultured and understandin' gentleman; his papa is a very rich New Yo'k broker. Right off, he appreciated exactly the way the intolerant and decadent democrats back home would look at my—my misunderstandin' with Hubie. In Russia little mistakes like that make no nevah-mind."

"True enough," North agreed. "I suppose the Russians are much more advanced than we. Is it true that in the Soviet Union illegitimacy is encouraged?"

"Not exactly—but they—they condone it so long's the children are brought up as good Party members some day. At least that's what Ben told me."

"Who?"

"Ben Gramont." Velvalee's eyes shifted uncertainly. "You've met him, silly!"

"Have I?"

"Didn't you see Eric at the dance? Give me just a little mo' of that cognac, Honey. Ah, Ah declah Ah'm cold as ice all at once."

North tossed his topcoat over her lap. "Tell me more about Gramont."

"Ah never took him for a Russian. He always talked with that Ivy League, Pa'k Avenue accent——"

If only the progress of this train could be checked; how exasperating to perceive that Edirne's suburbs' lights in increasing numbers were winking and blinking through flying snow clouds.

He came to sit beside her and patted her hand in an encouraging fashion. "You surely have had a rough time of it."

"Really, Honey, Ah don't know why Ah bore you with all this. Ah cain't believe you're really interested."

"But I am."

"Well, you've got a mighty kind face and Ah feel Ah can trust you. You don't think Ah'm bad, do you?"

"No. Certainly not, if you were truly in love with this Texan."

She slipped her arm through his, leaned a little wearily and forlornly against him. "Ah was, like crazy. Hubie sho'

took me in—just a little fool from the po' relation State."
Her head came to rest against his shoulder. "You can see
how it was—all at once Ah had a car—Ben gave it to me—
and two maids. Ah had it better than eveh Ah got it at
home." She fell silent briefly, then said, "How wrong we
are. When Ah look back on the way we mistreat the nig-
gers——"

"We always called them 'colored people,'" North murmured. "Tell me, Sweetness, do you think Phoebus will
meet the train?"

"Phoebus? Ah don't expect so." Suspicion re-entered her
manner and she pulled out her compact. "Reckon you'll
think me a terrible little chattuh-box. Ah don't generally
talk too much, but Ah reckon Ah'm upset ovah Steve's dis-
appearin' like this."

The locomotive's whistle shrilled like an angry slut
twice—three times then the train began to slow.

The express commenced to buck and rattle its couplings
as the air brakes went on and presently it halted just within
the outskirts of Edirne. The reason for this soon became
apparent; at the crossing a troop train was passing. Complete with a sleeper for the officers, numerous flat cars
charged with light tanks, field pieces and some rolling
kitchens, it clattered by, soon to be followed by a second
section composed of third-class coaches crammed with
troops on their way north.

North experienced a reminiscent twinge on glimpsing
American-cut uniforms and World War II helmet linings
crowding the smoky interiors of this Turkish troop train.
The artillerymen, as soldiers will, were smoking and gambling, or else snoring in the aisles, disposed in grotesque,
distorted attitudes.

"Um. Things are looking up," North thought. "This is the
third troop train I've seen." Obviously, here was Turkey's
undaunted reply to Soviet diatribes hurled at the United
Nations Security Council.

Probably, all along this restless border dividing the Iron Curtain countries from their frightened neighbors, other troop trains were in motion; there'd also be truck convoys and troops afoot, moving through this bitter night towards the Turco-Bulgarian frontier.

By consequence, the express panted into the dim, gassy and chilly gloom of the railway station at Edirne a full half hour late. Here, despite the late hour, grimy platforms were jam-packed with weary peasants, red-eyed commercial travellers and soldiers returning or departing on furlough. Fortunately, the hour was too late for the usual hawkers, hotel runners, pimps and procurers.

In silence Velvalee watched North pick up her bag.

"Come," he directed, "and don't attract any attention because there'll be Secret Police on hand. I presume someone will be here to meet us?"

"Oh—Ben—I mean Eric!" Velvalee called out, waved frantically, and to North's un-surprise there appeared out of the crowd that suave and well-dressed individual who was pleased to name himself Eric Brecon-Fyffe.

"Will you shut up, you little fool?" he drawled and treated North to a curious alert look. "Ah—a pleasure to welcome you, Major. I trust you had a comfortable trip up?"

North was summoning a friendly and guileless smile when in the background he recognized the chunky figure of Captain David Larkin disappearing into a steam-clouded café opening off their platform.

CHAPTER 20

Gray Clouds over Vaisal

DURING his career North had on occasion experienced some fairly expert grilling, but nothing previously could be compared with that interrogation to which he was subjected hour after hour in a drafty, ill-furnished dwelling in the Karagatch Quarter of Edirne. Largely inhabited by Bulgarian expatriates, this quarter occupied the right bank of the Maritza River which, together with the Tunga River, trisected the ancient and Oriental-appearing city of Adrianople. During a speedy motor trip North judged that Karagatch must lie somewhere between the railroad station and the center of Edirne.

Only a threat of immediate physical violence thus far was lacking from his inquisition. Brecon-Fyffe and a pair of stolid, brown-faced Slavs occupied chairs immediately behind a student lamp which had been turned full into North's visage. Alternately, singly, or all at once, this trio flung question after question at him in varying tones. A beetle-browed individual who spoke fluent English marred by a thick Russian accent, appeared to be in command.

"Exactly what did Petrie say when he left you?" he demanded for the tenth time. "Repeat, word for word."

Without in the least varying his account, North supplied the information.

"What were these men wearing?"

North shrugged. "I've already told you, so for God's sake stop wasting valuable time. Brecon-Fyffe, please tell these gentlemen that I'm telling the truth, and that they have nothing to gain by all this, except to tire and annoy me."

Subconsciously he began wondering how best to exploit his solution of the Mata Hari message. Very likely these gentry must know where Phoebus could be found; probably more accurately than any of Colonel McKenzie's operatives. Could he, if he bribed them and won some of their confidence by explaining his interpretation, so manage the situation that Eric and his friends would remain a few strides behind?

"Very well, Georgei, I believe we had best postpone further inquiries."

So this tall, red-blond fellow with the reddish guardee mustache was the notorious Gramont! Odd, he looked not at all dangerous seated across this cheerless and smoke-fouled apartment. Indeed B. Arnold Gramont at the moment resembled, to an embarrassing degree that originally ruthless and later philanthropic tycoon who had sired him.

Velvalee, too, had been questioned until she had dissolved into tears and threatened hysterics—much to the disgust of that oak-faced Russian thus far known only as Georgei. It became evident that this Comrade Commissar remained suspicious of the travellers with typically Slavic tenacity. In Russian, of which language North was once more lamenting his ignorance, the third inquisitor, a sloe-eyed Bulgarian known as Dimitri, violently protested, shook his shaven head, tapped the holstered pistol at his belt and so warned North that a crucial moment was at hand.

"I say, Brecon-Fyffe, could I beg one of those cigarettes?"

"I don't fancy you'd like one."

"Rot! Ever since I served with the French army I can smoke anything. Incidentally, do I gather that you and our new friends here still haven't doped out what that unwashed joker at Melek Effendi's party was driving at?"

"Don't be a wise guy," Breton-Fyffe snarled in an unmistakably American voice. "Sit down!"

"Like hell I will. I'll do as I please," North retorted. "You and your dumblock team bore the be-Jesus out of me. Since you seem so abysmally stupid as to pay the Party's good money for a smart man's help only to threaten, insult and refuse to play ball with him, I quit and I'll bet that, in spite of your Ivy League education, you'll be voted 'least-likely-to-succeed' by the Muscovite Team."

"Why, you goddam, insolent——" Features flaming, Brecon-Fyffe gathered himself.

"Be quiet, *Tovarich*. You are being too hasty, perhaps." The man named Georgei held up a thin hand then, pursuing a mannerism, stroked his short black goatee. "Yess. Major North is quite right. Sixty t'ousand dollars of Party funds iss not to be thrown away. Vot you t'ink, Dimitri?"

The Bulgarian, a thick-bodied, bullet-headed individual, grunted, sucked hard on the stub of a cigarette. "Maybe, *mostranet,* he is so good a liar we can use him. Maybe he tell truth."

"Now we're getting somewhere," North commented. "Suppose, Eric, you turn that damned light out of my eyes and get rid of the notion that you can scare me. You can't, even if you've a gun and some pals on hand.

"Incidentally," the Intelligence Officer moved boldly out of the lamplight, "the next time you want to interrogate somebody with brains enough to pound glass down a rat hole, I'll give you some pointers."

His show of arrogance was succeeding, North realized, and he barely suppressed a smile at having so deftly maneuvered Brecon-Fyffe into a defensive position. The former American pilot obviously was ruffled, but evidently possessed considerably more self-control than the late Stephen Petrie.

Grating like a piece of chalk on North's mental blackboard was that glimpse of Captain Larkin. What the hell was he doing in Vaisal? Why should he show up so promptly?

Eric demanded abruptly, "Well, what about this Mata Hari business?"

Aware of the value of a stage wait, North coolly helped himself from a box of Regie cigarettes on the table and quite deliberately lit it.

"You have an agent named Phoebus."

"How did you know that?" Georgei demanded in his unusually soft voice.

"If you will call in Esmé Murfee she can explain that point." He wondered whether Esmé was in this drafty, crudely furnished dwelling or not, but suspected so.

"Yes. The Major here," Eric explained, "decoded a message from him."

The Bulgarian belched and then eased the broad leather belt containing his black peasant shirt. "So this man has already been of use, no?"

"What has Phoebus to do with the Mata Hari problem?"

"The explanation lies in the Javanese translation of Mata Hari—it means 'Eye of the Morning.'" North seemed to hear once more the rhythmic clatter of the night express, to see that automatic levelled above Petrie's lap. Praise God he'd had the wit to throw away the Walther! If ever a man had been thoroughly searched he had been on arrival from the railway station.

Georgei leaned forward. "Get on with this. Time iss growing very short."

"Phoebus was the Grecian sun god. The sun rises in the morning. It's my contention that the message concerned Phoebus, Phoebus Skoularis, and that we must look for him in Vaisal."

"*Ousht!*" burst out Dimitri. "That sounds sensible."

"Yes, that's a sound bit of reasoning," Eric conceded.

Georgei's pince-nez glinted as he arose. Lean and cadaverous, he was wearing an ill-fitting coat, paper collar and brown serge pants stuffed into typically Russian boots. He glanced inquiringly at Dimitri—a typical, half-educated Bulgarian peasant with dirty, lumpy hands tipped by broken and yellowish nails. In four days he could not have shaved, nor had his greasy black hair been touched by a comb any more recently.

"Unfortunately, Comrade Major," Georgei said softly, and North was infinitely relieved by his use of the title, "your so clever solution does us little good."

"Why not?"

"Because," Brecon-Fyffe explained, "our friend, Phoebus Skoularis, fell, mortally wounded, in a border skirmish on the frontier two days ago. Yesterday they buried him in Vaisal."

Phoebus dead? The wind, rattling at a loose window frame, and the blizzard's moaning about the roof corners were disconcerting, yet North's mind had never worked more intensely. Here *was* a bad break and no mistake, a serious setback to those plans commencing to take form in his mind.

"Where did he die?"

"In a tavern in Vaisal," Eric told him, "where Turkish border guards brought him. He took his time apparently and lived for nearly a day with a bullet through his belly."

"He was searched?"

"Do you t'ink de Turk Secret Police fools?" demanded Dimitri. "He vass stripped and all his belonkinks took avay——"

"Are you sure about that?" North wanted to know. "It's most important."

"*Da,*" Georgei asserted. "Iss only natural. Ve, too, haff agents, many off dem along dis frontier."

Like the slow ticking of a metronome the phrase, "Eye of

the Morning, Eye of the Morning," reverberated through North's subconscious. He got up and took a turn over a gritty old Ukranian rug.

He halted, faced Georgei, not Eric. "We must go to Vaisal as fast as we can and, somehow, examine Skoularis' effects. Can that be done?"

"*Da!*" Like an overgrown toad Dimitri bobbed his blunt and hairless head. "In Vaisal iss vun corporal off rural police. Maybe for a little vhile dose clothinks and papers he could brink."

Georgei ceased staring at the American's lean, rather Indian-like countenance and stalked over to a door and called "Andreyev! Order the big auto. Make sure there iss of petrol a sufficiency."

Eric translated the fellow's anxious protestations that the road, a rough country one, had become impassable because of the blizzard.

"Besides, *Tovarich,*" Dimitri pointed out, "Turkish frontier guards patrol dat road. During darkness efferyone iss halted. *Da.* Too often dose fellow shoot first and question later."

"In that case I fancy we must wait till daylight," Brecon-Fyffe admitted. "Suppose we eat, it's nearly three."

By consequence North presently was offered a bowl of *mamalega*—a coarse cornmeal mush, and some hideously acid bortsch, followed by tea brewed strong enough to float a steel helmet.

For the Intelligence Officer there was no bed, only a lumpy, coverless couch that suggested itself as a haven for innumerable insects. They left him crouched on a wooden stool feeding damp billets into a small iron stove that proved quite incapable of coping with frigid drafts eddying so strongly as to make his lighter's flame bend.

His trench coat plus its liner, however, proved adequate and he could pull up a muffler to warm his ears. Of course

Georgei et al. had confiscated his suitcase and in all probability at this very moment were going through his luggage with the proverbial fine-toothed comb. Whether he ever again would behold his soft wool socks, Jaeger underwear and other warm clothing seemed problematical, to say the least.

Eye of the Morning? The more he mulled over the translation the more he felt convinced that he was on the right track. What he needed was an opportunity to examine the late Phoebus Skoularis' effects.

Very much he wondered, as he sat there, feet propped against the stove, gloved hands locked back of his head and watching minute scarlet patches of light shimmer and wink against the stained and flyblown plaster beyond the stove, whether by tomorrow night Walewski might be brought to safety. Where was Jingles now? A mighty useful gal—the warm sparkle of her eyes, her golden-brown complexion, her easy stride, her rich and ready laughter kept obtruding themselves in his thoughts.

Maybe she could have helped him understand the true status of swarthy Captain Larkin. Like Banquo's ghost the A-2's barely familiar figure flitted against the background of the situation. Most likely it seemed that the Air Force officer had been posted by Brecon-Fyffe, otherwise Gramont, to check on others of the same plumage—this being standard MVD practice.

North sighed, belched as, in a silvery vapor, the bortsch backfired. It was growing colder, so he fed more willow billets into the stove. By listening hard he could recognize an undertone of voices in the next room, but found it impossible to distinguish what was being said. He could, however, recognize Eric's clipped pseudo-English inflection, Dimitri's growling voice, and Velvalee's drawl mingled with Esmé Murfee's metallic accents. He heard several slaps, immediately followed by the Southern girl's wails.

Esmé's edged voice suddenly rose loud enough for the solitary eavesdropper to hear. "Of course, you should have checked on him, you damned, lazy slut. What the hell do you think we pay you for? You're supposed to think, besides wriggling your hips and rolling your eyes at whoever you're told. Now get smart or Dimitri will give you a test of his belt. I won't tolerate such stupidity, see?"

"Oh, no! Don't! *Don't!*" Again Velvalee cried out under a resounding slap, then a door opened and several persons emerged and descended to the ground storey.

CHAPTER 21

Reminiscences

HUGH NORTH waited fifteen or twenty minutes, refuelled the stove, then on quiet, but not furtive feet went to try the lock on his door. He didn't expect to find it locked and it wasn't, so he walked quietly over to a door from behind which sounded a dreary sobbing.

His soft knock resulted in a gasp infinitely descriptive of a woman's terror-stricken apprehension.

"Please go away! Ah swear Ah did the best Ah knew how. Honest to God Ah did. Oh!"

"Quiet!" North entered and by the light of a single candle beheld a room quite as cold, bare and uninviting as the one he had just quitted. The only improvement was a small iron bed set in a far corner and some dingy hangings of Rumanian origin.

Velvalee Petrie was seated at a bottle-marked table, and crying into the crook of her arm, for when she looked up the candle flame gilded the course of tears over cheeks that looked red and swollen.

"Go 'way," she begged. "You're the cause of all mah trouble. *Please* go 'way."

The dishevelled creature's eyes widened fearfully when, firmly, he reclosed the door. "Velvalee, any trouble you find yourself in," said he not ungently, "was caused not by me—but by yourself. Did they question you about Steve?"

The Petrie girl emitted a moist sob and then nodded. Because she made no effort whatever to repair her appearance North judged her to be truly distrait.

"I hope they haven't hurt you too much?" His manner was deeply sympathetic.

"N-n-no, n-not much Ah reckon, but that damn' Esmé can pinch like a blue fin crab." Reminiscently she rubbed first an arm and then her left bosom. "She's the meanest low-down bitch evah Ah saw. Wonder what she uses fo' a heart?"

North offered a cigarette then seated himself across the table from her. "Eric and his playmates gave me a bit of a grilling, too, but they didn't get physical. You poor kid, they surely gave you a bad time."

"You heard?"

"Only the slaps and your crying out."

His instinctive sympathy suddenly became chilled. "Better go slow," he warned himself. "Remember, Chum, they've used this Mississippi mocking bird as a come-on before." No, it wasn't inconceivable that once more Eric and Esmé were testing his loyalty. Even in her distress, despite a pink nose and inflamed eyes, Velvalee remained undeniably alluring in a pale blue jersey that did nothing to disguise the perfection of her bust. By the candle's dancing gleam her pale blonde hair yet shone like a coif of shimmering gold.

"They didn't lock my door," he reminded himself. "Nor have they posted a guard in the corridor. Does this mean that I'm right at last?" No telling.

Suddenly Velvalee ran around the table and, sinking onto her knees, clung to him like a frightened child. "Please be kind to me, Hugh," she whimpered. "Ah—Ah'm so terribly frightened and all—all mixed up. Mah haid hurts. Oh, please, Honey, cain't you get me out of this? Ah didn't know what Ah was doin' when Ah joined them."

From his back pocket North produced the now familiar silver flask and smiled into her still strongly flushed features. "Take a pull of this, and for God's sake lower your voice. They'll hear you." He emphasized the word "they."

For several minutes Velvalee clung to him, her slight but plump body a-quiver to the violence of her weeping. Were she acting, North decided, she was putting on a superlative performance. But then, the MVD was not given to employing clumsy actresses.

Their breath vapors mingled and, gradually, her weeping diminished in violence until, at length, she stopped crying and at long last turned to her purse for lipstick and compact.

"You won't let them hurt me any mo', will you, Hugh? Please, Honey, tell me what to do." Her eyes narrowed. "If you could know how Ah just hate all—all this cold, all these mean, cruel people and their everlastin' suspicion of everythin'. Oh!" she wailed. "Ah'd do 'most *anythin'* to be back in Bolivar County, sweatin' real hard and just watchin' magnolia leaves shine under the sun and listenin' to noises down in the bayou below our place."

"It must be lovely there," he whispered above a sudden fierce rattling of the windows. "Why did you change your allegiance?"

"Oh—oh, it was Ben Gramont mo' than anythin' else. He swore he was in love with me and he knew how miserable Ah was there in Berlin." She pressed herself even closer to him. The candle light magnified their shadows to gigantic proportions against the plaster wall upon which were sketched grimy rectangles caused by the removal of pictures which had hung there long ago.

"Ah really loved Ben till we got to Moscow." She sensed his unspoken inquiry. "Then he changed and got so mean and hard; Ah tried to change with him, but Ah reckon Ah still loved America. Up till now Ah've always done like Ah was told—and did mah very best. But," her eyes, so preternaturally bright that he wondered about it, sought his, "but now, since you've showed up, a real clean and honest-to-

God American, well, Ah don't want to go on any longer."

"Then, you don't believe I've really turned my coat?"

Velvalee looked him squarely in the face. "No, Ah don't; not that Ah'd evah ask you, point-blank," she added hurriedly.

"I'm glad of that," said he, slipping his arm about her shoulders. "I'd hate to disappoint you," which was by way of being the most ambiguous answer possible.

"Please don't go on," he continued, "if it makes you unhappy. Here. Tell me, to change the subject, what do you make of Captain Larkin?"

"Oh, he's sweet, but he's Esmé's boy friend, not mine. Honey, Ah've nevah had such a miserable headache in yeahs. You haven't an aspirin?"

"Yes, but they're in my bag, which I can't get at it seems. Here, have a cigarette instead."

"Honest, Honey, d'you know what it means," she sighed, "to meet an honest-to-God American again? My, you're good-lookin'."

North settled back in his chair, watching his breath create a brief, gilded miasma. "You keep forgetting, my dear, that I am under contract."

He would never forget the peculiar intensity of her wine-colored eyes, their pupils enormous because of the faint light. "Please, don't say you haven't been playin' a game. Fo' God's sake don't you make the same mistake Ah did."

His shadow mimicked the way he ground out his cigarette. "Oh, stop that damn' snivelling," said he angrily. "I don't know about you but when *I* make a bargain I stick to it, so when I said I was finished with the United States Army I meant it."

"Ah'm sorry. Forget what Ah said."

The way her expression crumpled and the dejected way she stared at her cigarette almost convinced him.

"Suppose you were right about me and I—well," he suggested very softly, "I asked you to help me, would you?"

"Oh, darlin' yes, yes!" she murmured. "Just ask. Ah—Ah'll do anythin' you tell me, Honey, anythin'."

He patted her cheek and was surprised to feel how hot it was. "That, my dear, we shall presently find out."

CHAPTER 22

The Red Tide's Edge

THE village of Vaisal, it appeared, lay only thirty miles to the northeast of Edirne, but on the very outskirts of the latter city evidences of unrest were plentiful. The party set out in a stout old Benz and an Alpha-Romeo which had seen much better days. Painfully the two cars bumped along over a miserable and snow-choked secondary national route.

All the travellers were aware of Turkish patrol planes droning back and forth, keeping unbroken surveillance over the frontier. Expressive of the tense international situation was the presence of a heavily armed infantry detachment in nearly every hamlet. Smoke from their camp fires hung low for, during the night, a warm wind off the Black Sea had blown away the snow clouds to cast brilliant sunshine over the treeless and gently rolling countryside. North estimated a fog might set in before long.

It was a revelation to see how busy were the eyes of his companions once they overtook a column of American-built trucks laden with all manner of military supplies. Dimitri and Georgei slumped low on their seats but Brecon-Fyffe waved to the drivers in friendly fashion and even tossed out some packs of cigarettes. By good luck this convoy had halted on the roadside, else the Benz would never have succeeded in passing it. From two jeeps heading this mud-spattered column they were subjected to sharp scrutiny by a group of Turkish officers who were warming their hands and heating coffee over a G.I. helmet full of blazing gasoline.

The further the Benz progressed towards the frontier the more desolate and forbidding grew the terrain. Bare, snow-covered hills were numerous here, many of them surmounted by the ruins of some ancient fort or castle.

The presence of North's American Army trench coat and Eric's British "warm" probably contributed to the comparative lack of inspection with which the two automobiles progressed towards Vaisal. Twice, when American Army staff cars bearing the insignia of the Military Mission came ploughing by, mud-splashed and dripping, Brecon-Fyffe fixed a shrewd glance on North, but read nothing save a casual interest.

Too bad that none of those red-faced officers in sheepskin coats and sun glasses could know that, at this moment, they were passing leading actors in a drama the dénouement of which would profoundly affect their careers.

"God, what a hind-end of a country," grunted Brecon-Fyffe, rubbing eyes grown red from glare off the snow fields. "Why anybody should want it escapes me." He turned suddenly. "By the bye, what were you and that dumb blonde discussing last night?"

"Only the going-over you and la Murfee gave her. She wanted sympathy and company."

He shot North a penetrating glance. "She didn't talk out of turn?"

"No. She was too scared, even if she'd wanted to. Which I doubt."

"She'd better straighten out. I was all against taking her to Turkey in the first place, but Esmé thought she'd earn her salt pumping the boys on the Military Mission."

North felt prompted to mention the enigmatic Captain Larkin, but at the last moment restrained himself and was glad because, a moment later, Brecon-Fyffe observed, "Damned if I'm sure, even now, whether to give you a free hand or not."

"What do your friends Georgei and Dimitri think?"

Brecon-Fyffe grinned wolfishly. "Dimitri is all for knocking you off, but, for some reason, Georgei's convinced you're to be trusted."

"Kind of him. He's clever enough to sense that I really intend to earn my salary."

"Maybe he's right," Brecon-Fyffe admitted. "After all, for years you've slaved for the dear old Jew-nited States and for what? Ten, maybe eleven, thousand a year—minus taxes. No wonder you'd be ready to make a change."

The old Benz churned to the top of yet another rise revealing Vaisal perhaps half a mile distant, a typical poverty-stricken Turkish village. Dominated by the single minaret of a mosque it appeared to be a helter-skelter assortment of buildings, the largest of which appeared to be three gray, grim-looking barracks and a pair of untidy factories, the chimneys of which were belching yellow-black smoke. These were dye works, Dimitri explained.

The Benz and its companion car encountered little traffic beyond farm carts, a drove of cattle and innumerable stray curs. A majority of such troops as previously had been garrisoned in Vaisal must have been moved nearer to the Bulgarian border lying a scant ten kilometers distant, for only a scattering of soldiers plodded about on duty and an occasional officer in long gray-green overcoat and chapka was visible when the Benz turned into Vaisal's ill-paved and narrow central street.

To Hugh North it came as a revelation that their chauffeur, a thick-necked, silent individual wearing a flat leather cap and worn coat, without hesitation drove to a tavern called The Tartar's Head and situated a block off the village's shabby main square where stood the usual statue of Mustafa Kemal Ataturk.

There could be no doubt that, despite the dye works and the presence of an Army post, Vaisal had remained wretchedly poor. Most of its houses were of but a single storey and lurked behind ragged wooden fences originally designed to afford protection from wolves. Under this unexpectedly warm sunlight their eaves dripped steadily upon goats, geese and chickens foraging hopelessly among rutted alleys and muddy side streets.

A path had been shovelled granting access to this forbidding-appearing hostelry's garage, so without pause the Benz was driven inside then, in military precision, both doors were immediately shut by a pair of peasants in long white linen smocks and heavy leather boots.

"Come this way, Major," Brecon-Fyffe directed, "and pray God we'll get thawed out."

The Bulgarian turned, heavy brows merged. *"Tovarich,* vot vas that you said about prayink God?"

Brecon-Fyffe flushed. "Merely a catch phrase, Dimitri. Of course I didn't mean it."

Came Georgei's soft accents, "You really must take care, Comrade, some people might not understand your use of such a 'catch phrase.'"

Strong odors of cooking entered North's nostrils, set his mouth to watering; after all, he had not consumed a real meal since leaving Istanbul. Once the travellers had traversed a refuse-heaped stableyard they were conducted into what proved to be a most unsavory kitchen. There they lingered until Esmé, Velvalee and Nestor came in, blue-lipped and surly of mien. Velvalee, in particular, looked badly. Her usually lively eyes were dull and, minus make-up, her features appeared faded and drawn.

Served by a pair of huge-busted women wearing elaborately embroidered headkerchiefs, very full black skirts and heavy red leather knee boots, the new arrivals lunched on scalding tea, a lentil soup, boiled onions and slices of greasy sausage so lavishly spiced with garlic that North was forced out of self-defense to eat some himself.

Dimitri wolfed his food, muttered something to Brecon-Fyffe, then hurried out in company with Nestor.

"Come, Velvalee," said Esmé, "let's go and unpack and maybe you'd better take some Empirin for that headache of yours. You'll come up presently, Eric?"

Thus North and Georgei were left alone in the low-ceilinged, pine-panelled dining room, grateful for the billows of heat given off by a great, flat-topped and porcelain tiled stove. It was large enough to occupy a whole corner of the room. Still resting upon its broad surface lay the thin mattresses and rough blankets in which certain of the hotel staff were accustomed to sleeping.

Georgei lit an enormously fat and long cigarette, inquired, "What do you make of our friend Eric?"

"Seems able, if a little impetuous. Thanks for shutting him up."

The Russian tugged at his little black goatee. "He iss a fool—but a useful fool."

An hour dragged by, an hour during which the Intelligence Officer drowsed. Lacking any rest the night before, he welcomed this opportunity. God knew that soon he would need every smidgen of alertness he possessed.

He was roused by feet hurrying in from The Tartar's Head's main entrance. Brecon-Fyffe appeared simultaneously from upstairs. Like a wrathful gorilla Dimitri came shuffling in and levelled a hairy forefinger at North.

"Thiss man must be shotted," he growled at Brecon-Fyffe.

"Why?"

"I haff learned several counter-agents haff just arrived in Vaisal. Two of them are off Americanski Intelligence; one belongs to the Turkyi Secret Police."

Nauseating apprehension invaded North's being. How in God's name could McKenzie have been so inept as to send identifiable agents? What a fine thing if a piece of inexplicable carelessness were to encompass the destruction of the one person who might yet reach Josef Walewski!

"I assure you," North broke out in convincing vehemence, "I have absolutely nothing to do with the arrival of these agents. As you should damn well know, Eric, this whole border is in a perpetual turmoil." He appealed to the Commissar. "Surely you understand that this is merely a coincidence? Intelligence agents come and go all the time."

Georgei frowned. "Iss thiss true?"

The traitor hesitated. "Yes. Other Turkish, Greek and American agents have appeared here in addition to many of our own. Let's talk to our local man."

A gaunt, heavily mustached individual appeared, wearing the uniform of a gendarme corporal and saluted the group across the dining room. "Yes," he told Georgei, "they come. They go. More come. More go." The police corporal's brown face was bright with sweat engendered by his heavy overcoat, the lapels of which bore brilliant red tabs ornamented by brass unit insignia.

Under his left arm the policeman was carrying a large cardboard box to one end of which was attached an official tag stamped with a serial number and some dotted lines filled in with purple ink.

That which instantly captured North's attention was the sight of Phoebus Skoularis' name typed large across the reverse of a bright yellow tag. Fervently, he fell to praising the late, great Ataturk for having instituted Latinization of Turkish written speech.

North continued to tilt back in a straight, rush-bottomed chair and smoke unhurriedly. At one time the conventionalized flowers painted on each wall panel, now so smokedulled and chipped, must have appeared gay and graceful.

Not having been invited to participate he watched Dimitri and Brecon-Fyffe unpack the reinforced cardboard box. Some of the contents proved to be grisly; a striped blue and white shirt and an undershirt plentifully stained with unmistakable rust red splashes which could only be dried blood; a detachable collar, a new and gaudy green and red knitted necktie and other items of men's wear.

To restrain himself proved difficult. Somewhere among the deceased's effects might lie the clue to Walewski's whereabouts. From where he sat he could see fairly well. In the collection were only a mere handful of papers, a Greek passport, frayed and greasy from continued handling, a few old hotel statements, but quite an imposing sheaf of banknotes in various currencies: Turkish pounds, Greek drachmas, Rumanian lei and Bulgarian dinars. Last, but not the least interesting, was the sum of five hundred dollars in crisp new American notes.

As unobtrusively as he might, North studied Phoebus Skoularis' possessions. That which he sought in particular was a spectacle or eye-glasses case; presently, sure enough, it was placed upon the dining table. North was reminded that he had top-calibre enemies at hand by the eagerness with which Georgei reached for that glasses case and commenced to examine it so thoroughly, and leisurely, that the border police corporal spoke up.

"What's that?" Brecon-Fyffe wanted to know.

Dimitri translated, "Thiss *onbasi* swears he must return evidence to hiss *karapol* very quick."

"Very well," came Brecon-Fyffe's impatient agreement. "Georgei, let me see those spectacles."

Leaving the Russian to explore the worn velvet lining of the spectacle case with the point of a knife, the traitor carried Skoularis' glasses over to a window and North's breath halted in his throat while watching Eric produce a soft lead pencil. With great care the tweed-clad figure circulated the point first over the inner and then outer surfaces of both lenses.

"Don't let that bastard find anything. Oh God, don't— please don't let him," North breathed. This, he knew, was a turning point. All at once he noticed a small cylindrical object of red rubber and felt better.

"*Tovarich,* only ten minutes are left," Georgei grunted. "And we dare not compromise our friend the *onbasi* here."

"Damned if there's anything significant here." Brecon-Fyffe by now was sweating profusely. "Major, suppose you try your hand? Perhaps we've overlooked something."

"Thanks." North permitted himself a brief chuckle and a smile of contempt. "Dear God, Eric, how dare you preen yourself as an expert? Really you should go back to Lubliana Street for a refresher course."

Brecon-Fyffe looked really dangerous. "You're right, Dimitri, we've had enough of this fellow's insolence."

"And I of you." With two quick strides North crossed to the table. "Look, you idiots, *look!* See this rubber cup?" He held up a hollow red rubber contrivance which much resembled an amphora.

"*Da.* I wass wondering its purpose," muttered Georgei, tugging once more at his little black beard.

This was North's moment; he made the most of it. "That I'll explain when you give me an opportunity to examine Phoebus Skoularis' body."

The other occupants of the room stared.

"Can you get him exhumed?"

Investigation revealed not only that the Greek's remains occupied a grave in Vaisal's Greek-Orthodox cemetery, but this walrus-mustached corporal of police was aware of its exact location. On the other hand, the frontier guards and secret police were so alert that to effect a removal of the corpse would be impossible.

North let them wait a little, enjoyed Eric's discomfiture and Georgei's Slavic imperturbability despite what must be a nearly unbearable anxiety. "No need to remove the corpse. I need only to examine Skoularis' body."

"Why?" Brecon-Fyffe demanded.

"If you'd been less obnoxious I'd tell you now. As it is, I'll have you worry—and wait. Maybe sometime you'll learn not to irritate me."

He examined the deceased's garments, noted among other things that they were of excellent quality; the dead man's linen—a most important pointer—also of fine quality was clean for a Greek traveller. A fastidious fellow, this.

"Any of you know this chap Skoularis?" North inquired while running an eye over the late lamented's passport. That credential had been remarkably well-used. While leafing through many liberally stamped and cancelled pages of visas he learned some interesting revelations as to that individual's recent travels. Um. Belgrade, Saloniki, Sofia and the secret police stamp of a place called Kavakli.

"*Da,* him I knew," Dimitri admitted, chewing on the stump of a thin Macedonian cigar. "A vain fellow he wass. Effery voman in the world most be in loff with him."

North fingered the spectacles. "Did you see him wear these often?"

"Only at vork," grunted the Bulgarian. "He not see vell, bot pretty girls he not vant see hiss glasses."

"Most significant—eh, Eric?" he taunted the traitor now so angry that the scar across his chin shone dark red.

With half an eye the Intelligence Officer could tell that Skoularis' glasses had been ground to suit an extremely short-sighted person.

"There's nothing more to be done about this until we can view the remains, so may I clean up?" he demanded.

A miserable day ensued for North. There was no blinking the fact that he was, to all intents and purposes, a prisoner. In the afternoon Esmé Murfee appeared, mannish in a jacket and corduroy slacks. She could not have been easy in her mind if those pale brown half-moons lurking under her eyes meant anything.

"Here, Comrade." She offered a half tumbler of vodka. "Maybe this will brighten life for a reformed drunk."

"You're so considerate, Esmé, I'm touched. Really, I am—I was feeling almighty dry. How!" They clinked tumblers.

"Did you know that Georgei has been called back to Edirne?" Her gaze flitted restlessly from one point to another. "The pressure upon us is becoming—well—terrifying. So——" Those now familiar small dark blue eyes wavered aside. "Please—for all our sakes—make no mistakes."

A long swallow of vodka sent color back to her unpowdered cheeks. Possibly that drink, plus some secret fear, could have accounted for the almost incredible breach of security she then committed.

"If only you could find this fellow Walewski," Esmé said, picking a bit of tobacco from nearly colorless lips, "we could all return to Russia and breathe easily. What a damned pigsty of a town! Back home you wouldn't——" The sentence died, but Hugh North appeared not to notice, only inquired.

"Tell me, Esmé, are we expected to cross into Bulgaria?"

"If it becomes advisable."

"But? The Turks have pillboxes every quarter of a mile and a patrol every yard of the frontier day and night."

"We'll get across, never doubt it."

During the late afternoon Georgei reappeared from Edirne and laboring under some badly-disguised emotion. Behind the pince-nez his watery and red-rimmed eyes shifted endlessly as one after another of the whole group assembled in the inn's common room which smelt of mice, dust and insecticides.

"You appear agitated, Comrade." Esmé looked apprehensive.

"With reason. Dyakov iss furious. He hass heard of the arrival here of the American agents; also they are reported keeping thiss inn under surveillance."

"Was Dyakov sure on that point?" snapped Brecon-Fyffe.

"Not entirely," Georgei admitted. "But you know how fearful he and Tarelkin are.

"Where is that *mozhno* girl—the empty-headed blonde? We will send her to visit these Americans."

"That's out. She's in bed with chills and fever," Esmé explained. "No, she's not faking. Right now her temperature is up to a 102 and still climbing."

"Vhat iss wrong vith her?" Dimitri's bass voice demanded.

"It's hard to tell. Maybe she's coming down with 'flu— I hope not, because there's a serious form of it—something like the Spanish 'flu—spreading westward from Rumania. On the other hand, it might be typhus, or only the abominable food we've been eating."

At length North, who had been at pains to remain both unobtrusive and indifferent, inquired whether the exhumation of Skoularis' corpse still would take place.

"*Da.* After dark," Dimitri replied. "A veather report promises more snow; that iss goot."

CHAPTER 23

Dead Dandy

THE WEATHER was proving strictly pro-Communist, thought North when, at about eight of the evening, he and the men from Istanbul, accompanied by a pair of broad-shouldered and stupid-looking young Bulgarian peasants, stepped out into a glacial wind. This rising gale and clouds of dry, very fine snow had emptied the squalid streets of Vaisal. Were the inn indeed being watched the surveillants must be thoroughly miserable.

Dimitri led the way, slipping and cursing softly at those flakes stinging so viciously, relentlessly at his face.

North walked in this shadowy column abreast of him who once had been Ben A. Gramont. When, every once in a while, a particularly vicious squall would black out houses and fences Brecon-Fyffe inevitably moved closer, an entirely absurd precaution because North easily could have tripped him before vanishing wraith-like into the snow-filled darkness.

It was well that Dimitri knew his way, since landmarks were few and obscured once the party quitted the village and commenced climbing a deeply rutted road.

"Whoever they've got doing the digging," North reflected while pulling the khaki muffler higher about his ears, "certainly are earning their bortsch and *mamalega*."

Presently the snow thinned and North was able to discern, not far ahead, the outlines of several monuments; most were topped with the double Cross characteristic of the Greek Orthodox Church. Some of the headstones, long neglected, canted drunkenly sidewise, while the outlines of others, fallen flat, barely were visible beneath the snow carpet.

Presently Dimitri's dim figure halted in an area where cheap wooden crosses or simple headboards were the rule. He growled, "All off you stay here."

In the past North had found himself an actor on many an eerie scene, but none had ever been more bizarre than this. Without looking, he knew that the two young peasants, as well as Brecon-Fyffe, were carrying automatics ready for instant use.

"Well, Eric, hope you're partial to winter sports," he commented. "Pity we haven't any skis or a mug of hot, buttered rum waiting for us at home."

Brecon-Fyffe coughed and used his cuff to scrape snow from his brows. "Why couldn't this job be over on the Black Sea Coast or in southern Greece? Next time I'll put in for a warmer assignment."

"Funny, I was thinking just now you're finding the assignment plenty hot enough."

"You kill me," came the other's acid comment, then fell silent because Dimitri reappeared to conduct the party into a little hollow where a number of raw wooden crosses attested the existence of recent graves. North noticed a chink of light and presently became aware first of a tent fly rigged low over the ground, then of shovelfuls of raw earth showing inkily against the snow.

Two brawny ghouls must have been at work for some time since tendrils of malodorous sweat-vapor were rising from beneath their thick sheepskin vests. These workers wore no shoes, only ungainly strips of cloth bound around their feet and half way up to their knees. By the light of a kerosene lantern they reminded North of the giants, Fafner and Fasolt, in Arthur Rackham's wonderful illustrations for the *Nibelungenlied*.

Dimitri pointed at the tent fly. "So, go in. See vot you find—and make no mistake." The Bulgarian now was wearing a holstered pistol belted about an ankle-length overcoat.

"Good God," North complained wearily, "don't you ever trust anybody?"

"A thoroughly reactionary remark," Georgei commented, "but let us get to work."

Before him unfolded a scene that North could visualize until his last hour; the snow edging up into the tautly stretched canvas, an oblong gash in the earth, the two ghouls all yellow and black by the lantern light.

Kneeling, he peered into the grave and recognized the outlines of an un-coffined human body shrouded only in coarse brown cloth secured by cords.

"Hold the lantern lower." Then to Dimitri he directed, "Tell them to clear away that dirt around his head."

One of the peasants tossed aside a short-handled spade and commenced to claw aside the earth, for all the world like a dog digging a hole.

Hugh North's whole attention became fixed upon a rectangle perhaps two feet by three feet.

"Now expose the dead man's head," he directed.

One of the diggers groped at the back of his belt and produced a huge knife with which he slashed cords and fabric until the shroud loosened.

"Tell them to get out of the grave." Standing in the pit he became aware of a ring of lamplit faces.

Had his reasoning been well founded? There was nothing like finding out, so he pulled apart the burlap even as a handful of snowflakes propelled by a particularly vicious blast eddied in under the fly, settled stark but cleanly upon a mop of black hair. Another tug of this ignoble shroud exposed Phoebus Skoularis' head to the lantern's yellow glare. North reinforced it by the pitiless radiance of an electric torch.

During a long instant North studied the dead man's yellow-gray features and came to understand why Skoularis had been vain. The colorless contours and planes of his features reproduced the classic beauty of a good cameo and the dead man's nose was straight as a sculpture by Praxiteles.

Perforce, he stripped off his gloves and gently brushed the corpse's long black hair back over its forehead. Because the body so recently had been buried it had not yet become frozen; nevertheless considerable effort was required to repress the dead man's eyelids. Reproachfully they stared up at the Intelligence Officer when, straddling the body, he inserted the point of a metal pencil into the corpse's left eye at its inner corner. A wave of unspeakable relief surged through him when his pencil's point caught under something hard. Employing great delicacy he then lifted slowly, slowly, until, all at once, the chill flesh yielded and the edge of a transparent glass oval materialized.

So this was the Eye of the Morning. Mata Hari.

"Contact lenses!" burst out Brecon-Fyffe's useless explanation.

"Wonderful!" Even Dimitri grunted his praise.

Presently the other lens was freed and, perspiring gently, North straightened.

"Give them to me," Brecon-Fyffe directed. "You're a very lucky man.

"—And you're the most complete swine I've ever met." North indulged in a rare exhibition of exasperation. "Comrade Georgei, I'll not work for this—this fool any longer. From now on I'll listen to no one but you!"

"As you wish, *Tovarich*," replied the Russian, his lean features for once animated. Firmly, he took the lenses from Brecon-Fyffe. "As for me, I shall propose you to receive the Order of the Red Banner. The Proletarian Army knows how to reward its geniuses."

CHAPTER 24

Surprise Raid

ALTHOUGH Hugh North was aware that once the enigma presented by the contact lenses became solved, his danger would continue great, it would not be as immediate as formerly.

Georgei, Brecon-Fyffe and Esmé Murfee—he estimated their seniority to rank in that order—confronted by this, the second proof of his acumen and integrity, had indeed warmed to him, and even Dimitri appeared a trifle more affable.

"How is Velvalee getting on?" North inquired once they had shaken the snow from their clothes and stood scarlet-faced before the great porcelain stove.

"She's not any better," the Murfee girl informed shortly. "Just like that silly little *mozhno* to take sick at this time."

"What does '*mozhno*' mean?"

"Literally it means, 'You may if you wish.'" Georgei removed his pince-nez and wiped condensation from them. "We of the MVD find frequent use for such girls around the embassies in Moscow, in Vienna, in Berlin, in fact anywhere there are *nagranitzky,* especially American troops."

"Do they earn much?"

"*Niet!* Only for brains do we pay well. A little vodka, Nestor, that was cold work."

North insisted, "Is Velvalee seriously ill?"

"Yes. Her temperature's up to 104, and she's growing

delirious. There's nothing can be done except send her to the hospital in Edirne——"

"You'll do that, won't you?"

"No," replied Eric harshly. "With these damned agents in town it'd be too risky."

"But," North looked incredulous, "she's a member of our team!"

"—An unimportant one. Any-time trollops like her are a sixpence the dozen." His close-set eyes were expressionless, devoid of sympathy. "Now let's get to work; we've got to move fast."

Under the light of a powerful flashlight North revolved the contact lenses first one way, then the other. One lens proved to be devoid of any inscription, but lampblack applied with a camel's hair brush from Velvalee's make-up kit easily developed into the most important five words Major Hugh North would ever read. In microscopic characters was written: *"W'ski est Novak en Kavakli."*

"Ousht!" broke out Georgei excitedly. "At last! At last we have that supreme enemy of the people!"

"Where is Kavakli?" Esmé demanded, and North could have embraced her for it.

"Offer Bulgarian border," came Dimitri's prompt reply, "about thirty kilometers north from Vaisal."

Novak? North felt an overwhelming excitement. All at once his course of action lay clear and unmistakable before him. In a few minutes now, he would ease out of some window, run to the local *karapol* or border police station and from there direct an immediate round-up of The Tartar's Head's patrons. To delay quietly in that malodorous dining room, drinking tea sweetened with honey out of a tumbler, proved an onerous precaution.

Brecon-Fyffe said, "Congratulations, Major. I own myself mistaken in your respect. You as good as have the Order of the Red Banner in your pocket. Yes, my friend, with me to teach you the ropes, you'll go far in the MVD, else I miss my——"

The renegade never finished his sentence because people commenced pounding on the back door as if they meant to break it in. "Open! Open!" voices were bellowing in Turkish and Bulgarian.

"What——?"

Everyone indoors spun about, aware of another set of blows being rained on the inn's ponderous front door. As completely taken aback as everyone else North floundered in miserable indecision. Surely McKenzie and Razib Albey would not have jumped the gun like this?

"Scatter!" snapped Georgei, pale eyes glittering. "Get out any way you can. Make for the frontier. Quick!"

Brecon-Fyffe snapped out the light and drew that automatic he was so fond of displaying. Feet pounded about, furniture went flying and then some windows and shutters banged open. Louder sounded the impact of logs against the hotel's doors.

"Open or we shoot!"

"Ha! There goes——" A volley rattled just outside, staccato and vicious in the chill air.

Still dumbfounded by this disastrous and unexpected raid North remained in the dining room and, venting a bitter curse, lay flat as he could on the cold gritty floorboards.

"Çŏk fena! Haltez-là," someone shouted, then a pistol cracked in the front room, broken glass jangled, a man screamed in agony an instant before there sounded a crashing fall. More yells, orders and shots followed by a brief and complete stillness. The snowstorm still must be raging for blasts of icy wind and a few snow particles came sailing in through windows shattered on the ground floor.

He who had been struck in the front room now was gurgling and emitting those coughing gasps so distinctive of a man hard-hit.

Down from upstairs floated Velvalee's frightened outcries. "Oh-h. Help! Help! Ah'm so sick. Esmé, wheah are you? What's goin' on? Please somebody come and help me!"

The back door yielded first, went slamming back on its hinges. A swirl of snow billowed in, became transfixed as a flashlight was turned into the kitchen; it came to rest first, of all things, upon the still serenely singing brass samovar.

"No fools, these lads, whoever they are," silently observed North. "A bunch of greenhorns would have come bursting in, risking annihilation from a burp gun."

More lights glittered, then in Turkish a voice ordered, "Come out!" Then someone directed in English, "You're surrounded and haven't a chance. Come out with your hands up. You, on the floor there." A flashlight shone blindingly into North's face. "Are you hurt?"

"No," North replied without moving, "and I don't want to be, so don't shoot."

"God! By God, we're lucky! We've at least caught that rat North." The Intelligence Officer's bewilderment increased at the sound of that unmistakably American voice.

North got to his feet. "Who's that? Did you get the rest?" he called. By God, if there'd been no escapes all wasn't lost after all.

"Shut up!" snarled the unknown, an indistinct figure outlined against the whirling snow. "Come out through this door with your hands up."

"I will, but for God's sake don't let any of the others get away. Everything depends——" Somebody hit Hugh North so hard on the top of his head that all the world exploded into a great flash of white fire.

CHAPTER 25

The Unpredictable Captain

NORTH, recovering consciousness, found himself sprawled
on a pile of damp and foul-smelling straw. As soon as his
reeling senses steadied somewhat he became aware that
not only had he been handcuffed, but that gyves were
locked about his ankles, the chill steel of which bit into his
flesh like the jaws of an icy trap.

His head hurt—and no wonder. Barely had his scalp
healed from those injuries administered by Steve Petrie
and his cohorts than it had been lacerated a second time;
it must have bled considerably since the whole back of his
shirt felt sticky and stiff.

It was merciful that only gradually came the awful reali-
zation that Georgei and his satellites might have got clear of
The Tartar's Head and have evaded pursuit. Damn, it
seemed all too likely; if ever a night had been designed
by Nature to permit safe crossing of the perilous Turco-
Bulgarian frontier, this was it. Had any of the cell escaped?
Not to know would mean irretrievable disaster. Something
must be done and swiftly.

"Guard!" he tried to shout, but only produced a feeble
croking sound and so was forced to remain quiescent for
several minutes more before regaining sufficient strength
to raise a real outcry.

At length a light wavered beyond the bars and presently
a heavy-faced Turkish policeman carrying keys belted about
a most respectable stomach came waddling up.

"Ne istiyorsunuz?"

"Send for your officer!" North pled first in French and then in German. "I must, I must talk with him. It is most important."

Aside from Turkish and possibly a native dialect or two, this jailer understood neither French, German nor yet Spanish, he merely shrugged, stared from beady black eyes at the haggard individual swaying behind the bars like an animated scarecrow. Finally he nodded and, keys jingling softly, disappeared, presently to return carrying a cracked earthenware jug of water.

"No! No! *Officeri!* I must talk to your officer, *officeri.* Oh God, please let me make this dumb lug understand," North groaned. If only Jingles had been here to make this dull brute comprehend.

Serenely unimpressed by North's frantic pleas, the fat jailer shrugged and shuffled off.

Evidently he occupied a cell especially designed for holding prisoners incommunicado; only the damp gray stone walls replied to his weary cries. The more he reflected upon the disastrous consequences that were bound to ensue, should even one of Eric and Georgei's group reach Kavakli, the more he wondered over this extraordinary and completely unpredictable catastrophe.

If indeed Colonel McKenzie and the Chief of Secret Police had, for some reason, anticipated the agreed arrangement to wait for North's signal, why had he been thus beaten and imprisoned? No, it couldn't have been McKenzie. Who then had tipped off frontier guards and some American agent? Where had this raiding party come from? Certainly, Eric's men would have spotted so large a contingent the moment it arrived.

To pass the time and so preserve his sanity North attempted to cleanse his face, but found it difficult because of the clumsy, old-style manacles. Damn! His split scalp began slowly to bleed once more; he could make use of a doctor's services.

What time was it? By now just enough light penetrated the window bars to warn him that sunrise was not far off—around seven o'clock—the raid, he judged, must have taken place around two and he'd been out like a light for nearly five hours. That certainly had been a mean lick someone had dealt him.

Again and again he yelled for the jailer, with the net result of straining his vocal cords and setting his head to aching.

Dawn was giving way to true daylight when voices sounded down the corridor and presently the floor reverberated hollowly to the tread of several men.

An explanation of the disaster, of all that had chanced dawned on North with absurd swiftness when the compact figure and dark features of Captain David Larkin appeared beyond the bars.

"Larkin!" he choked. "For God's sake get me out of here! Quickly! Quickly!"

The A-2 of the Military Mission, looking weary and unshaven in a civilian suit, hooked thumbs into the belt of his trench coat. He smiled grimly. "Well, you low-flung son-of-a-bitch, it's just fine to see you where you belong."

Rage such as seldom had shaken Hugh North flared in his usually well-disciplined mind. "You great, blundering jackass! You incredible meddling moron! You've done our country the greatest disservice since——"

"Shut up!" snapped Larkin. "From the day you landed in Istanbul I've had you watched. Think I don't know about your holing up with your Commie friends in that villa on the Rue Top Hané?" His teeth glimmered to a smile of triumph.

"Oh, you incredible idiot!" North fumed. "How dare you stand there patting yourself on the back?"

"There's some satisfaction, my friend," Larkin observed to a short and moon-faced commissaire of gendarmes, "that we caught this bastard so red-handed there can be no doubt about his treachery."

By a vast effort North controlled his fury, spoke in a low and even voice. "Larkin, for God's sake tell me—*did any of the others get away?*"

For a moment the A-2's smug expression faded. "Yes. I expect you'll be tickled to learn that a woman, your dear pal Brecon-Fyffe, and another man shot their way out."

A groan rose from the depths of North's soul. "Get after them, man! For God's sake hunt them down. They mustn't get away! Bring them back!"

"So you'd sell out your new frends too. Christ, how low can you sink?"

The battered knuckles of North's hands turned white above the bars. "Listen to me, Larkin. You've *got* to. Can't you understand I'm working for G-2?"

"Really? How interesting," Larkin jeered. "Good thing it's not A-2 that you've been selling down the river. Yeah, we've been thinking it's time you had a house cleaning over in G-2. What you need is some fresh blood, some new ideas."

Like a wild animal driven into a trap which offers no avenue of escape, North raged once more. How appalling that this blow should have been dealt by a fellow American. "Larkin, isn't there anything I can say or do to make you realize that, by holding me like this, and refusing to act, you're causing our country more harm than—than a Soviet block buster on the Pentagon?"

Utterly unimpressed, the A-2 from his overcoat produced a package of cigarettes. "Nuts! Anyhow we've killed two of your bright Red playmates, have captured two more and some sort of an MVD Axis Sally. By the bye, Sister Velvalee has proved mighty useful to me." Through a haze of smoke, he added, "Wench seems to be down with a fever of some kind."

"Look here, Larkin, if you'll let me at least communicate with Colonel McKenzie I'll remember it at your court-martial."

"Me, court-martialled?" Larkin roared with laughter.

"I tell you you've made a horrible, a ghastly mistake. Please let me contact the Embassy, then."

"The hell I will. Soon as this storm lifts I'm fetching you back to Istanbul where I'll turn you over to the Provost Marshal. You can tell him whatever you've got on that rotten mind of yours. I'll send in a sawbones presently to mend your head."

That there was absolutely no convincing this fellow had become unmistakable. The fact that the passage of each moment was diminishing whatever hope remained of reaching Kavakli and contacting Walewski, proved all-but intolerable.

"At least," North pleaded, "have these damned irons taken off."

Major Larkin hesitated, was pleased to appear magnanimous. "All right, I'll order off the manacles, but you're still to wear those ankle irons. You can take it as a compliment that I think you're too damned resourceful to be left completely unsecured."

"For the last time I beg you to listen," North pled in terrible earnestness. "I swear, on my honor as an American officer, that you're interfering with G-2 in its most critical assignment since V-J Day. This is a last opportunity to save your scalp."

"I'm told you always were a smooth talker—so was Benedict Arnold," Larkin grunted, then turned on his heel and stalked off, followed by the commissaire.

All morning long the blizzard—apparently one of unusual duration for this time of year—hurled snow furiously against the cell's unwashed window panes. Hunched on a three-legged stool North tried not to surrender to an altogether unfamiliar sense of despair. What could have become of the agents Razib and McKenzie were supposed to have posted here in Vaisal? Why had they proved so completely useless?

How long he remained crouching miserably in his cell he did not know—or care—but eventually he heard the broken link of a tire chain slatting to a diminished tempo and then a car must have pulled up before the jail. In the far distance sounded the shutting of a door, voices and then nothing more.

Meanwhile Captain Larkin was receiving guests. Sight of the first one to enter the *karapol* made him start incredulous to his feet. "Miss Lawson! For God's sake, what brings you to this dump?"

"I'm on a story," Jingles replied shaking snow from her coat.

"Then you're sure shot with luck!" he cried. "You've stumbled on the best spy story since the War—even though you won't be able to break it right away. Who's with you?"

"Colonel Razib."

"—Not the Chief of Secret Police?" She nodded. "Boy, what a break for A-2."

"Maybe," Jingles said and turned as the door opened to admit Razib Albey and Colonel Alexander McKenzie. Both men wore mufti, were snow-powdered, wind-bitten and grim of expression.

Captain Larkin stiffened to attention. "Good day, sir. I——"

The Military Attaché cut him short. "What in hell have you been up to?"

"Been rounding up some Soviet spies, sir."

"Indeed? You haven't, by any chance, arrested Major Hugh North?"

"Quite correct, sir. We caught him red-handed, too."

"Then you've committed *the* Intelligence blunder of all time."

"Oh, no! No!" Jingles burst out. "Captain, you've sure put all ten feet in the trough!"

Razib Albey glared about, exploded with staccato Turkish that froze the commissaire gray-faced in his tracks.

"B-but, sir," Larkin had commenced to stammer, "I tell you I c-caught North working hand-in-glove w-with the C-Commies."

"You impertinent smart-alec!" McKenzie thundered. "Hugh North's no more a traitor than you are! Probably less. Where is he?"

"Here in the cell block. He's——"

Footsteps rang in the corridor again and North looked up thunderstruck to watch Jingles Lawson appear at a run.

"Oh, Hugh!" she gasped when she recognized that battered figure beyond the bars. "Hugh, dear, what have they done to you this time?"

"Nothing compared to what I aim to do to a certain jackass of an A-2," he growled, and, undoubtedly, North would have taken at least one swing at the A-2 had his gyves and Colonel McKenzie not limited his furious lunge.

Larkin made no effort to avoid the onslaught; he looked like a parent helpless to prevent his child's drowning before him.

While the ankle irons were being unlocked North managed to regain a measure of equanimity—after all, the damage had been done. What really counted was to learn whether anything might be accomplished to retrieve the disaster.

Colonel McKenzie was searching his memory as far back as the Philippine campaign to find adequate language in which to express his wrath.

"A-all I can say, sir," stuttered the unhappy A-2, "I thought I was d-doing a fine job."

"I suppose so—if you never heard of liaison or official channels," North snapped, rubbing at the reddened areas on his ankles. "We'll worry about your stupidity later."

"My apologies." For the first time North noticed Razib Albey looking smaller and thinner in civilian clothes than in his colonel's uniform.

North offered his hand. "It's fortunate you're here, Colonel. If there is anything to be done it must be initiated right away."

"Please," Larkin begged, "isn't there anything I can do to make up a little for this?"

"How did you find out we were here?"

"Had you tailed from your hotel, sir."

"Then your men warned you, and your raiding party drove over last night from Edirne. Is that it?"

"Yes. Please, isn't there any way I can help?"

"Yes, either drop dead or get to hell out of my sight." Seldom had North been so ungenerous—and later regretted it.

In the Commissaire's office a conference was called over hot tea and a belated breakfast and during it North described the sequence of events aboard the night express and in Vaisal.

Razib nodded. "The body of Stephen Petrie was discovered beside the railway lines yesterday morning. Of course, news of the fact was suppressed by me."

Colonel McKenzie broke in, "On account of her language abilities and knowledge of the country, I agreed to allow Miss Lawson here to accompany us. It was her idea. Further, she is unsuspected by Soviet agents."

North thought a moment. This might be true, provided Petrie and Nestor hadn't talked—both of them were now incapable of further mischief-making—Nestor being one of the prisoners.

"Seemed like a sound scheme," Jingles offered. "Besides,

when I'm not around, the Major seems prone to get into trouble. What about that blonde babe they're holding at The Tartar's Head? Heard tell she's pretty sick with something like typhus."

North pushed back his chair. "In that case we'd better amble over and talk with her. Might be she could tell something about what gives around Kavakli."

Razib Albey jerked an abrupt nod and over the empty tea glasses exchanged glances with McKenzie. *"Bon.* While you are gone, the Colonel and I will question these stupid sons of bears and arrive at some better estimate of the situation. Tell me, what do you intend?"

"Cost what it may, I *must* get into Kavakli before those people of the MVD. Please see what can be done to get me there in a hurry."

The Chief of Secret Police strode over to the window and stood looking out on the falling, wind-driven snow. "There could be only one fashion—to fly."

Colonel McKenzie's balding head glistened. "Correct. I suppose a plane might fly over the border if the weather moderates a bit. It will be a terrible risk but we'll start laying on a flight."

It was a very pre-occupied Hugh North who, trying to forget the throb of his newly bruised scalp, supervised a quartet of experts in ransacking the hotel. Jingles aided in a detailed examination of Esmé Murfee's luggage.

"Maybe," she encouraged, "your ex-pals got lost in the blizzard? Maybe right now they're lying frozen stiff somewhere along the border. It isn't impossible, you know."

"I suppose so." North glanced over his shoulder. "But that would be too perfect. Incidentally, I could wish la Murfee back here. She's a trained nurse."

"Is Velvalee worse?"

"Don't know. She was asleep when we got here so I've let her rest and asked the police to send to Edirne for a doctor—a real one—the local practitioner looks as if he had trained under Lister."

"I don't know much about such things," Jingles continued, "but from what I hear it sounds suspiciously like pneumonia."

North straightened above Esmé's ravaged suitcase. "In that case maybe we'd better look in on Velvalee." North sighed, added softly, "In some ways she's really rather pathetic."

"If your little magnolia blossom had her health," Jingles announced evenly, "I'd make her a lot more pathetic. Her sort of soft-headed, floozie treachery somehow sublimates my more lady-like instincts." The Lawson girl closed Esmé's suitcase with unnecessary vigor.

As they reached the staircase Jingles slipped an arm through his. "Please, Hugh dear, don't look so utterly woebegone. This fiasco wasn't in any way your fault." She hesitated, her faintly golden face raised. "Hugh?"

"What is it?"

"Of course, I've no idea what your mission is, but an astigmatic mole could tell that it's supremely important—critical. Incidentally, when you cross the Bulgarian border, whom are you planning to take along?"

"No one," he announced while peering out a broken window onto the snow-shrouded carts and autos standing in the hotel's court.

Jingles' fingers tightened on his arm and her expressive gray-blue eyes widened. "But how'll you manage? You don't speak Turkish, Greek or Bulgarian."

"That's a lamentable gap in my education," he admitted with a quick smile.

"Wouldn't Razib Albey lend you someone?"

"Gladly. But this—er—mission is purely a U.S. affair—so damned delicate we can't let any foreigners in on it all the way, not even people as friendly as the Turks."

"But, dear, how would you find your way about? You've never been in Kavakli, have you?"

"Not even in Bulgaria, but somehow I'll manage," North predicted. "You can help though."

"How?" Jingles' expression became radiant.

"God knows I hate charades worse than poison, but in a little town the size of Kavakli, these duds would stand out like a beacon, so," he made a wry face, "I'll have to get your help on a disguise and a cover story that will stick."

"Of course, dear, a fine cover story you'll tell—in Spanish —or maybe a lovely, West Point English?" Jingles jeered. "And just when do you expect to start?"

"Soon as Razib figures a way of flying me in. Don't worry so, I'll make out——" His arm went about her shoulders. "My dear, you'll never know how wonderful it was to hear your voice this morning—not that it's ever unpleasant."

"Such diplomacy, my sweet, earns dividends." Eyes closed, Jingles raised bright lips and, all of a sudden, he was kissing her hungrily.

"Imagine getting romantic among the ruins." He smiled presently and stepped back. "Must be that rap I took on the pate."

"Watch out I don't fetch you another clip," Jingles retorted. "Come on, let's go see this Velvalee baggage. Even now I can't believe it's her real name."

They found the sick girl still wearing her travelling blouse, bright-faced and semi-delirious. A gray-haired crone sat helplessly beside a white-painted brass bedstead. Greatly disturbed, she immediately addressed Jingles in Turkish, at which Velvalee's sherry-hued eyes opened a little; they were luminous with fever.

"Thank goodness, you're heah at last," she greeted in a feeble voice. "Esmé's swiped my make-up, so Ah reckon Ah look a fright."

"You look fine." North seated himself beside the lumpy brass bed. "How do you feel?"

Velvalee's small hand made a febrile gesture. "Ah'm burnin' up. Hugh, Ah want—Ah need to talk to you, Honey. Please send the others away."

"Miss Lawson is quite dependable," North assured, but in weak stubbornness the stricken girl shook her head. "Please do like Ah ask. Ah'm really bad off and Ah—Ah've got a feeling Ah won't——"

"Nonsense!" He bent, passed a wet cloth over lips dry as chalk. At the same time he signalled Jingles to leave. Without comment, she beckoned the wrinkled old crone and went out.

After he had propped her head higher, Velvalee stared fixedly at him. "The others—they got away?"

"Dimitri was shot and killed along with a couple of the hotel people, and Nestor and another were taken prisoner. The others escaped."

The patient's flushed features contracted and she turned aside her head on its coverlet of candy-blonde hair. "Oh deah, and Ah was prayin' they'd all get killed. Honey, please take my hand a while, will you? Ah—Ah'm kind of —of scared. Ah've never felt so alone befo'. There, that's better." Presently, "Hugh, Honey, what's wrong with me?"

"We don't know yet," he encouraged. "Probably it's only a touch of pneumonia."

"Reckon it's that. Ah feel so choked up and out of breath." Her fingers pressed on his ever so lightly. "Thanks for comin' to see me. Until you came along Ah'd forgotten how decent, true and kind most of our people are. What a fool Ah've been."

The girl's lustrous head rolled sidewise on her sweat-darkened pillow and a trickle of tears sketched shiny paths over the heated contour of her cheek. "Ah know Ah've been wicked, an'—an' selfish, an'—an'," she choked momentarily, "a bad woman sometimes. More often Ah was just a plain fool, most of all back in Berlin when Ah listened to Ben Gramont, gave up my American passpo't—an'—an' became a Commie."

North nodded, stroked her hand. "Would you feel happier if you know that, on the day we left Istanbul, I felt sure you wanted to clear out of this mess? I'm still ready to help you, Velvalee, because there's nothing approaching truth, honor or human decency to be found among the rulers in the Kremlin."

Velvalee's shallow breathing quickened. "Please go on. If you only knew how right that is."

Smoothly, he inquired, "Do you know anybody in a place called Kavakli?"

She sighed, wiped the sweat from her brow with the back of her hand. "Kavakli? All these foreign names sound alike."

"Try to remember, Velvalee, it's important to me—and America."

"Yes, once Ah did heah Georgei mention someone there called Brusov. Yes. Ah think he's commissar of police, there."

Again he wetted the cloth, wrung it out and placed it across her forehead. "I've got to leave in a minute, so I won't tell you what I think of people who'd sell out our country. We'll only talk about your having seen your mistake."

Her eyelids rolled back and she peered anxiously upwards. "Don't go, please, Hugh, Ah'm so frightened. Everythin' seems so—so strange. Ah wish Ah were back home in Mississippi—and Ah'll go there, no matter what happens, 'less Ah get sent to prison."

She brushed off the compress. "If Ah don't evah get home will you write my Pa?" Her voice became increasingly labored. "He's a preacher and his name is Cameron

—— and we live —— he lives—near to Rosewood. Please tell him Velvalee—it's really mah given name—is sorry fo' all the sorrow and shame Ah've caused him and my sisters."

The patient coughed several hard coughs, then shivered violently. "Please say—Ah—never really did despise—our country—it's the mos' wonderful——" She blinked, dug both hands into her eyes. "My, how Ah'd like to wear again—blue party dress with the frills—Aunt Daphne's dance. No, suh, Ah'm goin' with Carroll—next Tuesday, isn't it, or is it Friday? No, Randolph, Ah reckon you—— Letty, you cain't——"

North summoned the women waiting outside. "She's sunk into delirium. That doctor had better show up in a hurry."

"Poor thing," Jingles murmured. "Let me see if there isn't something I can do to help her."

There wasn't. Two hours later Velvalee Cameron died of a deadly influenza that was spreading westward from the Caspian Sea.

CHAPTER 26

Messenger from Istanbul

DELIBERATELY, Razib Albey put down his coffee cup, spoke in precise French. "One has surveyed the matter with the most competent of authorities. Colonel McKenzie and I are agreed that there is no possibility of successfully crossing the border on foot, as desirable as that might be. Colonel McKenzie has gone to Edirne in answer to a most urgent signal from your Embassy. He took that foolish Captain Larkin with him."

The two officers were occupying the Commissaire's quarters—that mournful-eyed individual, having been dispatched to make various preparations despite biting wind and persistent if diminishing snow flurries.

"Then I'll risk flying. I've got to get over there in a hurry," North reminded. "Main thing I'd like to learn," he passed a hand over a compress showing amid his crisp black hair, "is how long it will likely take Brecon-Fyffe or any of them to reach Kavakli?"

Razib Albey strode over to a yellowed and flyblown map. "Unless those Communists meet with extraordinary good fortune, they must have lingered in whatever refuge they could find, waiting for this storm to diminish. It is a wild and desolate country across the border; for yourself you can see practically no roads exist." Razib Albey frowned, used the tip of a tobacco-stained brown finger further to explain his discourse. "They must then either proceed on horseback along this track or attempt to cross this range of hills on foot."

The Turkish officer turned a furrowed brow and tugged at his reddish mustache. "Since the snow by now is nearly a half meter deep in the level places it will—how you say?— drift much deeper. One knows further that these fugitives were poorly clad and had no equipment therefore one might say the chances are fair that, so far, they have not even been able to communicate with Kavakli—unless they stumbled onto a post of the border patrol."

"Um, as you say, Albey, it looks a pretty wild country over yonder, and our agents report that the Bulgarians aren't 'cooperating' as they once did. Stupid as they are, they, too, are beginning to perceive the worthlessness of the Kremlin's gilded promises."

"True enough," agreed the Turk. "Were it not for the presence of Russian-officered units over there, to get you across would be no problem."

Razib Albey crossed to the table, helped himself delicately to a slice of sugared ginger.

Presently North inquired, "May I communicate with Edirne?"

"*Vallahi!* But of course. What is in your mind?" The Turk's blue eyes considered that lean, broad-shouldered figure standing before a tall, German-type porcelain stove. Immediately he added, "It is not that one would pry into your secrets, Major, but one has received instructions from one's Foreign Office to offer all manner of assistance."

"Thank you, Colonel, I've come across damned few governments so generous—and practical!"

To a timid knock Razib Albey called, *"Lutfen!* You may enter."

A maid servant wearing native costume entered and bowed humbly before the Colonel. *"Sabahlar haier olson—* may the morning be lucky, Effendi." She paused, hands clasped nervously under a dark red woolen shawl.

Following a brief conversation in some frontier dialect

Razib Albey turned with a puzzled, somewhat uneasy expression. "She says a native woman from up the valley seeks to speak with you, Major. Do you care to see her?"

"Of course."

A moment later there clumped in on clumsy muddied boots a thick-bodied creature hooded and swathed in shawls and wearing numerous grimy red and black petticoats typical of the region. In greasy black strands hair dangled over the caller's dull brown forehead. The Chief of the Secret Police addressed her sharply and the woman replied in a whining sing-song.

"She claims to be from Devletag, a village not far from here," the Turk translated. "The old witch swears early this morning she beheld a woman and two men struggling up her valley in the direction of the frontier."

"How far away is this village?"

A considerable conversation ensued, lasted until without warning North reached out and pulled one of the woman's hands from beneath her shawl.

"*Vallahi!*" burst out Razib Albey. "That is no peasant's paw!" It was deplorably dirty but small and well proportioned.

"Don't be a spoil-sport, Hugh," protested the visitor. From under the dingy head shawl Jingles Lawson's gray-blue eyes peered up into his.

"*Haman!*" burst out Razib Albey. "But that Rumelian accent: it—it was without fault. Lawson Bayan, what is the meaning of this doubtful pleasantry?"

Quite seriously Jingles pulled off her head covering and pushed the tangled hair from her eyes. "Merely a small demonstration to prove to a stubborn idiot called Hugh North that I can be of real service. You heard, Colonel? My voice and accent were just what they should have been?"

"*Aman Allah,* one was completely deceived."

North sighed. Save for the fact that she had not revealed her hands the imposture had been most convincing.

"Of course," Jingles continued quickly, "this is only a rough and ready get-up. When we go into Bulgaria my hands won't be soft and my eyes will be as red as if——"

"You are not going," North snapped.

"—Is it wise, or right, to deny my usefulness?" quietly demanded the shapeless figure. "Think again, Hugh, and recall that you don't know a single word of the local dialects. You'll get caught the minute you put your nose into Kavakli; then what would our side's chances amount to?"

Entirely characteristic of North was the abruptness with which he gave over objection. "Colonel, I am most reluctant to admit it, but Lawson Bayan is quite right. I *must* get into Kavakli and I—well, I can't do it alone. Again, her presence constitutes a hedge against the chance that I might get knocked off after getting what I want. She'd stand a fair chance of—of getting back with the information I'm after." He frowned at her ecstatic burst of delight. "Can you find us Bulgarian identification; labor permits, ration books, army draft cards, et cetera?"

"In Edirne that will be easy to arrange by nightfall."

"What costume do you suggest?"

"Why not ask Lawson Bayan?" demanded the Turk.

"We should appear as peasants from Eastern Rumelia. Their general build and coloring is more like Major North's than any other. You, Hugh, would have to wear a wig. Most East Rumelians wear their hair long and—and——" To North's surprise she blushed furiously, went scarlet to her neckline.

"What's wrong?"

"Well." Jingles gazed at the floor. "To be entirely convincing you and I will have to shave off every bit of body hair. It—it's an old Rumelian custom—keeps off vermin I suppose."

"Well, I'm damned," and for the first time in hours North laughed right out loud.

Typical of Razib Albey's tact was the fact that he appeared lost in speculation. He spoke as to himself. "Of course, such a leap would be perilous in the extreme, but under cover of darkness it might be accomplished. Tell me, Major, have you parachuted much?"

"Enough not to hurt myself." North nodded. "How about you, Jingles?"

Between steady fingers she picked up a cigarette and lit it. " 'I'll try anything once' as the chorus girl said. When do we leave for Edirne?"

CHAPTER 27

Charades

NEVER during recent years had Hugh North employed a disguise, but so perfect were his preparations that none would have suspected it. He and Jingles spent a full hour rubbing heavily muddied water into their faces, hands and necks. Several applications of a dark brown oil were then applied, then more mud, then the exposed skin was towelled so vigorously that it grew thick and red. Scissors and a razor shortened, and so gave an effect of thickening, Jingles' brows. The razors also had been applied in the most approved Eastern Rumelian fashion. It was a shame to shorten the luxuriant length of her eyelashes, but this also was done.

Colonel McKenzie warned that North's hair must be clipped very short, else his wig of eight-inch-long tangled brown hair would never fit. Further, the Intelligence Officer's nails first were chipped then yellowed with iodine before he dug fingers into a dirt box so thoroughly that surprisingly soon his hands looked as if they had not met a wash basin in days. Only an absence of calluses marred the perfection of the conversion.

Baggy trousers of thick black wool, and bare feet thrust into crude felt boots bound around with lengths of dirty linen were supplemented by a food-spotted and malodorous, red-embroidered shirt which also did service as underwear. A wide sash of black, crudely embroidered with orange wool served to secure these unlovely garments together. Above North's shirt was tied a greasy sheepskin vest, its shiny side turned out, and on top of all, rode a shaggy black and white goatskin cloak, which soon filled the room with a luxuriantly gamey aroma.

To fit the wig and its dangling hanks of oily hair into place proved a delicate matter because of the contusions resulting from that crack Captain Larkin's minions had given him.

Again and yet again, North surveyed the contents of a frayed and threadbare wallet which were intended, conclusively, to identify him as Simeon Petroff, horse-breaker by profession, and a resident of the commune of Papaskoi.

Colonel McKenzie rubbed the pink beginnings of a double chin and predicted, "The most difficult part of your disguise will be acting deaf mute."

"I know," North admitted worriedly. "I tried it once before and nearly went crazy."

Razib Albey shrugged, spread eloquent brown hands. "How else to disguise your ignorance of the language? You, of course, are unable to read, but your wife—here— fortunately, is better educated. One thing more," Razib Albey pointed out, "please to stand not so straight. Get too short a walking stick, it will remind you to remain somewhat bent over."

"*Tovarich* Simeon Petroff." North assumed a vacuous expression and paused before one of the few full-length mirrors in Edirne.

What the onlookers saw was a swarthy peasant with eyes red-rimmed through an application of chemical peering stupidly from under a shapeless rusty-green and broad-brimmed felt hat. Dirt furrowed the faint wrinkles across that much of his forehead as was visible beneath a fringe of locks hanging over his eyes in a fashion suggestive of an English sheep dog. His hands, when he did not conceal them beneath his goatskin cloak, were as dark as his face.

There came a knock at the door and Razib Albey caught his breath before inquiring, "Is that you, Ludmilla?"

A whining sing-song voice replied that it was, then in shuffled Jingles Lawson. About the girl's head was coiled her thickly plaited light brown hair; over it an ancient kerchief had been knotted peasant fashion under her chin. Her blouse, elaborately embroidered at shoulders and neck, certainly had been designed to accommodate breasts infinitely more ample than those of its present wearer; therefore it sagged loosely above her wide sash of blue and yellow dyed horsehair.

A rather short, faded and often-mended skirt of light blue wool flared far out because it concealed no less than half a dozen coarse linen petticoats. The shapeliness of those slim ankles North so often had admired was concealed beneath heavy, white wool stockings and ponderous red leather knee boots. Cheap brass jewelry gleamed at this peasant woman's wrist and a heavy chain of the same metal supported an amulet over her uncleanly neck.

At the sight of each other the two burst out laughing. "How's this, umpire?" Jingles demanded.

"You'll do," McKenzie admitted. "If anybody can get through it should be you two."

Razib Albey sighed. "One is pleased that merriment can be found at so grave a moment," he observed. "You Anglo-Saxons must be mad, completely so; but please to accept my profoundest admirations."

Still shaking his gray-brown head the Chief of Secret Police led the couple over to a map. "Please to remember this well." He spoke slowly, incisively. "You will plan to cross the frontier somewhere between Valaif and Bojuk; our guards along that sector will have orders to admit and to protect you, if necessary. Should you be pursued," Razib Albey paused for emphasis, "carry this red handkerchief in your left hand, and the blue one in your right as you run."

Colonel McKenzie looked very grave. "We have arranged

with the Turkish authorities to attract, to divert rather, Bulgarian attention to a nearby point."

"That's excellent," North said. "Either we'll show up within the next thirty-six hours or you'd better write us off."

Razib Albey offered his hand first to the Lawson girl, then to Hugh North. "As we say in my country, *Allaha ismarladik!*"

"*Güle, güle,*" soberly replied Jingles.

CHAPTER 28

Police State

MORNING SUNLIGHT, flashing red-orange over snow-covered hillocks, created such an all-but unsupportable glare that a pair of peasants pausing on the summit of the last rise of a frozen, little-travelled road could hardly see the bulbous church towers rising above Kavakli. Ludmilla Petroff fumbled for a handkerchief.

"No! Blow your nose with your fingers," warned her companion. "It's fashionable in these latitudes."

"But I've *got* to," complained Jingles, "I'm snuffling like a heartbroken schoolgirl. Well, all right—I know how."

Despite a biting north wind they paused to catch their breath, the Intelligence Officer bent over a crutch-like shepherd's walking stick produced by Razib Albey.

To recognize lovely and graceful Jingles Lawson in this red-nosed, dumpy and frowzy peasant wench standing beside him would require more than a dash of imagination, North decided. The wind struggled with her jerkin of rusty black lambskin and drew tears from eyes already swollen and red from the sun's glare; eyes that could become redder still, upon necessity, thanks to the judicious insertion of snuff into their corners.

Half a kilometer away to their left sable rooks were circling about the stark, yellow-gray remains of some ancient castle. The ragged outline of its keep thrust upwards like an obstinate fist rising above snow concealing the balance of the ruins.

By North's estimation, Kavakli's low roofs might, in times

of peace and plenty, shelter as many as fifteen thousand inhabitants; after all, the place was one of Eastern Rumelia's principal market centers and was located on a railroad.

They had landed quite unhurt, thanks to the deep snow, which also made it easy to conceal their parachutes. Since four of an uncommonly black morning, North and his companion had managed to cover at least twenty kilometers—five kilometers more than they needed to travel, for, of course, they had taken the basic precaution of striking off in a direction opposite to which they now travelled. Not until they had been able to lose their tracks among the hoof-prints of cavalry patrol overtaking them on the highway, had North been willing to face about and start towards Kavakli. And now the goal lay before them, gray-black in the floor of a glistening white valley.

"Hardly as dramatic as Nuremburg or Rothenburg is it?" North commented.

"It looks like no ogre's castle—more like Greybull, Montana," panted Jingles, scraping snow out of the top of her boots.

"May as well realize now, my dear, that despite lugs like E. Phillips Oppenheim intelligence work is a damned unglamorous profession."

"Maybe you're right," Jingles admitted, a taut look on her wind-bloated features. "I'm just coming to think that perhaps it isn't quit as gay and gaudy as they'd ask you to believe along Broadway or in Hollywood."

They lingered a little longer, studying the terrain through watering eyes. There would be need of such knowledge later.

"Now remember," said he, after retying his leg covers, "we certainly will be stopped on entering the town. What are you going to do then?"

"First ask where to find the Police Commandant, then insist on being brought before the Chief of the local MVD. Correct?"

"Check. Let's go."

They exchanged brief glances, smiling no longer; that danger which, at a distance, had appeared a brilliant challenge, was now settling about them like a chill and poisonous miasma. Bitterly now, and in vain, North was cursing his acquiescence in accepting Jingles for a confederate. Well, come what might, there now could be no retreat; in a moment more their feet, clumsy and malodorous in felt and heavy leather boots, would convey them closer to —Josef Walewski—or the clutches of the MVD? Let either Jingles or himself make the slightest false move—he couldn't bear to dwell on what would follow.

From the depths of his jacket North produced, of all things, a package of chewing gum. Jingles was too tired to comment when, hurriedly, he commenced to masticate. Back in Edirne he'd calculated that holding a wad of gum clenched between his teeth would lessen the chance of being startled into some betraying comment.

When a huge cart drawn by a pair of black, slant-horned water-buffaloes came screeching and complaining along the road its drover called a salutation to which Jingles made an unenthusiastic reply, but nonetheless beckoned North to walk along in the wheel tracks.

On the edge of town the wayfarers overtook a couple of blue-lipped boys herding half a dozen big gray and white Sebastopol geese towards their doom in the market of Kavakli.

To walk bent over like this proved uncomfortable, but North managed to stump along, eyes on the dung-splashed snow until he felt Jingles' hand come to rest upon his arm. Raising inflamed and lack-luster eyes, the pseudo horse-breaker perceived that just ahead was a road block about which a party of fur-capped soldiers in red-frogged, ankle-length overcoats stood warming their feet about a brazier improvised of a well-punctured oil drum. Big, bearded fellows, they wore Tommy guns slung over their shoulders and pistols strapped about their waists.

The two young goose herds apparently were well known and together with their cackling charges were passed without delay. The drover, however, was required to halt. The peasant bowed humbly several times, then fumbled about a cossack-type hat until, presently, he produced identification papers.

A big five-pointed red star decorating the front of a corporal's cap glared bright in the brilliant sunshine, but North kept his eyes on the ground even when the huge, two-wheeled cart creaked on towards the ancient walls of Kavakli.

Of a conversation which ensued between the sentries and Ludmilla Petroff he understood nothing. One of the soldiers suddenly shouted something into North's ear; he turned, shrugged, smiled vacantly. Not to have reacted at all would have invited suspicion; the deaf soon learn to sense such surface vibrations as are caused by a loud sound nearby.

Jingles, jabbering all the while in Rumelian, made signs for him to produce his papers. Then indeed did sweat start trickling down his back. According to the most recent information received by G-2 this identification should be complete and up-to-date; yet *had* there been some minute, but fatal, omission? Humbly, patiently, as became their role, the two wayfarers waited at the edge of a slushy circle formed by the brazier until, after a seeming eternity, the corporal, a small, gimlet-eyed fellow, returned their documents. He spat, and made some observation, to which North responded only by gurgling and manufacturing an idiotic grin. Then Jingles elbowed him and together they shambled on towards an ancient or medieval gate guarding this entrance to Kavakli.

Like persons lost in the woods, they found it difficult not

to quicken their pace. Jingles, while tightening her dull red kerchief, muttered, "That corporal's looking after us, but I think it's all right. Brute wouldn't tell me where the MVD headquarters are located, but that's no matter since we must report our arrival and have our circulation permits stamped at Police Headquarters."

Once they had passed the gates and found themselves actually within Kavakli they noted a surprising activity in its narrow and snow-choked streets; apparently this must be one of the town's fortnightly fair days. In Kavakli's inevitable central square and in the shadows of a third-rate Orthodox Cathedral sprouting curious, onion-like steeples, peasants and small shopkeepers were shovelling snow aside in order to raise portable booths. Goats yatted, cattle lowed and sheep bleated under a pall of acrid wood smoke rising from dozens of braziers and open fires. Every now and then a half-hearted dog fight broke out. No one paid any attention.

Somberly clad townsfolk, tall-hatted Orthodox popes, pinched-looking private soldiers in shabby uniforms jostled rosy-cheeked peasants wearing a variety of gay, if soiled, costumes, or eyed apprehensively the numerous pairs of police, stalwart and well-fed, who swaggered about like the lords of creation.

Police Headquarters, a grim, brown stone structure, lay just off the main square and directly behind the mayory. It proved easy to find for, waiting in the snow outside, stood a long queue of travellers and other unfortunates having business there. Among those who waited were not a few frightened-appearing peasants, some figures in uniforms that meant nothing to North, and a trio of weeping women who, huddled into shabby cloth coats, stood red-eyed, clutching rags to their noses.

Humbly, unobtrusively, the pseudo horse-breaker and his wife took positions at the tail of this unhappy file, and in it

shuffled along, a few inches at a time, until near noon. To
the Intelligence Officer, nostrils wrinkled at the body smells
of an old rabbi preceding him, it proved easy to sense a
sharp contrast in the atmospheres of this town and of
Edirne. In Kavakli townsfolk, military, and peasants
shambled along and kept their gaze on the ground if they
were not casting quick, apprehensive glances over their
shoulders.

No one looked up even when another flight of planes
roared over this dingy little town; they all-but cringed at
the appearance of a long convoy of camouflaged tanks—to
North they looked like old German Mark III's—clattering
by splashing manure, mud and melting snow far and wide.

Still North and his companion waited and presently were
forced to flatten themselves against the muddied front of
the police station to avoid icy slush spurting from beneath
the wheels of an endless column of infantry transport trucks.
In them rode fur-capped soldiers huddled into vari-colored
mufflers and great coats, at the same time steadying rifles or
sub-machine guns on their knees. At least two regiments,
North estimated, must have roared through Kavakli and
down that valley which ended near the Turkish frontier.

Meanwhile still more formations of pursuit ships and
light bombers—Yak-3's and Lavochkin LA-9's, North
thought them—streaked overhead. On street corners numbers of military police appeared and began to check the
passes of casual soldiers.

His inability to converse with Jingles was proving more
serious a handicap than he had anticipated. Proving herself
a consummate actress, Ludmilla Petroff merely huddled
into her clothes, wiped mucus from her nose onto her sleeve,
hawked and spit quite as loudly as any of the bedraggled
females in her vicinity.

Imposing store window offerings proved largely to be
mere samples at which the dun-colored citizenry peered

mournfully a moment before shuffling on towards the market. Was it possible that Josef Walewski moved among them?

Eventually, the Intelligence Officer and his companion found themselves in a long, cold, whitewashed room. There they were instructed to halt before a low dais above which were arranged huge photographic portraits of Gottwald, Stalin and Ana Pauker's simian profile. Below these sat a big mustached and shaven-headed police sergeant.

Shoulder boards of tarnished gold braid gleamed briefly when the police sergeant held out his hand for Jingles' identification. She broke into explanation, pointing to the stupid figure standing, stoop-shouldered and fearful, behind her. Also in this cheerless apartment were a couple of clerks seated at a desk and a civilian—obviously a detective. This last had his black, fur-lined coat unbuttoned and sat tilted comfortably back in a chair with feet propped against a big cast-iron stove. On the floor around him lay a wide semicircle of cigarette butts.

"Yonder," North warned himself, "will be Mr. MVD." Equally taut moments he must previously have experienced, yet he could not recall them.

The man in the fur coat did not turn his head nor lower the cigarette poised between pale fingers, only traversed yellowish eyes to inspect those frowsy figures cringing before the police sergeant's desk.

North's relief was enormous when suddenly the shoulder boards gleamed once more and the sergeant passed their travel permits to a clerk who selected a stamp from among a large collection and, in bright green ink, surcharged the permits. Then, employing a purple indelible pencil, he filled in spaces left for such inscription.

North guessed that Jingles now was explaining the alleged purpose of their visit to Kavakli, that of reporting a secret radio which, presumably dropped from a plane, had been set up in a barn near their farm at Papaskoi.

The sergeant straightened, then sent for a lieutenant who fired a veritable volley of questions at Jingles. God send that she found prompt and plausible answers to them! Peering cautiously from behind the lank bangs of his wig, North felt shaken; sweat was standing out in bright little patches all over Jingles' cheeks and forehead.

The MVD man still made no motion, but both clerks, sly, brutal-looking fellows, gave over writing in order to survey this pair of peasants looking so forlorn in the midst of that big, cold room.

Utterly exasperating was Hugh North's inability to understand anything of a conversation so vital to his mission. Yet there was nothing to do but to stand there, making gargling noises, shrugging and waving helpless hands.

A pang as if a steel icicle had been plunged into his back stung North when, quite unhurriedly, the MVD man got to his feet, seized Jingles by the arm, and then, exactly as if he were inspecting a new horse, pulled back her head and pried apart her lips. This was what he had been fearing, all along; both his and Jingles' teeth were far too white and sound to be found in the mouths of Rumelian peasants.

Over his shoulder the MVD man barked a command to the police lieutenant. Jingles emitted a thin wail of fright when from an adjoining room tramped a pair of brown-uniformed policemen. North made no effort to resist when his arm was twisted behind him. The other grabbed Jingles, then hauled the suspects into that room from which they had appeared, a room ominously devoid of furniture save for a bench, a desk and a sturdy straight chair to the arms and legs of which heavy straps hung loose.

Once the prisoners had been pinioned by handcuffs secured behind them the pallid MVD man sauntered over and remarked in French, "My friends, may I congratulate you on almost perfect disguises?"

North rolled his eyes, made inarticulate noises.

"Alors, vous ne comprenez pas? Then I shall try English. Why not speak now and save yourselves—er—inconvenience? Sooner or later you will talk. Do not doubt it."

"This time you're fairly up against it," North thought. "Usually there's something can be done, but not here." The windows were heavily barred; the doors solid and even if he could regain the use of his hands it would avail him nothing. Their only hope, therefore, was to cling to this imposture to the bitter end. And to think that Walewski, clever courageous Walewski, might be hiding somewhere within a quarter of a mile.

The MVD man straddled a chair, lit a fresh cigarette and left it tucked between two of the thinnest lips North had ever beheld. His was a long thin nose which divided little, yellow-brown eyes that looked as cruel as dagger points.

"From your build," observed he to Jingles in English, "I would say that you, *Baboushka,* are either English or American. Shall we converse?"

Angrily, Jingles retorted in Bulgarian.

"Very good, in Bulgarian then," commented the MVD man.

Jingles began to sniffle and to tremble so violently that her numerous brass bracelets set up a perceptible tinkling.

"You say you are a Rumelian woman from the Papaskoi region? Let us see—there are local customs of interest."

Languidly, he turned, called in a short, wolfish-appearing fellow. At the same time he signed the two brown-uniformed men to strap North into that grisly chair; the prisoner submitted as if dazed.

"Istvan, search and thoroughly examine the woman."

Involuntarily North's body contracted when one of the detectives jerked away the scarf covering Jingles' braided hair—two others were holding her steady. She screamed, cursed in dialect and wrenched at her handcuffs when one of them pulled out a heavy silver pin securing the sash about her waist. Employing great care he scrutinized both sash and pin, then placed them on the table. Next he jerked undone the tie strings of the blue petticoats.

It was well that North had been strapped down, else certainly he must have suffered physical violence through efforts to prevent a systematic disrobing of his furious and scarlet-faced companion. Each garment as it was removed was passed over to the MVD man who, with a magnifying glass, studied seams, hems and embroideries.

At length a final petticoat was reached, whereupon the MVD man chuckled. "Good teeth, eh? And now another error in your masquerade. So you come from the Papaskoi district? Proceed, Istvan."

Another jerk of tie strings let the ultimate covering fall, disclosed the symmetrical length of the suspect's pearl-hued figure from free-flowing light brown hair to the tops of her heavy white wool stockings and dull red boots. Jingles gasped, stared fixedly before her, then stood straight and proud, as if ignoring the existence of onlookers.

For a first time the MVD man appeared disconcerted. "This woman has been most carefully prepared," he commented. He ordered the manacles removed, which permitted blouse and a coarse chemise to fall free, then flung Jingles her clothes and in some unintelligible language ordered her to dress.

"And so, Monsieur, we come to you." The MVD man turned to North, sweating, panting, but helpless. His wig, he anticipated, immediately would be recognized as such and ever more fervently he cursed the folly of having attempted disguise.

"My deaf friend," murmured the MVD man standing before the strapped prisoner in evident enjoyment. "I hope you will not object," he produced a heavy revolver, "if I make a small test." He spoke, pale features a scant foot from North's angular countenance. "I shall fire a shot and we shall see what we shall see."

Silence filled the room when he stepped behind the prisoner, a silence relieved only by the girl's dreary sobbing as she fumbled back into her clothes.

Apparently a past master in the use of tension, the MVD man waited. Clearly, from beyond the examination room's door sounded voices in the police court. All at once North stiffened. Had he recognized one of them? Gambling on all or nothing, he yelled at the top of his voice.

"Brecon-Fyffe! Eric! For God's sake come here!"

CHAPTER 29

Comrade Commissar

THAT anyone possessing Eric Brecon-Fyffe's evident limitations should wield so much authority among his Soviet confrères, came to Hugh North both as a shock and as a rather pleasant surprise. Here in Bulgaria, apparently, the traitor evidently outranked Georgei, a fact puzzling enough in itself.

It had been pleasurable to watch that MVD man in Kavakli Police Headquarters positively cringe before the erstwhile Ben Gramont. For a fact, the fellow had become quite terror-stricken, whining, he excused himself again and again for having undoubtedly carried out his duties with tact, if not with restraint. He even offered the most abject of apologies to Simeon Petroff's lovely wife. The rapidity with which Jingles Lawson re-estimated the situation and acted upon that estimate was nothing short of inspiring.

"See that this dolt, this imbecile, is punished," she demanded, cheeks still flaming over her humiliation. "Send him away so far that he never can brag of having humiliated me!"

Eric Brecon-Fyffe proved most solicitous and, over tall glasses of vodka served in the police commandant's quarters, seemed entirely content to postpone queries. Instead, he related, how he, Esmé Murfee and Georgei had braved the blizzard and just won their way across the frontier when Esmé's strength had given out.

"What did you do?" North inquired.

"We left her lying—freezing is not a painful death and,

most certainly, we could not carry her through those terrible drifts."

North nodded. "Of course not. By the bye, you should know that Dimitri was killed and Nestor captured. Velvalee died soon after the raid of Spanish 'flu, or something very like it."

"Did she?" Brecon-Fyffe sighed. "Velvalee was really a good-hearted little fool—and pretty. She was terribly in love with me, did you know?"

"I suspected as much."

"In a way I'm glad to hear Velvalee's dead. She'd been softening up recently and I've no tolerance of weaklings."

Later, while reclining upon the comfortable cushions of a limousine, Brecon-Fyffe put the inevitable question concerning North's presence in Kavakli.

"I came to catch Walewski," North explained, truthfully enough. "I'd no way of knowing whether any of you had lived to cross the Border—and this Walewski fellow was still to be found."

"By the way, how did you get across the frontier?"

"During the blizzard. You know how it was."

"Yes." Brecon-Fyffe indicated frost bites on his cheek. "Where does Miss Lawson fit in on this?"

Feverishly he wondered whether Steve Petrie had confided a report of that tender scene at the Pera Palace. "I brought her along because she's good on local languages and I'm not. I knew we'd have to talk our way through and she could do it. She's reliable—I'll vouch for that—and can be very useful back in Istanbul."

He was immensely relieved when Brecon-Fyffe merely nodded. "Okay. But I doubt you'll be ordered back into Turkey. I know now what you're worth. Yes, when this shindy is over, I think I'll fetch you to Moscow."

"Then you admit that I've earned my pay?"

"—And then some," came the hearty rejoinder.

"Incidentally, did you find Walewski?"

The traitor hesitated, glanced over his shoulder at Jingles, now huddled silent and sleepy-looking on the seat beside the chauffeur, then, apparently having made up his mind, caused a dead sensation in North's soul by saying, "Yes. He was arrested last night, two hours after Georgei and I got here. The, er—interrogators are working on him right now."

At the thought of the enormities undoubtedly being inflicted North felt sweat break out on his hands.

He tried to weather this disastrous intelligence by inquiring, "So Georgei got through?"

"Yes, but he's got some frozen toes."

To North this information was something of a relief, but best of all was the fact that hard-faced Esmé Murfee was no longer a factor; she had lent the impression of never fully crediting his sincerity.

The limousine's brakes squealed and its driver turned into a narrow street lined by very old houses.

Not to inquire further about Walewski proved difficult in the extreme. Had he been tortured already beyond endurance? Had he yielded the all-important microfilms?

Brecon-Fyffe suddenly leaned forward. "Comrade Lawson, did you ask to be taken to the MVD?"

"The police sergeant and that idiotic MVD detective will tell you so."

The traitor rubbed his scarred chin. "That's the trouble with these lower-level operatives. We should have been notified immediately at headquarters. He took too much on himself in searching you that way."

"I'll say he did!" blazed the girl.

"Think I'll have him shot," Brecon-Fyffe remarked. "—A salutary example for boys who get too big for their breeches."

North passed a hand over the close-clipped contours of

his head and pointed to the adhesive. "Those damned Counter-Intelligence swine gave me that. Knocked me cold."

"How did you get out of jail?"

"Remember that gendarme corporal who brought Phoebus' clothing?"

"Yes."

"He made it possible."

Brecon-Fyffe pulled out a notebook and wrote a few lines. "There's a good man. Ah, here we are—our little red home in the East."

The limousine had halted facing the solid-appearing sheet-iron valves of an arched gateway. To an imperious tooting of the horn a soldier appeared through a small door. He cast one look at the car, then vanished and a moment later the ponderous gates swung back to admit what North was beginning to think of as a tumbril.

"—And these," Brecon-Fyffe explained, "are Comrades North and Lawson." He used English.

A yellow-bearded and florid individual behind a handsomely carved oak desk merely nodded. "Goot! Goot!"

"This is Alexei Brusov, Commissar for Kavakli," Brecon-Fyffe remarked, dropping into the chair Brusov promptly had vacated. Pleasantly he turned to the new arrivals. "I presume you people haven't eaten in some time? Correct? Well, we'll remedy that in short order."

The assured way in which Eric pre-empted the Bulgarian's desk was encouraging; despite his previous subordination to Georgei he must indeed occupy a lofty position in the Party organization.

Eric offered Jingles a cigarette and lit it for her. "You'll have no further need for that ghastly rig you're wearing. Presently you may help yourself from a quite considerable wardrobe collected from certain bourgeois ladies who, in the Trans-Urals, no longer have need of such finery."

"Well, I must say, you top brass Party members don't do at all badly for yourselves," North commented running an eye about the handsomely panelled library. Some excellent French landscapes and even a good Gaugin were in evidence, as well as thick rugs and heavy furniture upholstered in rich, dark green leather.

"Why suffer when it is not necessary?" Brecon-Fyffe demanded, stroking his red-blond Guardee mustache. "This mansion formerly was the property of a wine and liquor dealer who, fortunately for us, was discovered trafficking in the black market." The renegade smiled. "It may surprise you, my dear Major—and Miss Lawson—that the rewards for occupying certain responsible positions in our Soviet democracy are well, considerable."

An hour later North was feeling much better, thanks to an excellent roast of veal, pilav, buttered onions and delicious black bread spread thick with fresh white butter, washed down with some really distinguished Rhein wine.

Jingles, at North's covert urging, had delayed changing, but with hair combed and most of the dirt removed from face and hands, she looked uncommonly pretty. Lipstick and a touch of eyebrow pencil further had restored the familiar colors and proportion to her faintly olive-hued features.

Quite suddenly Brecon-Fyffe put down a long Havana cigar. "I presume that by now the West knows that we have taken Walewski."

"Why?" North demanded innocently. "How could the news get out?"

"In the MVD we don't deceive ourselves. The American and Turkish Intelligence Services are a damned sight more effective than anybody believes—except us. Tomorrow," Brecon-Fyffe settled back and put his feet onto a chair, "the radio will speak of a Soviet ultimatum to the Western Pow-ers. They'll truckle," Eric predicted. "They've got to, now that we've captured Walewski."

"That is so," Brusov broke in, "but in spite of our most skillful questioning he has so far made no talk. He admits to nothing——"

Jingles winced and looked away, nevertheless, like a warm flood thawing a frozen river, relief engulfed North. But how much longer could Walewski hold out?

"A most difficult case," Brusov continued while picking his teeth with a fork. "The question has been applied until there is danger of death."

Brecon-Fyffe started up, purple with rage. "You great idiot! You haven't let them go that far?"

"Why—why, Comrade, I——"

"Why didn't you tell me of this earlier?" snarled the renegade. "If you've gone too far the pack of you'll take a trip you'll be a long time returning from!"

Brusov went white. "B-but Comrade. We were confident we would succeed; unfortunately this reactionary proved to be not as strong as——"

"Perhaps," North suggested evenly, "if you'll permit me to employ different methods I can get him to talk, provided —well, if he's not too far gone."

CHAPTER 30

Josef Walewski

THAT the former wine dealer's mansion, in more ways than one, was supremely well suited to the purposes of the MVD became unmistakably evident within the next few moments.

Along the course set by a moon-faced underling, wintry afternoon sunlight soon gave way to the harsh glare of naked electric bulbs. He led the way down a long flight of stone steps at the foot of which he produced a key then unlocked and slid sidewise an iron door. From beyond the gloom beyond came rushing up such a combination of telltale odors as to set North's close-cropped hair on end.

A good thing Jingles had at last been left behind with orders to repose herself. God knew that she needed rest; neither she nor himself had enjoyed more than a very few hours of sleep out of the last forty-eight. He felt like a nonagenarian, as if his eyes had been packed in sand and pickled in vinegar.

Following their guide, he, Brecon-Fyffe and Brusov descended a second well-constructed stone staircase, one which, in the days before the Red Terror, had led to an imposing wine cellar. Arches and vaults had been well groined in dull yellow brick. These vaults which once had sheltered only the choicest of vintages now had been served a new and less agreeable purpose.

A series of dull bulbs illuminated rows of bars protecting the former wine vaults; now they imprisoned the most wretched specimens of humanity to be imagined. Both sexes lay supine and all but lifeless on trusses of straw, weeping feebly, crowding as far away as possible from the men in the corridor. North fetched a slow breath. So this was what an MVD prison was like?

"Brusov's efficient in one thing at least; he's got a nice collection here," Brecon-Fyffe commented.

An old man upon whose fine face tragedy had sketched deep, ineffaceable lines, advanced to the bars and held out hands hideous because devoid of fingernails, and begged something in piteous tones. The jailer merely spat in his face.

"He? Oh, former landowner," Brecon-Fyffe explained, then indicated a wretch lying with vacant eyes fixed upon a miniature gray stalactite forming on the vault. "That is a doctor who was so unwise as to treat a Yankee flyer who crashed a few miles away. A fool, because the flyer, er—died anyway."

North, looking at the traitor's overly handsome countenance, wondered how anyone could so callously refer to a former fellow countryman.

There must have been at least ten vaults giving off an effluvium composed of stale sweat, excrement and bodies too long unwashed.

The far end of this gallery was blocked by another iron door guarded by a Mongoloid soldier, who, in addition to the usual holstered revolver, carried a heavy, short-stocked whip tucked into his belt. When he noted the approach of Brusov's party he ground out his cigarette, pulled on a peaked cap adorned by a huge red star and stood up, flat and expressionless features golden in the lamplight. Upon a signal from the Bulgarian he saluted then slid back the bolts of an enormously heavy door.

This cellar proved to be much smaller, less well ventilated and sub-divided into two compartments. Without any preliminary Brusov pushed upon a door to his left and revealed that spot where the MVD extorted secrets from even the most determined lips. In Nazi Germany, North had seen similar chambers, perhaps more elaborate but no more complete. There was the usual icy bath, the clubs of varying size, all loaded with lead and, of course, a complete set of knives and electrical soldering irons.

In here the atmosphere was hot and musty and the light so dazzling that North did not notice immediately a fine spattering of fresh blood drops staining the floor about a chair identical to that in which he himself had been strapped at the police station. The two executioners, brutes undoubtedly, were undistinguished because of high Slavic cheekbones, broad pug noses and sloping skulls. The third man appeared more intelligent; he gave over writing at a small portable desk and jumped to attention.

"I have received your message," Brusov announced harshly. "You have done badly, Doctor Marcowicz, very badly."

The doctor winced, blinked, then explained hurriedly, "Your pardon, Comrade Commissar, but the prisoner has a heart condition not immediately to be recognized. His strength gave out quite without the usual warnings. I am not to blame."

"Like hell you aren't," Brecon-Fyffe snapped. "What is wrong?"

"He has developed a coronary condition——"

"—Thrombosis?"

"Yes. The clot must have been very small or he would not yet be alive."

"Has this bastard talked yet?"

"Not even the hot irons on his soles, nor the loss of an eye has shaken him."

Great God, it was Josef Walewski these swine were discussing. To plunge hands deep into his pockets and grip the lining of his mouth between his teeth were the only means by which North could restrain himself from a fatal outburst.

Poor Joe Walewski! For no particular reason he recalled going to a ball game with Joe—yes, it had been the Senators and the Red Sox and homely, friendly little Joe had eaten nearly a full bag of peanuts whilst razzing the umpire; it had been such a masterpiece of that gentle American pastime that he'd never forgotten. Um. What would Joe look like now? He shuddered at the prospect.

"Where is the bastard?" Brecon-Fyffe demanded. "Come along, Doctor, and you'd better pray that you haven't let this business go too far; dead, Walewski isn't worth a hoot in hell to me."

The thin-bearded medical man's plump features went scarlet then gray-white. "But I tell you, Comrade, there was no knowing. How could I tell he has a weak valve?"

"You are supposed to check heartbeats every ten minutes, are you not?"

"But I did," Marcowicz protested. "First it was normal and then, with no warning at all, it weakened. It was not my fault, Comrade, really it was not."

North pulled himself together and spoke in a low voice. "If he's in such bad shape hadn't we better look at him immediately?"

An odor as of badly scorched beef grew strong when the doctor opened still another steel door. Almost incredibly flat upon a blue and white striped mattress, gruesomely stained by rusty brown splotches and revealed by a single bulb of blinding intensity, lay the wreck of him whose silent courage might have changed the course of history. Well-set-up, blond and of medium height had been that half-naked figure lying motionless beneath a coarse blanket. Beside the cot stood a stool and metal table upon which reposed a tray of hypodermics and a row of bottles.

So cruelly disfigured, beaten and burnt was this old friend that an impulse to vomit became nearly overwhelming.

"Have you ever seen this man before?" Brecon-Fyffe demanded in a sibilant undertone.

"Yes, but only once or twice. He used to work at the War Department." North now was scheming furiously. "Eric, I can't hope to succeed if you don't send these butchers and that damned quack out of here."

Once his suggestion had been complied with, North bent low over his friend, tried hard not to notice how the swollen lid of the left eye sagged uglily in upon an empty socket; lucky that the blanket concealed most of Josef Walewski's colorless form.

"Eric, right now I must be the only person he's to be made aware of."

The very personification of Suspicion Brecon-Fyffe went over to stand near the door and growled, "Get on with it."

North dropped on one knee beside the cot, groped under the blanket until his fingers closed over a chill and sticky wrist. There was no perceptible pulse.

"Joe," he cried in a desperate undertone, "Joe! It's Hugh North! Can—can you see me?" He had to repeat the question thrice before the uninjured eye's lid quivered. "This is Hugh North," repeated the Intelligence Officer in a low voice. "Joe, do you know me? We used to go to the ball park."

Hesitantly, the eyelid rolled back exposing a clouded blue eye—then the victim's head turned slightly on a filthy gunny sack serving as pillow.

"Anything to tell me? I'm still your pal."

A low gurgle manifested itself in the American agent's throat. Brecon-Fyffe started forward but Walewski must have seen him for he closed his eye.

North rasped, "Damn it, Eric, I can't accomplish anything if you don't stay back. It's my frank opinion that he'll be dead in a few moments more; his pulse isn't noticeable.

"Joe, old friend," he resumed, "can you still cuss an umpire?"

The faintest of plucking at the corners of hideously swollen lips brought reassurance that indeed Walewski had recognized him.

"Tell me, Joe," he invited, "what's the score?" Even as he spoke the Intelligence Officer leaned forward as if to test Walewski's pulse again.

Faint as a sound of a night bird's wing came the ghosts of three words: "Key—my room," followed by a paroxysm of weak coughing which in a fine spray blew blood into North's face. A slight pressure of Walewski's hand indicated that the coughing had been intentional. God! What a man.

"Did he recognize you?" Brecon-Fyffe demanded from across the room.

"I think so."

"Did he say anything?"

"No. He only sighed."

Key—my room! North straightened, wiping the blood specks from his features.

"You're sure?"

"He's too far gone. Get that horse doctor in here and tell him he'll have to work fast—not that I think anything can be done." He pretended a profound disgust. "This is as badly a bungled job as I've ever seen. Thought you had only experts on your team."

Cursing at the top of his lungs, Brecon-Fyffe ran over to the door and hauled in the doctor. "If that man dies, Doctor Marcowicz, you can pack for a long trip—a one-way trip!"

CHAPTER 31

The Key

As HOUR AFTER HOUR dragged by with the prisoner Walewski alternately gaining and then losing strength, tension
mounted about MVD headquarters—a much larger place
than Major Hugh North at first had suspected. The mansion proved to be quite as huge as it was luxurious and
occupied by a veritable battalion of executives, secretaries,
agents and guards.

During the afternoon North, from the window of a small
sitting room he was sharing with Jingles Lawson, watched
several closed cars roll into that very same courtyard in
which they had dismounted, but he was not able to see
who alighted. Further expressive of a hectic atmosphere
was the sound of telephones jangling almost without cessa-
tion and, somewhere, a radio sender was buzzing and whining, operating at full speed.

The two impostors still were wearing their peasant costumes because, apparently, the pressure of events had become so great the promised European clothing had not yet
been forthcoming—an omission over which North rejoiced.

Now they sat on a sofa decorated with a gay blue and
yellow Ukranian rug; Jingles' head was resting against his
shoulder as she spoke in whispers.

"When do you think we'll try to get out, I—I can't stand
much more of this, I'm afraid. Every time that horrible Eric
looks at us I break out in duck bumps. What a fancy stinker
he is!"

He put an arm about her, murmured, "Sometime during

the night, and the earlier the better. Tell me, dear, were you able to find out where Novak lived?"

"Only just a little while back," Jingles whispered. "I sweet-talked that little horror Brusov—even gave him a kiss —until he actually thawed and bragged a bit. When they took your friend Joe, he was living under the name of Novak in a cheap boarding house at 34 Tarnapol Street."

"You're tops," North breathed and kissed her so soundly that color went streaming into her cheeks. "I'd surely have been lost without you, but I'll never forgive myself for having exposed you to such—such misery."

"Ixnay on the self-reproach," she interrupted. "Just remember one thing—when I asked to come along I knew very well what I was risking. But thanks for that kiss." She smiled. "What's your scheme?"

"I'll tell you, but sing a little song while I talk," he said. "I expect they've hidden more microphones around here— though I've neutralized two already."

Whilst very softly she sang, "Back Home in Indiana" he detailed his plan—and on this occasion North's lips moved hardly at all.

"It's imperative that we get to Joe's room and find a certain key."

"The key to a code?"

"No, just a room key. I'll know what kind to look for," he reassured. "Once we've got it we'll make our break for the frontier. With luck we should get a fair head start. Without it, well, neither of us is to be taken alive."

"But you've no weapons."

"There's a collection of handy-looking rods in Brusov's desk drawer."

The tempo of the song decreased, but Jingles sang on, fingers caressing his forehead.

"I note that your bedroom lies across the hall from mine and looks out onto a street." He spoke slowly. "Have you noticed whether there are any signs of wiring or electric alarm connections about?"

"No, but I will."

When a burst of angry discussion beat up from downstairs, North grinned.

"Our dear friend Gramont is in such a fine rage, I expect poor Joe's losing ground again." He sighed. "And they don't award Congressional Medals to civilians! Only hope Joe doesn't talk in delirium. What they did to him was simply God-awful," he told his companion. "It's getting dark. What time is it?"

"Don't know, dear, but I thought I heard a clock strike five a while ago."

The roaring purr caused by still another flight of jet planes momentarily terminated the conversation.

"—That was such a mighty nice kiss," Jingles reminded herself aloud. "Wonder if you'll do as well once the pressure's off."

"So long as you seem to appreciate my poor efforts," he chuckled, "here's a special one on accoun——"

Too late they sprang apart. The door had been quietly opened to disclose Brecon-Fyffe in the doorway. He must have been preparing to go out for he wore a gray astrakhan chapka, a black leather coat and a pair of high boots. "Pardon the intrusion. I see you're passing the time pleasantly, eh?"

"Since we couldn't play gin rummy," Jingles pointed out, "we compromised on post office. Want to get a gal and join in? It's fun."

"Bah!" rasped the renegade. "How can you be so frivolous when the final Class Struggle is about to break out?" Then he launched into a wild tirade against the Western Powers, the capitalistic system, private enterprise and the stupidity of his assistants, to which North listened in mounting disgust.

"How very true, Comrade," North agreed. "By the bye, what's on the schedule? I'd like to get some shut-eye."

"I'm leaving in a few minutes," Brecon-Fyffe announced, "to search that goddam Walewski's room!"

Quickly, but not eagerly, North volunteered his assistance.

"No!" the renegade snapped. "That's one thing I don't need you for. I'll want you to stay here; that damned reactionary spy may regain consciousness and for only a few instants."

"It's as you say, Boss." North smiled but his heart sank. Brecon-Fyffe to Joe's lodgings? That would be no help at all.

Jingles stopped re-braiding her hair, gave the renegade a winsome smile. "Say, Eric, when do we take off for Moscow? I've been wanting to get there for years."

"Tomorrow, probably by plane." He grinned, commenced to do up his overcoat's buttons. "One thing. Don't you two go nosing about. It's distinctly unwise. They'll bring up some supper before long; don't wait for me." He ran an eye over the room. "I'll have some cards sent up. This is no time for post office and amusements of that sort. By the way, your city clothes should be along any time."

North shrugged. "No hurry until I've had a bath. I suppose such a refinement can be arranged?"

"I presume so, although our local colleagues don't bother with such trifles." He wrinkled his nose. "They're a filthy lot of pigs." He hesitated, demanded over his leather-clad shoulder, "Tell me, Hugh, do you suppose that damned Brusov mismanaged the matter of Walewski simply to embarrass me?"

"I don't know. Why should he?"

"Brusov wants my job as Chief of MVD for the Balkans. I know he envies me and hates my guts quite as much as I despise his."

"It's wonderful," North reflected yet again, "how thoroughly frightened and suspicious everybody is in this Soviet paradise. Why, in God's name, don't our bright boys in the State Department play on that more effectively?"

Despite Brecon-Fyffe's announcement, supper was served in the library and proved an exceedingly grim affair. Brusov and another beetle-browed Bulgarian performed brisk operatic selections on an excellent lentil soup then sailed into a platter of roast veal. For all the attention Brusov paid North and Jingles they might as well have been items of furniture. At length, however, he flung down knife and fork, then proceeded to lick veal gravy from his fingers.

"Doctor Marcowicz reports that that damned bourgeois spy gains strength; the minute he sends word you will hurry to the cellar, understand? Pay no attention if the doctor looks badly; Comrade Eric decided to discipline him with a riding crop. He was much irritated." From a rank of cigars paraded across his vest pockets the Commissar selected a long perfecto upon which he chewed thoughtfully for a moment. He bent forward. "What do you make of Comrade Gramont?"

"He's an extremely capable individual," North supplied promptly and forced himself to fight off the soporific effect of this excellent meal, so greatly in contrast with the food shortage otherwise prevailing in Kavakli.

Brusov picked up a fork and used it expertly to dislodge bits of meat from between his teeth. "That is so, but sometimes I wonder if Comrade Gramont does not regret his upbringing and that society which he so wisely renounced?"

"His high position in the Party should answer that," North asserted.

Down the hall a telephone bell shrilled, preceding by only an instant the entrance of an excited-appearing flat-faced Mongoloid secretary. "Your pardon, Commissar, but for you is message of urgence."

"So? Come, Anton," Brusov flung to his black-browed companion.

Once the precious pair had clattered off down the corridor North sprang up. "Stay in the hall and warn if the waiter comes back."

He sped across the room and, praying fervently, opened the lower right-hand drawer of Brusov's desk which, praise God, proved not to be locked—a most reprehensible breach of security. From among half a dozen automatic pistols of varying calibre and manufacture he selected a pair of .38 Walthers and was pleased to note that each was equipped with an extra clip attached to the holster.

Less than a minute had been required to execute the maneuver, which proved just as well because Brusov's secretary appeared and ordered Jingles and her companion back to their rooms.

The headquarters teemed with such activity they found it difficult to make even a pretense of playing gin rummy until eight o'clock, at which time North nodded. "Enough is enough, eh? Well, sweet dreams to you and all that."

She collected the cards, winked, then crossed the hall into her own room.

The Bojuk-Dervent sector of the Turkish frontier—where alone they might hope to cross in safety—North had estimated from the casual inspection of a map gracing the library to lie all of twenty miles to the south-southeast of Kavakli.

By the time North had donned his goatskin coat and felt hat the excitement and activity had risen to a feverish pitch, perhaps because a radio below was blaring a speech. Jingles was listening to it when, in two quick strides, North crossed the corridor and stepped inside.

"Radio says there has been a terrific meeting of the Security Council today," she informed *sotto voce*. "Russia has issued an ultimatum."

"What is it?"

"War if the United States does not immediately with-draw our military missions to Greece and Turkey."

"Thanks to Larkin's chuckle-headedness! God grant I get my hands on that self-satisfied dope. Are you ready?"

"Yes." She was fully dressed, her kerchief back in place.

"What about your window?"

"I found it nailed shut, but this afternoon, while you were down with Walewski, I worked the nails free."

"D'you know you're a very wonderful gal?" He paused just long enough to prop a chair under the door handle; there would be no keys to guest rooms such as these.

"Duck the lights," he directed, "and let's go."

His heart checked at a loud, protesting squeak from the window frame, then biting cold beat into his face. Dark-ness ruled immediately outside, but a street light glowed perhaps a hundred yards away to his left.

Fortunately the original owner of this building had not fancied high ceilings, so the fugitives were confronted by a drop not exceeding ten feet into snow banked deep from the street-side. The street seemed deserted and, praise God, the lower storeys of this MVD headquarters always re-mained tightly shuttered.

North eased himself over the sill, hung at arm's length then, relaxing every muscle, plummeted down into the snow. "Okay! Don't stiffen—just fall loose!" Amid a flurry of petticoats and snow flakes Jingles landed beside him.

Tarnapol Street? From a study of that map in the gen-darmerie he knew it lay somewhere off to their right. Praise God, Jingles could read the Bulgarian and Russian alphabet. Heads bent, shoulders rounded, the two set off immediately, did not even wait to brush off snow accumulated by their falling.

"D-don't ever let 'em t-tell you p-petticoats are w-warmer than p-pants," Jingles chattered.

Their objective, if he recalled correctly, lay two blocks down this street, Klementi Gottwald Avenue, then one block over to the right. Even at this hour of eight-thirty, Kavakli seemed utterly lifeless and lightless save for some big buildings in which troops undoubtedly must be billeted. Slipping occasionally on new-formed ice the pair stumped along, stolidly enduring the stares of an infantry patrol returning from guard duty on the outskirts of town. They proved entirely too chilled and eager to regain their barracks even to call a challenge.

Number 34 Tarnapol Street proved to be a dilapidated and unpainted wooden structure, sharp-roofed, two storeys high and built flush to a narrow footway. The front of it once had been altered to create a small display window now dingy and devoid of merchandise.

How to gain entry? The question remained paramount. North noted a paper tacked to the door panels, questioned Jingles.

"It's a notice warning everyone away," she explained, after staring intently through the gloom. "The former occupants have been arrested for treason to the State." That the MVD, on seizing so choice a prize as Josef Walewski, had arrested everyone on the premises seemed entirely likely.

From the shelter of a doorway North patiently surveyed the environs of Number 34. Brecon-Fyffe must have come and gone for certainly the place appeared tenantless. No lights shown from any of the windows so, in all probability, the renegade no longer even was in the vicinity. Many fresh tire marks in the snow before Number 34 lent further support to this thesis.

"Push your skirts against the glass," North directed and used his boot to smash—none-too-loudly—a pane of a ground-floor back window and so permit a manipulation of its catch.

The inside of the house proved to be colder even than the street—which argued that Walewski had been taken two full days back. Because nearly all of the windows had been heavily shuttered it was impossible to see anything.

"Wish to God I didn't have to show a light, but there's no help for it."

"Here's a candle," came the girl's quick accents. "We can shield it with this bowl."

The veriest dolt could have seen at a glance that the house had been thoroughly, savagely ransacked. Picture frames, despoiled of their contents, spilled broken glass across the floor and, in what looked like the living room, shabby furniture sprouted springs and trailed upholstery padding like entrails from a slashed abdomen.

Reasoning smoothly, North wasted no time on the ground floor—Joe would hardly have been rooming there—and warily set foot to a worn staircase. Eerily their tread resounded in the emptiness. North halted, indecisive.

"Funny, Eric and his pals never thought to post a guard outside," Jingles commented. "I suppose even the smartest ones slip up now and then."

"I'm only praying that they haven't noted their mistake." He turned, Indian-like features craggy in the subdued candle light. "Jingles, you'd better stay below—watch the street and if you see anything suspicious, squeak like a mouse. Can you?"

"Sure. I've been called a mouse on occasion—not that I liked it."

Shielding his light, North made his way up the hollow-sounding staircase and presently discovered four doors opened off the little landing on which he was pausing. Which might have served as poor Joe's hide-out?

A very cursory examination revealed that, beyond a doubt, Walewski's had been the left-hand front room; how

else to account for such merciless ransacking? Although
turned inside out the other three bedrooms remained comparatively unharmed.

Hurriedly North examined first the hall door. No key.
Then he turned to a wardrobe—the only other place where
a key of the sort he sought might be employed. Damn!
The clothes press proved as completely devoid of a key as
the door.

Now he'd have to start a real search, so he made sure that
the old-fashioned wooden shutters were closed; of course, it
was too much to expect that they'd be anything approaching light-proof. First, he ran his eye over a pile of smashed
furniture littering a threadbare rug, then tested the little
iron bed's ripped and ruined mattress. No luck. He was
unscrewing some dull brass knobs on the bedstead when
a car entered Tarnapol Street and creaked to a halt not far
away. Dear God. Was there a key here somewhere? On
hands and knees he scrabbled among the dead ashes of a
fireplace. He felt himself perspiring furiously.

"E-e-e-k!" Jingles called then hurriedly scaled the stairs.
He blew out the candle.

"Car's stopped outside," she muttered from the landing.
"Two men have got out and are looking up at this room.
May have seen your light."

"Go below and watch them—squeak again if they don't
move on. Got to have more time."

"No key?"

"Not yet. Get going."

Obediently she returned below.

Even as he struck a match to rekindle the candle a gleam
of metal caught his eye; it originated from beneath a section
of the room's warped and battered baseboard. Stooping,
North jerked out a plain wrought-iron key of antique design. A sharp humming sound filled his ears and his chilled
fingers tingled. This key was perhaps seven inches long

equipped with a stout shank and elaborate notching along the edge of its flange.

From below Jingles again squeaked shrilly then called upstairs in a stage whisper. "One of them's driven off in a rush; other's pulled a gun—he's watching from across—street."

Were this not the right key, there was nothing more could be done.

He tiptoed back to the ground floor and peered out, recognized that single figure across Taranapol Street.

"Stay close unless we're chased—then you're on your own," he breathed, pulled out his pistol and, very quietly, unbolted the rear door. Thank God, the snow in the back yard had been heavily trampled. Bent nearly double, he set a course for the shelter of a woodpile, from thence to the lee of a shed, and so gained an alley, all black and white in the frosty starlight.

"Remember to use that gun if there's no hope. You're not to let them take you alive."

As if it were glowing with heat he could feel the outline of that key pressing against his stomach; it should be secure inside his peasant's tightly bound sash. Somehow he felt certain that this old key was the correct one—the use of such had been one of the late-lamented O.S.S.'s most effective devices.

If only he had the opportunity to make certain; but he hadn't. In a few minutes Kavakli and the whole of Eastern Rumelia would be alerted and an inexorable pursuit set in motion.

With the wig's long hair flying in a stiff northerly breeze, North headed along a series of back streets and passages towards Kavakli's southwest perimeter. There, he knew, they would enter upon an increasingly critical phase of their flight. God above! They'd have twenty long miles to travel through snow drifts and over icy rivers; undoubtedly it would be unwise to use the roads—afoot at least.

Almost at once ill-fortune overtook the fugitives in the guise of a guard detail which halted awaiting its relief, and so held the couple motionless and shivering in the lee of a log cabin for half an hour. Soon there were evidences of turmoil.

"Alarm's out; here goes nothing," Jingles sighed and in the starlight her eyes sought North's.

A siren commenced to shriek like an hysterical woman. Dispatch cars, staff autos and even motorcycles commenced to roar through Kavakli's narrow and slippery streets. An N.C.O. came trotting up, overcoat skirts flapping wildly, and yelled at the waiting guard detail which stood so close that, to Jingles, his instructions were quite audible.

"Here's a break," she muttered. "They're setting this cordon closer in town," and, sure enough, the detail set off on the double towards the center of Kavakli.

"We've got to find transportation," North seemed to think aloud. "We will never get away if we don't get a real jump on 'em now."

They ran as long as Jingles could find wind, then at a hurried walk. By plunging at headlong speed through a gloomy pine woods, they paralleled a road leading southward for perhaps a kilometer. When they re-emerged into a bare and snowy plain the lights of the town shown but feebly through the strong starlight. To the fugitives it seemed as if every star in the firmament was fairly ablaze tonight.

"It's risky, but we'd better get back onto the road," North stated. "We're not covering enough distance like this. We can see the lights of a car in plenty of time to hide in the snow."

"Y-yes," Jingles gasped, chest heaving painfully under the shawls. "C-can't keep up in dee-deep snow."

Panting, sweat-drenched, they trotted doggedly onwards until, every now and then, some snow-concealed rut in the road would trip one or the other of them, send them sprawling.

"At this rate we'll never make it to the frontier by daylight," North was deciding.

Like curious yellow fingers the lights of a car suddenly commenced to probe down the road. Efficiently those twin rays picked out and gilded the low snowy hills all about and thin ranks of snow-powdered pines. North halted abruptly in the lee of some road mender's deserted cabin.

"Darling, I hate to say it, but our last and only hope is to take over that car."

Jingles' kerchief had slipped back and her softly brown hair clung in damp ringlets about her sweat-streaked cheeks. "H-how you g-get them s-stop?"

"You'll lie in m-middle of road," he panted. "Hold your gun ready under s-shawl. I-I'll pick off driver and anyone else from here. Course, if car's full of people we're out of luck."

"Okay, do I go now?"

"Signals over," he said suddenly. "I'll lie in road, you hide. Here's key—what we came for, so don't lose it—— 'F anything happens t' me, you get for Turkey."

"Oh, no, Hugh no!"

"Orders, dear, you've the better chance—getting through."

"But must we take this terrible gamble?" she gasped.

"No other way."

"All right, what am I to do?"

"You any kind of a pistol shot?"

"No, but I'm pretty good at skeet."

"Then if you have—shoot—don't try to sight, just swing on target and fire."

Aware that the dancing, wavering car lights now were much closer, he handed her the key, watched her conceal it deep in the bosom of her blouse, then effectively conceal herself amid a tangle of snow-covered shrubbery beside the road. Only then did he collapse—on his back of course —across those ruts marking the road.

The Walther automatic he held ready but concealed under his goatskin cloak. An odd, hitherto unfamiliar exhilaration seized him while the dazzling headlight beams gradually grew brighter. Apparently this road was too rough for speeding. In a few moments now some men surely were going to die—who?

Now he could distinguish the sound of the engine, the rattle of a loose fender. Subconsciously, his grip on the pistol tightened and he forced his eyes closed, for fear that the headlights might blind him during that crucial moment when the car ground to a halt. But suppose this car didn't stop, but ran right over him? The possibility was great; under similar circumstances he'd never have risked losing speed.

Near, *nearer* crackled the tire treads; he became positive they'd run him over when there came a loud squealing of brakes and the car halted not a dozen feet distant. Voices sounded in argument then a door banged back. North drew a deep breath, half opened his eyes and caught the pallid loom of a face bending above him.

Swiftly raising the Walther he fired squarely just below that seemingly disembodied face. At the same instant he rolled over, rose to one knee and, without sighting, fired point-blank at the driver. Unwisely for him the chauffeur— he wore a Bulgarian Army uniform—had started also to dismount. He had no opportunity to draw his gun before North's second shot caught him center line and spilled him stone dead beside the auto's running board.

The Intelligence Officer whirled and looked at the car. Praise God! There had been but these two persons in it. The man he had shot from the ground—a big Russian cap-

tain—must have been hit in the head judging by his squirm-
ing and threshing about, but he was making no outcry.
How quickly would his shots attract pursuit?

Hardly two minutes later he had hauled both the dead
and the unconscious victims of his marksmanship into deep
snow in the ditch. The Russian, too, would soon die, since
no man can live long with a bullet through the center of his
forehead.

When Jingles came running out of the underbrush he
yelled, "Take this fellow's hat and overcoat." He pointed
to the Russian officer.

For himself he appropriated the driver's peaked military
cap and overcoat—although it was somewhat soggy with
blood.

"Got key?"

"Yes. My God, but you can shoot," Jingles cried while
climbing into the front seat of this ancient Italian touring
car. "Never saw anybody move so fast."

"Thanks. But I hate gun fights—always have."

The motor never having been switched off, North had
only to put this aged Lancia in gear and attempt once more
to remember every detail of that map he had studied so
carefully in Razib Albey's office. Were he following the
road he thought he was, soon there should be a fork, and
they would find themselves on a well-travelled and therefore doubly dangerous road leading to the Turkish border.

CHAPTER 32

Border Incident

UNFORTUNATELY the sky remained clear, thererore around six-thirty the sky grew rosy with warnings of dawn. Thanks to a long delay on a side road, due to a clogged fuel line, North now was coaxing every possible bit of speed from the old Lancia.

"Do you want the key back?" Jingles demanded so faintly that he cast her a sharp sidewise glance. She appeared all-but exhausted and no wonder, considering that she'd had no sleep, no real rest in nearly fifty-two hours. Many a man would have caved in under the duress to which she had been subject. What a really wonderful girl she was! If they ever won through—well, he guessed he'd been a bachelor about long enough.

Said he quietly, "You've been superb all through this mess, I want you to know that, my dearest."

"Dearest?" She smiled. "Something new has been added, hasn't it?"

"Yes. Tell you about it later. About the key, no. As I said outside of Kavakli, you stand a better chance of getting across the border than I. You'll take that key straight to Colonel McKenzie *and no one else!*"

"You're sure this is the right key?"

He braced himself against the impact of the car tires on a frozen rut. The vehicle's whole fabric rattled and groaned.

"No, I'm not," he admitted, "but it was the only key I could find."

Seen as a series of planes shading from gray to black

the hovels of a hamlet loomed ahead. Yonder no lights shone but, as North guided the car hurtling down its single street, a flashlight wavered and a series of hoarse shouts rang out.

"Slide onto the floor!" North snapped then lowered himself as far as possible and stepped hard on the accelerator. Something struck the right door a resounding crack as a pistol blazed alongside. Shoulder muscles bunched, North guided his vehicle into a set of violent swerves, first right then left. More rifle and pistol shots rattled and a wicked star-shaped hole materialized in the Lancia's windshield. Had Jingles emitted a soft little cry? No telling now.

Jaws clenched, the Intelligence Officer whirled by the last tumbledown stone-and-thatch hut. He heard bullets twice more strike the Lancia somewhere.

"Jingles! Jingles! You all right?"

"Don't worry, I'm fine," she reassured. He didn't dare check by even a sidewise glance.

The alarm now would be out for fair! Anxiously he prayed that the Lancia's gasoline tank might not have been pierced. Every turn of the wheels now was fetching them closer to the frontier and to Bojuk-Dervent near which an ancient watch tower marked their point of exit.

There remained, he calculated, hardly more than five miles left to travel now that they successfully had negotiated Chaskoi, the village just left behind. Four miles, three miles. Lights now could be seen flashing in pursuit, lights that were paling in the increasing dawn.

"Soon we've got to ditch this car," he announced. "Hate to leave quick transport, but any minute now there'll be a swarm of planes looking for us."

"Whatever you say," Jingles agreed in a small voice. "You still have the red and blue handkerchiefs?"

"Praise God those roughnecks back in Kavakli didn't grab 'em. Ha! Here we are. Brace yourself."

What looked like a lumbering road veered away from the highway towards an evergreen forest, and up this North drove the Lancia as far as it would go before its wheels commenced to spin but by then dark green fir boughs had closed in overhead, effectively concealing the car from aerial observation.

North switched off the ignition, said, "We shed caps and coats. Come, first we circle back towards Chaskoi. We——" He broke off short; several ruby drops were staining the snow beside Jingles. "You're hit!" he gasped when, pulling off the outer shawl, he saw beneath it her left sleeve was sodden with blood.

"Not badly," she reassured. "Bullet only grazed my shoulder. Let's keep going. It doesn't hurt and I've nearly stopped bleeding."

This proved to be so, but despite Jingles' protests North applied a crude bandage before plunging on through drifts gone rosy with the dawn.

That his decision to back-track a little had been wise soon became evident. Hardly had he and Jingles emerged from the fir forest as a couple of peasants starting off about their daily labors than he took the precaution to break off some dead branches and tie them into bundles. All too soon a pair of observation planes came cruising along the length of the highway; these were not fast ships but old models which travelled slowly enough to permit a thorough inspection of the terrain.

"Everything depends on whether those chuckle-heads will notice our car tracks leading into the woods," North muttered. He and Jingles, he knew, must stand out against the snow like oysters on the half shell.

He felt better when the planes flashed by, bright red stars glowing on their underwings like danger signals, and made no effort to circle or to lose altitude.

Bent like any peasant, North stumped along, offered

encouragements to the silent girl at his side. It came as a relief to note that indeed Jingles' little wound was no longer bleeding, although she looked decidedly white, and her gray-blue eyes preternaturally large. This was not surprising considering the danger in which they stood.

"Don't look so worried, Hugh. I feel fine—really I do, probably better than our dear friend Brecon-Fyffe."

North couldn't resist a chilled grin when he considered the renegade's probable fate—should they escape. The Politburo up in Moscow would not likely overlook an error of such magnitude as that committed by Comrade Benjamin A. Gramont.

Not to hurry to the top of yonder hill proved hard work. From there, he estimated, they could sight that ruined watch tower over in Turkey marking the open sector. From its summit powerful glasses must continually be sweeping the generally bare and hilly terrain rolling down from the Chaskoi Valley.

"Some cars are coming," Jingles announced without raising her head and, sure enough, through the cold air presently resounded a muffled roar.

North made rapid calculations. "There's no use making a break, so we'll sit on those rocks as if resting."

Again a hundred doubts and fears beset him while beneath the malodorous goatskin cloak he readied his automatic. From under a black fringe of hair, and the brim of his shapeless felt hat, he watched an armored car and two sedans come speeding into sight and sucking billows of powdered snow along in their wake.

Would this motorcade slacken speed? He got to his feet, pulled off his hat, and humbly bent his head—as might a peasant of the old school. Jingles followed suit and they stood there beside their bundles of fagots, miserable, intensely commonplace figures.

North and his companion almost shouted their joy when the motorcade made no effort even to slow down. He wished he dared raise his head sufficiently to see who might be occupying those black sedans, but the risk wasn't worth it.

Jingles sighed while heaving the load of fagots to her back. "I hate to complain, but—I—I've never been so cold in all my life, and these sticks are so damned heavy."

"I know, dear, but, well, they're worth their weight in security."

"How far is the frontier?"

A confidence he came far short of feeling was evident in his reply. "It can't be above two miles more. Remember, darling, every single step brings us that much closer to our team—and to the preservation of our world."

They were hobbling along through ankle-deep snow when, from a side road, appeared a sledge drawn by a pair of great, wide-horned oxen, magnificent beasts, fawn-colored with white muzzles and brown noses. The sledge was largely loaded with hay but also carried some firewood.

In a quick undertone North cried, "Beg a ride will you? And for God's sake hide your left hand, it's still blood-streaked."

"Gladly," Jingles murmured. "I'm God-awful tired. What about you?"

"I'm okay, but my feet are near to freezing."

She hailed the ox driver, a wizened, gray-bearded fellow wearing an enormous sheepskin coat; he stared a moment, hesitated, but ended by nodding. A moment later the sledge resumed its sluggish progress with Jingles huddled in the warm hay and North sprawled beside her.

Deliberately the cattle set their broad splay feet and the sledge creaked on over the crisp white snow.

"He said he's going into Bojuk-Dervent," Jingles whispered. "When do you want to get down?"

"Once we get through Bojuk. The frontier can't lie half a mile beyond it."

Noon was a thing of the past by the time the sledge drew near to Bojuk. There, to North's immense satisfaction, a pair of Bulgarian soldiers, big, brawny fellows with flat Slavic features and untidy drooping mustaches, stood waiting by the roadside.

"Invite them aboard," North hissed. Jingles gave him one startled look, then waved, donned her sweetest smile and obeyed—to the driver's sullen fury. The infantrymen, of course, piled aboard and sat joshing this pretty *baboushka*.

Probably it was due to these soldiers' presence that the sledge escaped a thorough ransacking. As North had estimated, their fellow passengers belonged to the same unit of frontier guards—certainly they called enough greetings.

The wind had so burned North's face and inflamed his eyelids that to keep fully awake proved a real feat. Never had he felt so tired; he could feel his bones melting. Come to think on it, he really couldn't recall when last he'd enjoyed eight consecutive hours of sleep. No wonder poor Jingles looked so pinched and gray about the face, but what a story she'd have for her syndicate!

The sledge squeaked and bumped along in so leisurely a fashion that he settled deeper into the hay. By an effort he roused up and made sure that both the infantrymen were drowsing, with their old-fashioned Mauser rifles riding the sledge's floor.

Turning sidewise, he studied Jingles' haggard but suddenly rosy features. She should, if she'd have him, make a wonderful wife; certainly married life never could present more harsh and vital questions than those she already had met so staunchly.

He experienced an overpowering desire to take her in his arms, to kiss her, to tell her how eager he was to pass the remainder of his life in her company.

Ca-a-a! Ca-a-a! A long line of ragged ravens was flapping by, heading back into Bulgaria—for a feast at Kavakli?

The hay proved soft and the early afternoon sun so unexpectedly warm that North drowsed momentarily, but he reminded himself that he mustn't sleep. Soon he and Jingles must alight and face the supreme moments of their flight. The rhythmic gait of the oxen, the chill air and his own grinding fatigue nevertheless conspired to lull Hugh North into a comfortable half sleep.

Because its runners skidded on a patch of ice concealed beneath a layer of snow the sledge lurched sidewise, and with sufficient violence as to spill hay, firewood and all its five occupants headlong into the snow of the ditch.

"Damn it to hell! What's happened?" North burst out while scraping snow from his eyes. Only an unforgiving second later was he aware of two disastrous facts; his wig had become twisted crazily over one eye, and, for a deaf-mute, he had spoken with remarkable clarity—in a foreign tongue!

Even while floundering to his knees he jerked out the automatic, used it to gesture the two equally snow-bathed soldiers away from their rifles in the overturned sledge, and indicated the road back.

So unmistakable was the menace of the Intelligence Officer's steel-gray eyes that the Bulgarians hesitated not at all, but jerked mittened hands upwards and started running heavily away, stumbling on the road ruts with long khaki overcoat skirts flapping ludicrously.

The aged ox drover stood wailing, knobby hands raised heaven-wards in despair. Only the oxen seemed unperturbed by this misadventure; they stood, heads bent under their yoke, looking placidly through the regularly spaced puffs of steam rising from their nostrils.

"Get going!" he flung at Jingles. She was snow-covered and round-eyed but also handling her weapon. "Head for the tower—yonder. Be along in a minute."

It being nearly a kilometer back to Bojuk-Dervent, the two infantrymen could raise no immediate alarm; he lingered long enough to smash both rifle stocks against the runners. Over the necessity of deserting the unhappy ox drover, who had only been kindly, he felt a deep compunction—yet there was no help for it so, at a jolting run, he set out after Jingles.

"Key's all right?"

"Yes."

Wheezing and purple of face they started running down the furrows of a broad field leading downwards towards what appeared to be a frozen river—towards that ruinous watch tower on the further slope. How well were Razib Albey's men observing this little valley? How vigilant might be their watch? The going by turns proved difficult then easy as occasional drifts alternated themselves with wind-swept patches of frozen ground.

"Can't keep up. Too fast!" gasped Jingles and slumped onto all fours.

Aware that a droning of airplane motors was sounding more distinct, he grabbed her hand and dragged her onwards. Onwards they lurched towards the river. Now North could only draw breath in great, sobbing gusts and torrents of sweat poured down his face. Somewhere, far to their rear, could be heard the sudden, brazen shrieks of bugles.

Breathless and half-blinded by glare off the snow, they gained the end of the field. Then North's laboring heart gave an extra surge. Hitherto hidden in a small hollow stood a frontier guard's hut and outside of it were collected three or four figures. Obviously those bugles from the village had put them on the alert.

"Rest up—minute."

Wheezing for breath, and aware that the Lawson girl now was swaying drunkenly on her feet, Hugh North pulled out the red handkerchief, waved it frantically, then brandished the blue one.

Still carrying a handkerchief in either hand, he flung an arm about Jingles and half dragged her down towards the river, all the while angling away from the guard hut. Apparently, the border guards had not yet glimpsed them so he took advantage of a short fold in the terrain to gain another precious two hundred yards towards the hither bank of the frozen Chaskoi—it bore the same name as the town above.

Soon it became a dreadful necessity to halt every fifty yards to allow for Jingles' catching her breath. Her many petticoats must have weighed like lead. She had lost her shawl and the blood-marked sleeve showed plainly through a coating of snow covering her to the waist.

Only fifty yards from the river she sagged into a sitting position, fumbled briefly in her bosom, gasping, "You go— Hugh—I—done for—can't—more——" She pushed the key into his hand.

He took it, but also grasped her by the wrist. "Come on," he panted, "we've only—cross—river. Turkey's yonder!"

A shouting commenced off to their left, and was replied to by cries from the right. That snarling roar of airplane motors now was so close as to send a shiver down his back. God above! A flight of three patrol ships was racing down the Chaskoi; then, abruptly, he realized that these ships were not causing the uproar—they were still too far away. Wheeling he glimpsed a pair of Yak fighters, already low, preparing to dive on these two solitary figures so black by the river's edge.

"Dive under snow!" North yelled. "Then roll over."

They had been descending a gully into the bottom of which snow had drifted to a depth of three feet; it was easy to disappear completely from sight. Half smothered by powdery crystals, North spun over and over, away from

Jingles who, apparently was too exhausted to do likewise.

Idiotically he was reminded of the famous barroom tale about "Whirling Joe Jones." The ruse proved effective; the pilots, deprived of a clearly recognizable target, could only rake a wide area with their machine gun bullets.

The instant the Yaks had sped by, North yelled for Jingles to get up, and once more they plunged, staggering and reeling, out of the gully, and commenced to traverse that critical flat space some hundred yards wide marking the course of the Chaskoi and also the Turkish border.

So out of breath were the fugitives, so aware of the imminence of death, that they found their visions limited to a radius of some two hundred yards. Therefore, although North was able to distinguish a trio of Bulgarian frontier guards brandishing weapons, screeching orders and struggling in his direction through waist-deep snow, he had no notion of what might be transpiring on the Turkish side of the river.

"Here they come," choked the Lawson girl and this time needed no instructions to fling herself beneath the surface of the snow.

Once more the thunder of Yak III motors and the furious chatter of machine guns penetrated the too shallow snow covering the rise. A bullet rapped North's boot heel then, miraculously, the storm of machine gun fire ceased and there followed a screaming noise such as a plane causes when diving suddenly from a height.

Warily, he thrust his head above the surface, instantly to grasp what had chanced. Above the border not two, but five planes were maneuvering, engaged in a furious skirmish. Right now the two Yak III fighters were adopting evasive tactics to avoid perhaps purposely misdirected fire from three Turkish planes—stout American-Built P-63A's.

Jingles' head, pale and grotesque because of tufts of clinging snow, materialized.

"Get up," he begged, "we're almost safe!"

A resounding report ensued, then one of the Yak III's went into a spin and crashed in Turkish territory, whereupon its companion retreated hurriedly into Bulgaria. One of the Turkish planes, however, went speeding southwards trailed by an ominous comet's tail of sooty black smoke.

Quite suddenly Jingles fell and lay motionless. North hesitated, dashed the sweat from his eyes. To his left Bulgarian guards were running out over the river in an attempt to head him off. If the snow continued deep they wouldn't have enough time to come up; pray God they didn't decide to open fire. Then through the snow glare the Intelligence Officer glimpsed a series of black, ant-like figures descending the Turkish bank; there followed a thin scattering of rifle reports. The Bulgarian border guards halted and fell flat, obviously under fire from the Turkish side of the river. They, too, commenced to shoot—at the Turks not the fugitives.

North ran over to where Jingles had fallen, gathered her in his arms and staggered onwards.

More helmeted Turkish and Bulgarian soldiers appeared, joined in the skirmish, and began to blaze away with pistols, rifles and even sub-machine guns. A bullet hummed viciously past the Intelligence Officer's head, another, then from the Turkish shore sounded the deadly snarl of a heavy Browning machine gun. Ha! Over his shoulder North glimpsed the Bulgarian border guards falling back, firing all the while. Two of them lay still, sharply silhouetted against the snow.

An eternity seemed to pass before a stalwart Turkish lieutenant came running out over the ice and helped North to carry the girl's limp figure into the safety of a concrete blockhouse.

CHAPTER 33

Colonel McKenzie's Office

NOT THREE HOURS had elapsed from the moment Major Hugh North had been assisted onto Turkish soil than he found himself approaching Colonel Alexander McKenzie's office in the Galata Quarter of Istanbul.

For several reasons it was as well that the trip down from the frontier had been accomplished in an American A-26B —a twin-engine medium bomber. First, it had been possible to bring along Jingles Lawson; there could be no doubt that the girl had become very ill indeed needing expert medical care—and in a hurry.

Her wound was nothing to worry over, but to North's rising consternation, she had commenced to display many of those symptoms which had seized Velvalee Petrie. Second, he was afforded the blessed opportunity of catching an hour of badly-needed sleep. He had dozed even when Colonel McKenzie's heavily-escorted limousine detoured from Hadji Field long enough to deposit the girl, already light-headed and fearfully flushed, at the American Military Mission Infirmary.

"You'll do everything possible?" North pled once the semi-conscious girl had been placed upon a stretcher, her peasant costume looking very dingy indeed by contrast to the clean sheet beneath it.

"She'll have the best possible care," the Chief Surgeon promised. "This current variety of 'flu is tricky, but I don't believe you have cause for undue alarm. We've just received a shipment of aureomycin—a remarkable new drug."

"You won't experiment—take chances?" North gripped the lieutenant-colonel's arm. "If ever a girl has earned the right to a Congressional medal she's the one, and—and——"

"A bit fond of her, too, aren't you?"

North passed quivering hands over a lean jaw now darkly bristling with a four days' beard. "I—I really don't know how I could face anything going wrong."

The Chief Surgeon patted his arm. "Don't worry; incidentally, you'd better get some rest or you'll catch the bug yourself." He hesitated. "Pardon my asking, but for what is that key in your fist?"

"Key?" North's tired features relaxed into an uncertain smile. "Doctor, I hope that this key will unlock the gates of peace."

"'Gates of peace'? Just a minute, Major, I'm going to take your temperature."

But North turned away and began running back through the infirmary with a pair of stalwart M.P.'s clattering along in his wake.

Using great care Colonel McKenzie inspected the heavy iron key beneath a glaring electric light. He tried to unscrew the handle, then the flange and finally tried to pull the shank free of the head.

"I'm afraid you've made a mistake," he declared heavily. "I can't detect the least line or division."

North rubbed swollen and reddish eyelids and sighed. "You shouldn't, Alex. That key is one of several handmade by the very best master machinist in America."

"The hell you say! Then get busy and break this thing down. I'm holding open the scrambler phone to Washington for a final report."

Brow furrowed, North revolved the dull brown-black piece of metal between his fingers. "Send for a pair of pliers, will you? And keep your blood pressure down, even if I take some time. You see, there are several variations to this type of concealment."

Once an orderly had fetched in a pair of strong pliers and then had retreated, the Intelligence Officer set to work.

"This, Alex, is an uncommonly excellent bit of craftsmanship," North commented. "See? This shank or shaft of the key has been hollowed out, leaving a space large enough to contain the microfilm which I hope to God we'll find inside."

As had happened on certain other occasions of extreme tension, the world seemed to shrink about Hugh North until it ceased to exist beyond an area bounded by the top of Alexander McKenzie's desk.

This was really a magnificent job, so excellently tooled that even his keen vision failed to detect any hint of a break in the surface. A sudden and unbearable anxiety caused the sweat to spring out on his brow. North's grimy hands quivered. Was this key in fact no sham at all, only an uninteresting piece of iron?

Alexander McKenzie bent low, scalp glistening pink through sparse gray hair. He noted that three teeth of varying length and design constituted the key blade; and that the handle was rather ornate. Never had Hugh North's heart hammered and thumped more wildly than when he applied a gentle then strong pressure to the topmost tooth, attempting to turn it first to the right and then to the left. Despite strong efforts the projection refused to budge.

"Oh, God," breathed McKenzie. "It's the wrong key!"

Sweating violently now, North tested the short center tooth and when he applied counter-clockwise pressure a gasp of relief escaped him. The pin, ever so slightly, had yielded!

McKenzie confessed, "I have heard of such a device before but I've never seen one. On what principle does it work?"

"Beneath this tooth there's a spring," explained the Intelligence Officer, "a spring which forces a bolt into an inner core—within the shank. Unless one first loosens the control tooth and so relieves the spring exerting pressure on a little bolt it's impossible to unscrew this cap." North indicated a small ridge just below the tip of the key. "Now," he invited, "even if you haven't any special drag with the Almighty you'd better pray and pray hard."

Bracing the key with his left hand, North locked the pliers' serrated jaws about the top of the key. The application of considerable effort was required before slowly, smoothly, the key cap commenced to travel in a clockwise direction until at length it was completely unscrewed.

"What beautiful, beautiful machining," McKenzie sighed.

Out from the shank slipped a long, bright metal cylinder, one that with absolute fidelity fitted the core of the key. In no time at all North then uncapped the cylinder and held out his prize.

"It's there—it's there! I am sure it is!" A pair of tweezers deftly removed from the depths of the cylinder a tight roll of microfilm.

During an interminable instant the two officers stared across the table at each other. How impossible it was to comprehend the implications, the significance of that tiny roll of camera film. How many men had suffered unmentionable tortures, had died that this minute roll might reach its present destination? But how many millions more now might hope to live out their lives unafraid and secure? Conveyed with all speed to America, this little scroll soon would translate itself into thousands of all-important variphase multi-jet ejector units.

The desk lamp, the light swayed before North's weary eyes momentarily and he had to steady himself against the desk top. He thought of Josef Walewski and prayed that that hero might long since have won surcease in death.

"Sure as my name's McKenzie," predicted the Military Attaché, "you'll hear tonight that the Soviets have withdrawn their ultimatum. They won't dare to attack us now."

"I presume arrangements have been made for an immediate dispatch to Washington?"

"Of course, the minute we can get copies printed. Naturally, we'll not risk an only copy even in the best plane that was ever built. You have a right to look pleased," McKenzie continued, "but what the hell are you grinning about?"

"Oh, I was wondering just what's going to happen to a certain former American once known as Benjamin A. Gramont."

"It'll be nothing trivial, I hope," grimly added the Military Attaché. "And now I'm going to phone the Defense Department."

North got to his feet, feeling absurd in his Rumelian garments.

"Where are you headed? To bed?"

"No, over to the infirmary. There's someone there who should know that we've won."

Colonel Alexander McKenzie straightened, bowed a little. "Please convey to Miss Lawson my more than earnest congratulations." He broke off. "Oh, hell, tell her she's done a superlative job. Tell her that some day soon America will be informed of what she did. Tell her——"

But Hugh North already was through the door and striding downstairs.

CHAPTER 34

L'Avenir

AT SIX OF THE MORNING, Lieutenant-Colonel Lewellyn, Chief of the American Military Mission Infirmary, sent instructions that Major North might enter that small room in which Haïdi Lawson lay, once more fighting for her life.

"Good news, Major," announced the head nurse. "Our new drug seems to be taking effect in her case. Miss Lawson's temperature is down a little and just now she awoke entirely rational. I—I'm glad you're here."

"Why?"

"During her delirium," the head nurse's plain features flushed, "she kept calling for you. Here we are. You can go in, but you mustn't stay long."

"She's—she'll be all right?"

As usual, the head nurse evaded. "Doctor says we've good reason to think so. What we'll have to watch out for is a possible relapse; this kind of 'flu is terribly unpredictable."

A faint odor of antiseptics reached North's nostrils when he pushed open the door and ran over to the bedside.

How ridiculously small Jingles looked there on that stark hospital bed, perhaps because her soft brown hair had been braided into a little girl's pigtails.

"I'd give everything," Jingles said presently in a small, hushed voice, "if you could kiss me, but, darling, you mustn't—you mustn't even come close. They tell me this 'flu is terribly contagious."

Tall and gaunt but shaven and in his own clothes, Hugh North stood by her bedside, then drew a deep breath. "Before I say anything else, dear, I want you to know that we got the right key; it contained—what—what our country needed so urgently."

Jingles' eyes fluttered shut but a radiant smile lit her pinched-looking features. "Wonderful! How very wonderful! I was so afraid." She looked up at him, the gray-blue eyes intense. "Was there anything else?"

"Yes." He cast a quick look about, frowned and shrugged. "I suppose this is hardly the most romantic spot for a proposal of marriage—but, darling, would you be interested in the nonsense of becoming Mrs. Hugh North?"

"—For a great brain you ask some of the dumbest questions," she chided and held up slim arms. "Consider yourself accepted. Oh, God," she wailed. "And you can't even kiss me!"

"Bugs or no bugs," said he firmly, "that's just what I intend to do."